THE HT SUMMER OF 1968

Viliam Klimáček

THE HOT SUMMER OF 1968

Translated by Peter Petro

MANDEL VILAR PRESS   DRYAD PRESS

This book is typeset in Masqualero 11/15. The paper used in this book meets the minimum
requirements of ANSI/NISO Z39.48-1992 (R1997). ∞

Publisher's Cataloguing-In-Publication Data
Names: Klimáček, Viliam, 1956– / Petro, Dr. Peter, translator / Toth, Dusan, English translation
   rights owner
Title: The Hot Summer of 1968, A Novel
Other Titles: Horúce leto 68, Slovak
Description: First English edition. /Simsbury, Connecticut: Mandel Vilar Press (2021)/ Translation
   of the original Slovak: Horúce leto 68 by Marenčin PT, Bratislava 1,Slovenská Republika,
   2011. Summary: A novel about Prague Spring—the liberalization of the Communist regime
   in Czechoslovakia in 1968 and the subsequent crushing of this experiment by Soviet Bloc
   tanks and troops—and the impact of these events on the lives and families of ordinary Czech
   and Slovak citizens who, facing possible arrest and reprisals, quickly fled Czechoslovakia
   and became political refugees in Austria, England, Israel, Canada, the Arctic and the United
   States. It follows the obstacles and issues faced as refugees in foreign lands and how they
   rebuilt their lives in their new countries. It also follows the lives and experiences of those
   citizens who chose to remain in Czechoslovakia under the new repressive regime.
Identifiers: ISBN: 978-1942134-718 (pbk.) / ISBN 978-1942134-724 (eBook)
Subjects: LCSH: Languages and Literature: Slavic/Slovak 20th Century Literature/Fiction/English
   Translation World History: Soviet Union and Former Soviet Republics, 20th Century
   Czechoslovakia, 1960s, Prague Spring and its aftermath August 1968, Political Refugees in
   Austria, England, Israel, Canada and the United States. History of the Americas: Later 20th
   Century Social Sciences: Refugees and Immigrants in United States and Canada, England,
   and Israel.
Classification: LCC PG 5439.21 L56 H36 2021

Printed in the United States of America
20 21 22 23 24 25 26 27 28 / 9 8 7 6 5 4 3 2 1

Mandel Vilar Press, 19 Oxford Court, Simsbury CT 06070
www.mvpublishers.org/www.americasforconservation.org

Dryad Press, 15 Sherman Avenue, Takoma Park, MD 20912
www.dryadpress.com.

CONTENTS

THE HOT SUMMER OF 1968

Asphalt

Only one post-war car made in the people's democracy of Czechoslovakia bore a proud name reminiscent of an ancient English family: Škoda Tudor. That was what people called it. It looked like the ungainly iron-clad horses that carried the gallant knights of Albion in their battles for God, king, and country, although at the time of our story it was more like Stalin, Lenin, and Marx.

Bulbous and noisy, it sweated oil under a carapace that was more tin than glass. It offered gaudiness rather than elegance and commotion rather than performance. The word *design* was not yet in fashion, and the technology under the hood was also far from refined.

The time was ripe for surprises, however: Škoda designers, counting on the disappearance of classical education, named the successor to the Škoda Octavia model Felicia, "the happy one."

An elegant cabriolet, it glowed against the Czechoslovak asphalt like an orange on a pile of potatoes.

At that time happiness meant owning a fridge, a washing machine, and a television set. But for thousands of families this was only a dream, not to mention owning an automobile. And to own a Felicia marked one as truly exceptional—not as one of the powerful, like the top politicians chauffeured in Soviet Chaika automobiles or the local leaders driven around in domestic Tatra 603 cars, but rather as one of the unofficial elite, who acknowledged each other with a wink.

To drive a Felicia in June 1968, when this story begins, was no longer as exceptional as it had been a few years before, but it remained a car in which a citizen of a state enclosed in barbed wire could feel free, at least for a while, like James Dean on Route 66.

Alexander loved to drive. He felt no need to prove anything to the pedestrians who unfailingly waved at him every day as he passed; he always waved back. That was the proper thing to do in a country with a longstanding tradition of waving. Alexander, however, did his waving from a limousine rather than on the sidewalk.

Alexander held one of the top positions in Sanola, the only Czechoslovakian producer of medical equipment. He often gave tours of the production facility to exceptional people such as the surgeon Christiaan Barnard, who first transplanted a human heart.

It went without saying that Alex, as he was called at home, would one day own a car that attracted envious looks like a candle attracts moths at night. Corruption was inevitable in a country with a multi-year waiting list for cars, but Alex did not have to grease any palms. He merely arranged for the hospital that treated automotive plant workers to be the first to receive the new respirators that the whole country was waiting for. Payback was immediate in the form of a vehicle that teenagers pinned to their walls next to the tantalizing curves of Brigitte Bardot.

Sitting in his motorized jewel made Alex look as exotic as an orchid pinned to a worker's overalls. Needlessly provocative, it distanced him from his co-workers, but that did not bother him. He was no longer interested in furthering his career. He had achieved his ambition of becoming technical director, and another 5,000 a year was meaningless to him. Leave that to the multitude of climbers in their little Škodas or Wartburgs or on their Jawa motorbikes, with their hundred-square-foot vegetable gardens lined with carrots and potatoes and their children learning to become lathe operators or shop assistants.

Alex's daughter had finished her medical studies just a week before. In a small town a successful child was a source of jealousy, to say nothing of an extravagant car. When you pin your dream to a flag, you'll get a wake-up call before you can lift and wave it. Alex could afford to dream safely, however. No mere mortal, he was a member of the Communist Party. Without that red card with its little star you could not make a decent career in Czechoslovakia, or put your education to good use. Even so, when forced to say, "we Communists," Alex swallowed the capital C. His lack of commitment was not lost among the top comrades, and he had no idea how long his situation, best described as "unstable," could last. Teetering on the brink, Alex managed to remain upright for the moment, not thanks to his position but rather to an era of detente.

A distant province is far from heaven, and while the reformist thaw of the Prague Spring of 1968 finally managed to reach Stará Ruda, Alex felt he was socially still in 1965.

Even so, the weather was wonderful, and Alex was wearing a short-sleeved shirt as he opened the garage door to back his Felicia out. He shouted to his wife:

"Are you coming? Hurry up, we want to get there before dark!"

"Wear a pullover!"

"We'll drive with the top up."

"Never mind."

Anna brought out a yellow and black pullover that she had just finished knitting, looking at it critically for loose stitches, but finding it perfect. Then her gaze shifted to the family car. If her first look was a ray of sun caressing a blossom, this one resembled a bolt of lightning that burned everything to cinders.

She hated the car. She hated its retractable roof and eternal drafts. She would rather have kept the stodgy but airtight old Tudor they'd gotten rid of years ago. What does a woman who feels disgust at the word "convertible" look like? I will leave that to your imagination. I prefer to avoid descriptions of characters and landscapes as a service to you. As a reader, I always skim through them and imagine that, like me, you won't miss that kind of filler. It's enough to know that Alex's Anna was past her fortieth year, slightly younger than the man who pulled on his striped pullover with a frown.

"It makes me look like a hornet."

"Just put it on, it'll be windy."

In Czechoslovakia at this time people were always knitting, crocheting, making batik or even weaving macramé. Italians made homemade pasta, and Slovaks created crafts. Tin bottle caps were soldered together to form drumming rabbits, a wall was decorated with a nylon blanket featuring a setting sun, and a shelf was adorned with an unusual piece of lacquered wood that looked like a water nymph from Lake Balaton. The ceaseless effort to find joy in simple things was necessary to survive in such a country.

Anna and Alex engaged in their usual morning conversation about the astonishing success of their little Petra, who had successively put behind her the wooden preschool, the brick elementary school, the concrete high school, and the marble university, and was about to move out of her rented room in Bratislava with a medical school diploma in hand.

"Please, drive a bit slower."

"Don't pass!"

"Let him in. He's pushy."

"Watch out for that truck!"

"Did you notice he had no wipers?"

And so they re-enacted Beckett's *Happy Days*, with Anna playing the role of Winnie, but sitting in a car seat instead of being buried up to her waist in sand, while Alex played Willie, the silent recipient of his partner's prattle who every half hour gave her a smile that she interpreted as wishing her a happy day.

The freeway had not yet been built, and the roadway funneling a thickening stream of cars to Bratislava was called International Road E16, but the only international thing about it was the E. It was a narrow two-lane highway on which passing another car required a stuntman's nerve in a duel of egos. To pass meant to conquer, and to pass a shiny red Felicia with a light blue plastic Trabant bolstered the driver's self-confidence for at least a week.

A citizen of Czechoslovakia could overcome his claustrophobic frustrations in one of three ways: by having sex, stealing, or passing someone in his car. His practice was to engage in sex at home, pass cars on the road, and steal from his workplace.

Kept at a modest speed by Anna, Alex had to deal with the emphatic horn-honking of other drivers, but it should be mentioned that he didn't give a damn. After two and a half hours driving through dozens of town and villages, Alex broke his silence: "Bratislava."

The stench of the Dimitrov chemical factory welcomed them before a road sign signaled their arrival. More and more, the tin stars and concrete hammers and sickles flashing by had become intermingled with advertisements for peace and socialism emblazoned with yellow letters on red posters that enlivened the sagging frontages of buildings that seemed part of another era. Secession and classicism were foreign at the time, and instead of fixing the stucco walls and ceilings of palaces, the regime was focusing on the economy that was consuming the future of its people and their children.

A tram's warning bell clanged, and Alex slowed down.

Sublet

Petra didn't want to be a student anymore. Fed up with student life, she was miserable.

In the first and second years she was still friendly with the students in her group, going out with them to the wine cellars and missing the last transit connections so that they all had to walk home together, singing their way through the night streets. They came from all over Slovakia and lived in the student dormitories.

She liked studying. She enjoyed learning the Latin words that painted beautiful pictures in her mind even when they denoted painful diseases. Every semester brought thicker textbooks, but dormitory life distracted her. While the party warriors found themselves sent back to hometowns like Topolčany and Snina, the majority of students who made it through the examination sieve continued to divide their energy between studying and drinking. It was destructive, but who can take more than young people?

Alcohol was the marijuana of socialism, and twenty-two-year-olds need to have some fun from time to time. If she wanted to finish her studies, Petra had to move out of the dormitory.

On weekends she would escape to her parents' place, especially in the wintertime. Petra and the snow were a match made in heaven. She was an excellent skier and she managed to conquer the hills above Stará Ruda as a nine-year-old. She could have been a top skier, and was even offered a place on the national junior ski team, but she wanted to enjoy the sport, not make a living from it. She didn't want to commune with her body; instead, she chose her mind, and it was the right decision.

She had no close friends, only classmates, and in her fourth year she did nothing but study, sleeping with cotton wool in her ears to block out the nocturnal giggling of her dormmates. She began to get on people's nerves, and when her father managed to find a sublet for her, everyone sighed with relief.

She spent her last two years on Panenská Street 23. She was so eager for her student life to end that at graduation she almost ripped her diploma from the hands of the dean of the medical school. The hall was filled with parents who assumed the young doctor was suffering from stage fright, and they rewarded her with sympathetic laughter.

She just had to leave school as soon as possible. Six years is a very long time when you're young and don't know what to do with your youth. Petra didn't know what she wanted, but she knew exactly what she didn't want. She didn't want to be young. She was excited at the prospect of growing up, forgetting about textbooks and working the night shift in a hospital until she collapsed from exhaustion. Even so, she managed to ski occasionally in her free time.

Two years earlier she had gotten to know Tereza, the daughter of her landlord. Petra fell in love with their old apartment on the second floor overlooking the garden of a Lutheran church. She didn't understand why Tereza's father Ferdinand, a friend of her father, found the apartment uncomfortable. But it's one thing to be a boarder and another to live somewhere permanently.

The hundred-year-old building was showing its age, with cracked paint around the windows, stucco peeling off the walls, rusty pipes, and a coal furnace. The staircase to the apartment seemed endless.

Even so, Petra couldn't imagine living anywhere else. If Tereza became the sister she'd always wanted to have, then Tereza's mother, Maria, became a temporary substitute for her own mother, Anna. The household also included ten-year-old Janko, who admiringly shadowed the tenant buried in her books and would suddenly ask questions about things he read in them: "Osteomyopathy?" Then he would dart out of the room.

It would be hard to find two people more different than Tereza, who was like the sun, and Petra, like the moon. The apartment was not much quieter than the dormitory, and possibly even noisier, with five people occupying two and a half rooms, but the air was filled with a scent more precious than perfume smuggled from Vienna.

It was filled with tolerance.

From the big Lutheran church opposite the open window where the girls were studying came the sound of an organ. It was not a melody; the organist was practicing his fingering. A drummer practicing can make you feel like dancing, but an organ makes you meditative.

Tereza's voice interrupted Petra's reverie.

"That garden always seems so mysterious. And the music... it seems so special, celebratory. Greater than I. Do you think it's to make the people who go there..."

She nodded towards the fence, behind which young ministers were walking.

"Make them do what?"

"Make them fear God?"

Petra had drawn her own conclusions on religion long ago.

"I'm not a believer. When I was little, my parents told me: 'Look Petra, some people say there's a God, and others say there is no God. We're not going to force you to believe in anything, and if you want to go to church we won't stop you.'"

"And did you go?"

"Once. It was cold and airless. My father was smart. He sort of gave me a free hand, but he and Mom don't go there, just as they don't smoke. An example is better than a thousand words. That's why I don't smoke and don't know how to pray. How about you?"

Tereza looked at her.

"A bit."

"What do you mean, a bit? Either you do or you don't."

Tereza looked out the window at the future ministers walking around in the garden. They were still only theological students. She waved at them, and they looked up and waved back with a nod, and then continued walking without looking at the window again.

"See the one with the black hair? He talked to me for a long time. He was trying to persuade me."

"About what?"

"He told me everything about religion, but I only wanted to know about the organ."

"Was he flirting with you?"

Tereza smiled.

"I think you're getting too caught up in *Gynecology and Obstetrics*," said Tereza, syllabifying the title of Petra's textbook.

"And you, my dear, are tempting young pastors, and that's a sin."

Petra got herself a glass of water from the kitchen, while Tereza hugged her knees and gently rocked.

"Actually, they approached me. Apparently persuading a lost sheep is an *incredibly*, really *incredibly* good deed." Tereza drawled out the word "incredibly" with obvious pleasure. Then she asked, "What goes on in there, anyway? It must be nice when everyone sings together with the organ."

"You've never been in a church?"

Tereza shook her head.

"We're Jewish."

And so it was that three weeks after moving to Panenská Street, Petra realized that she was living with a Jewish family. While for Tereza it was the church organ that seemed mysterious, Petra felt the superficial, but nonetheless sincere, fascination with Judaism that often exists among people of different faiths. She recalled one night at bedtime, when her father told her how during the war all the Jews of Stará Ruda were taken to concentration camps, and none of them returned. Alex talked to her for a long time, and his eyes glistened in the dim light from the street lamp outside her darkened bedroom.

"Imagine Petra, if it happened to our family. One evening someone comes banging on your door, taking you from your little bed and driving your mother and father out into the street in their pajamas, herding us into a cattle car and transporting us somewhere for a week without any food, and then once we arrived, separating us from each other, and we would never see each other again..."

"Daddy, stop it!"

Anna appeared in the doorway like a storm cloud, thunderous with rage. Little Petra was hiding her head under her pillow, shaking her bed with her sobs.

"What on earth are you doing?"

Alexander looked at his wife and then hugged his crying daughter like a baby chick. He whispered to her for a long time that he would never give her up and that nothing would happen, since *that* happened such a long time ago. But a father's gentleness is like a steel file: it removes a layer and leaves the surface rough. That night Anna slept with her daughter, who clung to her like a tick even while she slept. Even so, Petra didn't regret learning that the most horrible crimes should never be forgotten.

Now she felt embarrassed that she hadn't noticed anything, even though the apartment looked like any other household, apart from a few small items on the shelf in the living room. Each Friday she would leave around lunchtime for her parents' home, so she didn't know that the family kept Sabbath. She recalled her father's words: "Come home every weekend. We can't impose on them too much."

She looked at Tereza, her face blazing.

"I'm so sorry... for being such an idiot! I came into your home without understanding anything!"

Tereza smiled and shook her head. She was used to having boarders.

Our Father

In 1956, when the Hungarians rose up against the Communist regime and Budapest burned under the attack of Soviet tanks, the apartment on Panenská Street became a home for thirty refugees. This happened gradually over time, but it took half a year for Tereza to get her room back from the visitors.

Her father had returned from the concentration camp with an unbreakable belief that one must always help others.

"Normally your room is yours, Tereza, but if there's a problem, we have to help."

It was because of this iron ethic that Petra eventually moved in as well.

Little Tereza was always perceptive and quick to understand, growing invisible antennae. She knew she was Jewish but didn't understand what that meant, except that she felt different from other children in school. She noticed that she understood some of them better because their parents knew her parents; she knew that some of them were "our people" and others were not, but why? That was too much for a child's antennae to register.

In the 1950s her parents often entertained visitors who liked to talk about politics. Sitting among them the child didn't understand everything they said, but she gained a sense of the context. The apartment was packed with two thousand books; Maria was the editor of Pravda Publishing House and would bring special books home for others, or lend them out. That gave Tereza access to books that her peers would never think of touching.

One night a noise awakened her.

Her father's friends were in the living room reorganizing the bookcases. They took some books out to the cellar and moved others from the front row to the back row. It was the year of the Slánský trial, when secret pogroms were carried out against Communist Jews. State Security conducted surprise searches, and possessing suspicious books could be dangerous.

A friend's father was locked up during the Slánský trial in the Palace of Justice, the same place as the legendary murderess Irena Čubírková, who burned her husband to death in a bread oven and tossed his head into the toilet of a train. These were times when a political prisoner was considered worse than a murderer. Little Tereza got used to always having someone they knew in prison, and knowing that he was certainly innocent. She never considered the possibility of her family's friends being punished for theft or violence; she knew they were imprisoned for words.

They visited her friend's father in Leopoldov Prison. His face, his conduct, his movements made it obvious at a glance that he was completely different from other prisoners. He was not a man who had taken the wrong path in life, but rather a man who lived for truth. Young Tereza was being educated in the lifelong school of being different, and these impressions were etched in her brain like hieroglyphs cut into a slab of marble.

Tereza's father was in charge of rail cargo at the main railway station. The railways were only slightly less strategically important than the army. Everything was transported through them: iron ore, coal, wheat, and armaments. Every delayed train was a reason for investigation. Doing this kind of work meant living twenty-four hours a day with the feeling that someone was watching you. Accusations could come at any time for any reason.

Like many Jewish intellectuals Ferdinand was a Communist; it was logical to join the force that stopped Nazism. Almost every Jewish family had at least one member of the Communist Party among their relatives, just to be safe. They no longer believed in anyone or anything except their own people.

Tereza grew into a beautiful girl, but she still remembered one night when she was thirteen years old and slept in a girls' dormitory during school camp. There were twenty of them in the room. As they settled into bed, the teacher checked in on them before wishing them good night and turning off the light.

The girls waited until her footsteps receded and then got out of bed, knelt on the wooden floor and secretly prayed the "Our Father."

Tereza knelt with them, not wanting to be different—not daring to. She opened her mouth and repeated after them, always with a delay and always wrong. The praying went on like that night after night, always with one girl leading and others following her. One day a girl maliciously turned to Tereza and said:

"How about if Tereza prays first this time?"

She kept her cool, saying: "Of course, but I'll start tomorrow."

There were giggles and whispers as the girls wondered what their favorite classmate would do the next evening.

Just to make sure, they asked her again during breakfast as she carried her warm milk and poppy seed roll on a tray to the table.

"Will you be praying today?"

She nodded. "Of course."

She mechanically bit into her roll but didn't eat the poppy seed filling as usual. Her body was invaded by a flush of panic. After breakfast she made a decision. She turned to the one teacher she trusted, who taught them physics. She confided her problem to him, and after looking at her for a moment that seemed to last forever, he smiled and nodded. Then he took her for a walk.

As they walked, he taught her the prayer, word for word, and Tereza repeated it. That was how she was able to kneel with her bare knees on the oil-scented floor and with a sure voice pronounce the foreign words that joined into mysterious sentences.

With these words she entered a mysterious island full of strange plants, invisible creatures, and threatening birds that circled menacingly above her. She did not come to the island barefoot; she came on her knees.

"Our Father who art in Heaven, hallowed be Thy name..."

In spite of her success, she felt she could not endure another such absurd situation if she wanted to respect herself. It was only the first of many tests that most people never have to undergo.

When the prayer ended, she stood up with aching knees, crawled into bed and covered herself with her prickly blanket. And then quietly enough that nobody could hear her, she began to cry. That was the price of her antennae.

Tunnel

hen Anna and Alexander entered the gate on Panenská Street they were awed by the short tunnel that led from the street to an inner courtyard garden. For a moment it seemed that the street was bathed in sunlight while the courtyard was drowning in twilight.

The tunnel brought them to another dimension where everything seemed upside down: light, time, and being. At the end of the tunnel was a swinging pendulum. Alex and Anna cautiously entered. After a few steps, the magic disappeared. From the courtyard came the shouting of children, a spotted ball flew by, and wind stirred the tree branches, admitting sunlight. The pendulum turned out to be a shiny pail of coal that someone was trying to lift from an upstairs window.

Winking at Anna, Alex grabbed the pail with both hands. The rope became taut, then relaxed and tightened again.

"Hey, let go!"

"What's the password?"

Anna scolded, "Alexander!"

She used her husband's birth name only when she was shocked by his childishness. A family man! An engineer! Almost a Director! The rope relaxed for a moment as if thinking it over. Then a loud voice boomed from above, "May your ass be pricked by a thousand injection needles!"

Alex released the pail, which flew up so quickly that some coal tumbled out.

"Sometimes I don't understand you, Alexander!"

Propelled by his wife's words, Alex sped to the second floor, where Ferdinand waited at his open door.

"Well, I should have known. Greetings, producer of enema instruments!"

"Hello, rail car switcher!"

Ferdinand removed the pail from the pulley. It was the same simple contraption he used to lift groceries.

"Are you heating your apartment in June?"

"Just imagine: we're cooking!"

"Hi Mom, hi Dad!"

With her kiss Petra dismissed the gentle invective that former classmates hand out to each other the way presidents receive honorary doctorates. Ferdinand was gasping for breath after the exertion of pulling up the coal.

"What's wrong, Ferdo?"

He just waved his hand.

"By the way, where's Tereza?"

A momentary silence descended on the apartment, and it seemed that even the clock with hands shaped like pencils stopped drawing the time.

"She left, you see? She didn't even finish her second year! She left with a group and postponed her examinations until summer."

"She's camping?"

"She's in Israel."

Tereza had joined a group of students organized by the writer Ladislav Mňačko. He and his wife had come up with the idea that young Czechoslovakians, Jewish or otherwise, should get to know the real Israel, so they organized a summer work camp in a kibbutz. Tereza had excitedly started getting her documents ready to join what were called Mňačko's children. That was in June 1968, and the ongoing reform movement made the formalities easier than ever before. Everything was getting better, and people were filled with hope. Tereza begged her parents to allow her to interrupt the second year of her university arts program, feeling that the trip was worth it. She longed to visit a place where she had never been and yet somehow belonged. She had no idea if she would find her roots, but she had to visit the Wailing Wall and the desert, and stand under the burning sun beside the earth's saltiest body of water, the Dead Sea.

Even as she spoke, Ferdinand knew he would not stop her. His incomparable fatherly love had a worthy target: Tereza, an excellent student and her family's hope, the center of so many universes around whom rotated the blurred faces of friends and acquaintances or other incidental bodies that entered her gravity field and contented themselves with being her satellites.

"Shall we go?" said Petra, trying to salvage the uncomfortable situation.

Alexander shook his head. "I need to stop somewhere..."

"Your little trains?"

These two friends had been dealt the wrong cards: Alex, the specialist in medical instruments who loved model trains, and Ferdo, the railwayman who loved literature.

"Listen, Ferdo, don't be irritated. You're around trains all day; don't they interest you at all?"

"That's work. Work is interesting in a different way."

"You've never wanted to collect model trains?"

"Are you insane? Have you ever seen a miner relaxing in the mineshaft after his shift?"

Alex had constructed a model countryside that took up half of their bedroom: signals flashed, tunnels wound through the landscape like snakes, and switches clicked. He had put the entire complicated mechanism together from pieces that he had bought for little Petra for Christmas until Anna rebelled. From then on, Petra found teddy bears, games, and electronic multiplication tables under the Christmas tree, while Alex bought himself a train. In order to give himself the pleasure of a small surprise, he gave the train to his wife to wrap: "Well, you know..." Anna re-wrapped the train in Christmas paper while selecting her own presents for Alex to wrap at his insistence. Their Christmas Eve ritual was to exchange presents after listening to carols on a scratched record, followed by a meal of sauerkraut soup, fried carp, and potato salad. Then they settled into their armchairs, eyes closed, and listened to *Eugene Onegin*, Anna's favorite opera. A quick peek at each other established that both were where they belonged, and then they closed their eyes again as Monsieur Triquet sang about the beautiful Tatiana. Listening to his dulcet tenor, no one suspected that Christmas 1967 was the last they would spend together.

The Prefab Building

The first prefab building in Slovakia was known as the experimental one. Those that came after, although not referred to in the same way, likewise embodied the regime's experimentation with how many citizens could be squeezed into a single square meter without protest. The exact number is uncertain, but it was certainly very high.

The first prefabs embodied a simple purity, constructed as they were at the outset of the Communist movement. They seemed progressive in the postwar misery: bright, warm, comfortable apartments complete with toilets—a true rarity.

In the 1960s they had not yet managed to become symbolic of mass housing estates where there had to be ten proletarians for each medical doctor. Bratislava was destined to become a workers' city: it had to think less and work more. Muscles were a better qualification than a university degree.

Notable among the buildings of early socialism, the first Slovak prefab was constructed on Kmeť Square in Bratislava. Its team of designers was led by Professor Karfík, who used pre-stressed concrete in a panel frame system—only architects know exactly what this means, and we don't have to.

The first tenants moved into the engineered building in January of 1956. They brought their modest belongings through two entrances, above each of which was mounted a work of art designed to beautify the building. Life had to be beautiful no matter what people thought, and no one commented out loud. The art consisted of a stone frieze of boys at play over one doorway, and of girls over the other.

It was under the girls frozen in stone that Anna entered the building. She was visiting her sister Erika and in her hand she carried a small parcel containing a sweater for Erika's son, which she had finished before starting on the black and yellow one for her husband. They had stopped only briefly in Panenská Street: Petra remained behind to help Maria cook Sunday lunch, while Ferdinand left for the railway station and Alexander headed off to the miniature train shop. They had arranged to meet back there in two hours.

Anna was in a hurry. She knew that Maria would hold lunch for them, and that there was nothing more humiliating for a woman than to spend her morning over the stove and then have guests arrive late, when the food is already cold. The only choice at this point is to rewarm the food when sentiment, and perhaps a fear of breaking the law, suppresses the impulse to hurl a knife at the offenders. For this reason Anna was out of breath as she rang the bell.

"Hello, my little one, can I come up for a moment?"

Erika would always remain the "little one," even though she was taller than her sister; she was a year younger, and that year mattered. Peter ran in from the kitchen.

"Auntie Anna, I want a hug!"

While lifting him in her arms, Anna sized the boy up, wondering if the sweater would fit.

"Oh my, what a big man you are! Look what your auntie brought you!"

"A car?"

Like many a woman before her, Anna disappointed the child with a practical gift. Boys dream of toy cars and air guns, but socks and shirts overrun their fantasies like weeds.

"It's not a car, but it will keep you warm while you play."

"I am warm!"

Erika shot him a stern look. "Peter!"

The boy obediently pulled the sweater on and grudgingly allowed her to drag him in front of the mirror. A red car embroidered in fuzzy cotton ran through the middle of the woolen mass. Anna had overcome her distaste for Alex's convertible to please the child, and Peter appreciated it. "Feh-lee-tsee-ya!" he chirped happily.

It was Sunday and the only shop in the world that Alex cared about was closed, but he could still enjoy looking at the window display and deciding what Anna would place under the tree.

Alexander was creating his own world. What the philosopher does with meaning, he worked into plywood and balsa, re-imagining his universe on a bearable scale. He had spent years building his model landscape with little houses next to little roads on which tiny cars drove next to miniature tracks along which electric trains hummed.

Anyone seeing Alex standing at the shop window oohing and aahing would have doubted his mental state. But other people were at home listening to the radio and waiting for their pork schnitzel with potato salad.

If your loved ones don't suffer from the same folly, all kinds of collector's passions are tolerable. Anna wasn't bothered by it; she was smart enough to have walked hand in hand with her husband across the threshold where romance turned into the mature love of a father and mother. Tolerating a partner's hobby became an opportunity to repay love with understanding. In practice, this meant that Anna tolerated more, and it can be said with assurance that Alex was a happy man, and knew it.

"So tell me, how are you doing?"

"I'm teaching at a high school and it's going fine. I keep waiting for a voice to come over the school intercom saying: 'Comrade Rola, come to the principal's office regarding the termination of your work contract!"

"Surely not!"

"It's fine, don't worry, but I still can't get used to the fact that they've allowed me to teach."

"Where's your husband?"

"At his parents' place in Modra. Oh God, I want to ask if you wouldn't mind taking us there..."

"I'll get Petra and we'll come back for you."

"Won't Alex mind?"

"He's looking at his miniature trains. He'll be in heaven."

"Thanks."

"We'll be back in an hour or so."

"Has Lajo called?"

"Not in the last six months. Has he called you?"

"No. What kind of family are we? I'll get some laundry done now."

"Bye bye, Peter! We'll be back to pick you up with the Felicia!"

The Vineyard

Like many couples, Erika and her husband fell in love during the May Day parade. Even a forced parade for happiness and peace couldn't deprive young people of their zest for life or capacity for love. Erika loved to watch Jozef, a skillful handballer, as he hovered in the air gripping the ball like an angel with a myrtle crown. They both studied with distinction in high school, but the moment Jozef applied to study theology, his grade ranking dropped from excellent to passing.

He graduated from the Lutheran seminary in his birthplace, and after passing the examination for chaplain he was assigned a post in Nové Zámky. Two days before he was scheduled to be ordained in Modra, the Deputy Minister of Education in charge of religious affairs summoned him for a meeting.

"Comrade Rola—but maybe I shouldn't address you that way... Let's get to the point. You come from a working-class family, right? Farmers with a vineyard? All right, fine. Your parents work in the vineyards, we know that. I rely on your understanding. Some sort of underground movement seems to have emerged in the church at Nové

Zámky. We need someone to keep us informed about what's going on there. We need someone reliable. You don't have to give me an answer right away. You have until tomorrow. Think about it!"

Jozef's face turned pale as he left the office, and he reached the street without knowing how he got there. Lighting a cigarette, he took a deep drag and released a cloud of smoke through his nostrils like a bull letting off steam. His initial fear turned into anger. His whole family was invited to the ordination, along with dozens of friends and hundreds of others for whom the young clergyman from their town had become a symbol of hope. Happiest of all was his mother, who had gone along with him from the beginning.

One day, as a child, Jozef had come home from school and run to the vineyard to find her.

"Did you know that there's no God, Mom? The world developed by itself, from matter!"

His mother put down her hoe, wiped her brow and smiled. "All right, tell me all about it."

She never contradicted him: she let him talk. And the child kept talking, but the longer the conversation lasted the more questions he found difficult to answer. The most important of those was: "Fine, but who created the matter?" Perhaps it was on this day that little Jozef's faith appeared. It never left him, and he decided to become a pastor.

Now as he slowly finished smoking his cigarette and felt it burn his fingers, he knew what he had to do. Standing out on the street, he summoned the courage for a step that would change his life.

For decades under socialism, many Lutheran ministers had cooperated with state power as members of the Peace Movement, while Catholics joined *Pacem in terris*—the Peace on Earth organization. Neither brought peace to anyone's soul.

Jozef stubbed out his cigarette, and five minutes later he stood in the office of the Deputy Minister. Both were uncomfortable as Jozef started to talk even before he closed the door. "I would rather be a layman than a clergyman informer!"

Three days later he received a conscription order to report to the army. Before he reported, he was formally hospitalized. He was not allowed to tell anyone that he had refused ordination, and in particular he was not allowed to give the reason. While he spent sleepless nights in the hospital, his parents had to announce the postponement of their son's ordination due to his sudden illness. It was never to take place in Czechoslovakia.

Meanwhile, before Erika took her matriculation exam, the high school's Party Committee declared that she would not be recommended for university study. The year was 1960, and she didn't fit the times because her father had once had a private dentistry practice and someone else in her family was a capitalist by virtue of owning a tailor's workshop. Although both the dental office and the workshop had long since become property of the state, the children still suffered the stigma of their parents having dared to work hard and achieve success in the past.

According to this perverted logic, Erika was not allowed to study at the university, but the daughter of a man who fifteen years ago had pranced around in the black uniform of the fascist Hlinka Guard, sewn from material that people called "the devil's skin," was somehow permitted a college education.

Erika wept, believing that her life was over. As the best student in her class, being denied her education felt like the heavens collapsing on her head and marble columns crumbling all around, burying her in the stucco of her broken ideals. Now she was nobody, a worthless and unnecessary person in an otherwise well-educated family.

Her sister Anna was also not allowed to go to university and instead took a course that allowed her to make a living as an accountant. Their younger brother Lajo made himself the exception to the painful rule. He had joined the Party early on and had graduated with a degree in economics. Now he sat in the pub with the kind of people you didn't want to talk to: informers, secret policemen, and collaborators with Public Security. Lajo didn't stay in his native Pezinok for long; he moved to Stará Ruda and ignored his sisters, and they in turn ignored him. He was making a career in district circles and aiming higher, for the Central Committee of the Communist Party, equipped with a golden telephone.

Erika finally made it to an adult education school, which was better than a mere high school diploma. She ended up collecting folk songs, which she enjoyed as someone who had always loved folklore. Everything seemed to be going fine. She became engaged to Jozef on a Sunday, and the following Monday her director called her to his office.

"Erika, are you engaged to a certain Mr. Rola?"

"Yes."

"Is he going to be a clergyman?"

"Yes."

"And you intend to marry him?"

"Yes."

"Listen, this is not my idea."

"Yes."

"As the wife of a clergyman, you cannot work in adult education."

So Erika gave up her folk songs and went to work in the laboratory of the military hospital.

The military was merciless to Jozef. He started as a laborer in a green uniform attached to the Auxiliary Technical Regiment, where politically untrustworthy recruits were re-educated with the help of a shovel and pick. Thanks to his experience with handball, however, he was seconded to the Sport Regiment and ultimately made the Red Star team in Bratislava.

He found it bearable because he spent a lot of time training and was able to play matches all over the republic. His superior, Captain Kořínek, became obsessed with the fantastic idea of turning the pastor into a Communist. This led him to agree to his guinea pig's repeated requests for long leaves of absence to visit his family: "Comrade Captain, I have to consult with my wife about this."

For her part, Erika was automatically promoted to sub-warrant officer in the military hospital without even knowing it, and began receiving visits: "Comrade Rola, we have a military task for you."

"Yes."

"What are we going to do with your husband?"

"I'll talk to him."

"He should forget all that nonsense.... Well, you know what I mean."

"Yes, Comrade Captain."

"Listen, we're going to turn your Jozef into a Communist. What do you say?"

"That will be difficult. Please understand, you'll have to be patient. He's awfully religious. He wants to cultivate the vineyard."

"But that's nice, isn't it?"

"The vineyard of the Lord, you see."

"You must talk to him!"

"The more he's at home and away from the barracks, the more chance I have. Give me some time."

"The Party has confidence in you, Comrade Rola."

"I'll let you know when he's ready."

But transmuting Jozef into a Communist was as unrealistic as turning iron into gold, for all Captain Kořínek's zeal as an alchemist.

Erika kept her promise and sent Jozef a textbook on Marxism. The reason was simple: she was once again preparing for the college entrance examinations and wanted her husband to underline the main ideas for her since she had no time. Jozef read Marxism with interest. He wanted to know his enemy, and besides that, he had a lot of free time and was glad to help his wife. He read the book everywhere, even while on kitchen duty. That was where Kořínek surprised him.

"Well, Comrade Soldier, what is that you're reading? Show me!"

The Captain was really looking forward to catching him reading some salacious novel, or better yet, the Bible, which would draw a harsh sentence in the brig. Jozef silently handed him the textbook.

When Kořínek read the title, he couldn't believe it. Just to make sure, he flipped through several pages, then he looked at Jozef and back at the book, and then he looked back at Jozef and again at the book for what seemed like a full ten minutes. Then he saw the underlining, and with ill-concealed astonishment he returned the book.

"Excellent. Continue!"

This episode led the army to believe that Erika was genuinely trying to re-educate her husband, so they left her alone for the remainder of her military service. They even accepted her second application to study German and Slovak at the university. Nobody was bothered by her past. She obtained an excellent recommendation, which she wrote herself at the request of the laboratory commander who was too lazy to do it himself. Erika followed orders brilliantly, creating such an impression of dedication to socialism that even the embalmed leader of the world proletariat in his glass coffin would enthusiastically approve. Nothing stood in the way of her university education now. She had a military ranking, however low, and she was going to the university straight from the lab, or as translated into socialist Newspeak, directly from the production line. Who could consider this young woman problematic after reading such a recommendation?

Her husband, on the other hand, was attracting controversy. A few years earlier the 900 ancient manuscripts known as the Dead Sea Scrolls had been discovered in a cave in Qumran, near the Dead Sea. More than 2,000 years old, they included a transcription of the Old Testament. It was clearly the most significant archeological find in the second half of the twentieth century. Scholars were opening the fragile scrolls very gradually, and it was almost impossible to learn anything about them in Czechoslovakia, so Jozef asked the Israeli Embassy for some information. The reply soon came from the barracks and counterintelligence.

Communication with the Israeli Embassy from a military unit was so dangerous and outrageous at the time that the counterintelligence comrades thought it must have been some sort of hoax. Then they went to work, but even their interrogations could not prove Jozef's connection to Mossad, the Israeli secret service. After a few weeks the interrogators left him alone, since accusing a Lutheran pastor of Zionism seemed patently absurd. The Army concluded that an exotic creature with no idea what it was doing lurked under that uniform, but whether Jozef had acted out of naïveté or unusual sophistication, it was still worth keeping him under observation.

Jozef had no sooner survived one catastrophe when another reared its head. Nikita Khrushchev, the Soviet leader who became famous for banging his shoe for emphasis during his speech at the United Nations, decided to send strategic missiles by ship to Cuba. American spy planes photographed the nuclear warheads the Russians planned to place a few kilometers from Florida. As the Cuban Missile Crisis spurred a countdown to the end of the world, all soldiers with the exception of those accepted by the universities had their service time extended in preparation for World War Three.

In a panic, Jozef sent applications everywhere, but with his political profile he did not even merit a reply. Finally he received an invitation from the College of Dramatic Arts, and having nothing to lose he applied for a short leave and traveled to Bratislava.

Soldiers in uniform were not rare among the students, but none were Jozef's age, or Lutheran ministers. Just ten hours after passing the tin guardhouse of his military unit he stood before the entrance examination committee, composed of the best Slovak actors: Chudík, Zachar, Záborský, Sládek, Budský...

To this day Jozef has no idea why they accepted him. An unordained minister, Jozef Rola became an actor.

Modra

odra, situated at the foothills of the Little Carpathians, was celebrated as the home of nineteenth-century scholar and politician Ľudovit Štúr and for its excellent wine. The drink of Bacchus fared much better than the father of Slovakian literary language, who remained under police supervision while residing in Modra to look after the orphaned children of his dead brother. When he needed to unwind, rather than drink wine Štur would go hunting, and this had fateful consequences. As he pursued game on the outskirts of Modra, his unsecured rifle misfired, and he died a short time later. Fortunately, the Slovak language survived him, and the local wine also continues to delight visitors.

Having married into a winemaking family Erika could distinguish the various kinds of wine, and not only by color, which is the sum knowledge of most of the population. It was only natural, then, for Erika and her sister and brother-in-law to spend much of their time on the road from Bratislava to Modra discussing barrels, grape varieties, and sanitizing.

Finally the Felicia stopped, much too soon for Peter, in front of a long, freshly whitewashed house. Vines embellished with grapes could be seen rising on the hill behind the house. This was the family vineyard, beautiful to some and terrible to others.

Jozef had toiled here from the time he was able to wield a hoe. You could say that hoeing was his school. He had no choice; he had to help his mother. Jozef's father was an invalid. Each morning he would sharpen the scythe, get the tools ready, and then return to his bed. In the evening he would check on how his family was doing. Little silhouettes would wave to him from the vineyard.

"My mother-in-law says you have to talk to the grapes and caress them all the time."

Alex didn't want to go inside, preferring to drive off and escape from Erika. "It's such a long way back to Stará Ruda, and driving in the dark..."

"You have to come in for a little while. What will it look like if you don't?"

Petra and Anna were stepping inside the house, and Alex reluctantly joined them.

"Welcome one and all, come in!"

Erika's mother-in-law shook hands with everyone, and then they went out to the yard pleasantly shaded by grapevines. The sun was still high but was on its way down.

"We won't stay long..." said Alex tactfully, but Anna interrupted him.

"How are you doing, Auntie?"

"It looks like we're going to have a good wine harvest, at least a ton. And the sugar content doesn't look bad either."

Erika knew her sister had no idea about winemaking, but in any case, her mother-in-law quickly found a new conversation partner. "Petra dear, are you a doctor now?"

"Almost, Auntie."

"You know, I have this nagging pain right here. What do you think it is?"

Petra seriously considered the problem. She had gotten questions like that from the moment she was accepted into medical school. People would stop her and share their diagnoses with her, and she spent many anxious moments cursing her own ignorance before she finally figured out that they just needed to relieve their anxiety. They didn't care that she was a mere student; they needed clarity.

Jozef returned from the vineyard and went to the faucet to wash his hands. His little son watched with curiosity as the clay disappeared from Jozef's hands in a stream of brown water. These were not the hands of a pastor or an actor, but of a hard-working man.

After his military service, Jozef had once again been refused ordination unless he met the previous condition of becoming an informer. He had to take care of his family, but no one would hire him. They wanted to starve him into submission. Without rhyme or reason he was taken on as a delivery boy for the printing plant. He studied acting during the day, and at night he delivered bundles of newspapers to the main railway station. He was permanently exhausted. During the student performance of Agatha Christie's *The Mousetrap* he dozed off on stage in front of the audience.

Otherwise, he had done well as a student and received scholarships for social reasons and for his excellent grades. He had no choice but to be good. In the first year as an actor he was invited to apply to Slovak Radio because of his excellent speaking voice. From then on, he regularly read the news on air at one and two o'clock in the afternoon.

When Viliam Záborský, the college's speech coach and future dean, recognized Jozef's voice on the radio, he was enraged. Who permitted this? How dare he? He'll spoil his diction! His speech will run to weed! How can he read in public without the permission of the university? The great actor Ladislav Chudík saved Jozef by saying that he had authorized the job and that Jozef could complete his studies. Jozef graduated but didn't join a theater troupe.

The setting sun gilded the courtyard where they were sitting. A similar light bathed the lives of Erika and Jozef that year. It seemed that the little weasel with invaluable fur called happiness had finally arrived on their doorstep. For people like them this meant that the authorities would leave them to their respectable occupations. What else could one want in the summer of 1968?

"Well, we should go. I don't want to drive in the dark. And you have a visitor."

Alex nodded at the man with whom Jozef's father had been debating for ten minutes, his hands writing entire sentences in the air while the guest sat with sagging shoulders, a pained smile on his face.

The man was a writer who lived nearby. As an invalid, Jozef's father had more time than anyone else and was a passionate reader, getting through a book every day. His preference was for contemporary Slovak prose. People brought him crates of literature, making him one of the best-read men around, although he didn't know it. He was able to analyze what he read in an interesting way and managed to grasp the substance of each work, not like the critics, but by using his own logic and the kind of shortcuts that only flash into farmers' minds.

If he had written book reviews he would have gained an appreciative audience, but he never wrote anything. Why should he, after all? He would lie all day near his window, and in the evening authors would come to visit him. His offers of sausage and wine ensured that he always had a full house. But some authors had to pay for their meal; if their book didn't meet with approval, the wine stuck in their throats. That was the case on this day.

Alex and Anna were saying their goodbyes. While Petra gave Jozef's mother her final medical advice, his father was gripping the prose writer's arm in a way that was clearly meant to be friendly, but still looked like he was trying to keep him from escaping. He had hypnotized the writer like a python hypnotizes a rabbit. "Jano, you're a good man but a shitty writer. Your latest book is simply no good. Please tell me, who is the main hero? What kind of man is he? I don't understand him. Why does he do what he does? Jano, you should have reworked the book."

The author was miserable. If he'd waited a few weeks to publish the novel he could have done so much more with it! To make things worse, the state press had cancelled censorship just a few days ago. Now books could be published without censorship! The writer was frustrated by what he had missed. Why did he rush his manuscript to the publisher? He could have waited! Who would have guessed that you would be allowed to write in a more courageous manner? Oh my God! There were some indications that this was coming, and some writers had actually become more daring, but he had preferred to remain cautious. His foresight had never failed him until now. But no matter! Beginning tomorrow he would write courageously in a new manner, and his characters would be people of flesh and bone and with their own minds. That was what he wanted to shout, but instead he was silent. The winemaker's critique had burned him like a premature frost.

Alex was glad to be sitting in his Felicia rather than under the vine-draped pergola listening to criticisms of his work, though he had never written anything. Finally the car loaded with Petra's things drove off in the direction of Stará Ruda.

Turbine

"Turn it up!"

"It disturbs your father when he drives."

"Then why do we bring the transistor radio with us, Mom?"

"All right, all right, turn it on, Petra."

"It's Uncle Jozef!"

"Is he broadcasting? We just said good-bye to him!"

"It's a repeat broadcast."

"Why is he doing *Watch Out for the Turn* when he doesn't even own a car?"

"In a normal country he would have one."

"Erika told me they're thinking of buying a used Škoda."

"What is a 'normal country,' my dear?"

"It's a country where people are allowed to study what they want to and what they have a talent for."

"For heaven's sake, stop!"

"Well, you're in medicine, Petra. It's an elite school. Many would have loved to make it in."

"I got in because you work for Sanola."

"They accepted you because you did the best in the entrance exams. You were the best of all of them. You didn't need Sanola."

"Don't make your father angry!"

"Still, it's terrible what they did to Uncle Jozef."

"If you don't stop, I'll get out."

"I didn't do anything to Jozef."

"I mean those who oppose the clergymen."

"I haven't destroyed a single clergyman."

"Not you, but your kind!"

"What do you mean 'your kind?"

"Watch the road, Dad."

"By the way, the Party acknowledged its mistakes. Now we can talk about anything. The Stalinists are gone and young people have taken over the leadership. Nobody has to keep silent about anything."

"Nobody? Nobody?"

"Won't you two just stop?"

"What have I done? I'm watching the road and driving! What do I care about clergymen?"

"Slow down. It looks like there's been an accident."

"That's not an accident."

"They're transporting something."

"Oh my God, we won't make it home till morning."

"It's a turbine."

"It's beautiful, isn't it?"

"How can anyone like a turbine?"

"You father likes model trains. Leave him alone."

"Do you think the poets of socialist construction get turned on by hydroelectric dams?"

"What?"

"I mean sexually."

"I guess I'd rather you talk about the Communists."

"Mom, come on!"

"Well, you raised a doctor, so get used to it!"

"When someone is turned on by a dam they're sexually deviant. A Soviet psychiatrist named Lesnitsky first wrote about it when he was treating the builders of Soviet hydroelectric dams."

"You're making that up."

"They would get an erection as soon as they heard water rushing through the discharge canal."

"I'm worried about you, Petra."

"You can't take a joke."

"I'm actually finding this interesting."

"It's called hydroelectrophilia."

"Can't we take a shortcut?"

"No."

"If we'd set out earlier, we'd be home already. Every night there's some kind of convoy on the road."

"I know my sister bothers you."

"What bothers me is the turbine ahead of me."

"You've always been against my family."

"I like Erika, and I also like her husband, as well as Luther, Calvin, and Hus, all of them."

"Sometimes I don't understand you, Alexander."

"Mother, don't argue."

"If I have to drive another ten minutes behind this turbine, I'll get a stroke. Or I'll get that hydro...whatever."

"Hydroelectrophilia."

"Right."

Masaryk

The first President of Czechoslovakia, Thomas Garrigue Masaryk, was an icon not only for the majority of the population, but also for those who left the country for various reasons and spread throughout the world. Some, accepted by Israel, founded kibbutzes.

One kibbutz was named after the President Liberator. Lithuanian settlers, mostly women, had originally founded it under a different name in 1932. The group needed men so they teamed up with Jewish settlers from Czechoslovakia. Later some Polish Jews joined them. The farm found its definitive place and name in 1940. Kibbutz Masaryk, or Kfar Masaryk in Hebrew, was where Tereza and the rest of Mňačko's children were headed. It took several connecting flights for them to reach Tel Aviv. When Tereza got off the plane and stepped down the stairs, she felt as if doused with a bucket of water. The humidity combined with the high temperature was a shock to young people arriving from a mild climate.

"It's so hot here, we don't even feel like kissing."

Before their departure, they had been confined to a hotel on the outskirts of Vienna for security reasons. This was a time of terrorist attacks on anything related to the Star of David. Those days in the hotel became an endless party, with everyone agreeing to sleep it off in Israel. They fell asleep on the plane and woke up in Tel Aviv. Buses waiting at the airport took them north, to near Haifa.

The kibbutz most resembled a giant garden, and the program for the next few weeks reminded them of their favorite school subject—working on a farm, except no one could take it easy here. They met some kibbutzniks soon after leaving their buses, but the rest were laboring in the fields, and they didn't meet them until evening.

Tereza noticed how surprised the locals were at the sight of the well-dressed young people. The last complement had arrived after the Communist putsch of 1948. When one is forced into exile, one's place of origin becomes frozen in time. Memories tend to become idealized, while one's new situation seems incomparably bleak.

The kibbutzniks expected the new arrivals to be poor; people could not live with dignity in a country taken over by Communists. Every emigrant subconsciously wished that it was terrible, however loath they might be to admit it, because that lessened the pain of leaving.

They knew that young people full of joy and laughter would arrive, but they didn't expect them to arrive dressed in the latest fashion and carrying elegant handbags and stuffed suitcases. Tereza wrote to her parents, "They're surprised at how nicely dressed we are. Did they expect us to live in trees and eat earthworms?"

The kibbutzniks wore khaki-colored shorts, t-shirts and sandals, along with the notorious pointed headgear dubbed "the madman's hat." Tereza recalled the recruiting posters inviting Jews from all over the world to come and live in Israel, which showed exactly these kinds of kibbutzniks with wide smiles and a clear goal in life.

The guests were assigned housing in pairs in wooden huts, and the very next day they were taken to the fields. Working there is how they came to know Israel. Within a few days they all began to resemble the characters in the posters, except Tereza, of course, and a few other individuals who wore at least one unusual piece of attire to the fields. Tereza put on the biggest earrings she had been able to squeeze into her luggage, which she called her hula-hoop rings.

The locals gradually became used to the new arrivals, who in turn got used to the locals. Initial misgivings about city kids from a distant country being dropped off on a farm vanished as they began to fulfill Ladislav Mňačko's plan of getting to know a mysterious country with a contradictory reputation.

Paradoxically, the kibbutz was ideologically similar to Czechoslovakia, an island of socialism in the middle of capitalist Israel.

All kibbutzniks were equal and had the same standing. Everything was distributed according to need—work, food, and money. Kitchen duty and working in the kindergarten or in the fields were organized by rotation, and everyone had to take part. The money the kibbutz made paid everyone's salary, a sum too small to take a girl out in the city. But why would they? The kibbutz had girls and every other necessity. Everyone was given two pairs of pants and three shirts per year. It was a modest life.

They would get up at five thirty in the morning. The day started in a common bathroom followed by breakfast in a dining hall, where they were presented with more fruits and vegetables than any of them would ever see again. After a healthy breakfast they would pile into trucks that took them to the fields. Tereza worked in a pear orchard; others cultivated vegetables and grapes, and some helped out at the fishponds. On weekends, the locals took them to Haifa for a taste of city life.

A few days after their arrival they experienced a *khatuna*: a wedding. The whole kibbutz celebrated the marriage of a young pilot who was about to leave for military duty. Slovak girls seemed much more conservative than Israelis, who started going out with boys much earlier and also started their sexual life earlier. The women also had military duty. In a country permanently at war, one never knew when one would be sent to fight, so young people wanted to experience as much as they could in the little time left to them. They matured faster and also lived faster.

Tereza observed the Israeli women with interest. Back home her impression had been that they were mostly darker women with black hair, but the street was full of beautiful blondes, their figures slender from military training or the dietary restrictions of their faith. They all seemed experienced and confident. To the Israelis, on the other hand, the Slovaks seemed too high strung. Tereza and the other girls felt that the Slovak boys were bound to drop them in favor of the local girls.

But their jealousy passed a few days later as news came that the recently married young man had been killed in action. As they all gathered in the dining room Tereza was astonished by their cheerfulness. Rather than mentioning the young man's death they celebrated his life: the kind of man he was, what they'd experienced with him and all the positive things he'd done. After all, he wouldn't want them crying for him.

They got along very well with David, who was called Corky because of his small stature and short arms that made him look like a walking cork. Slovaks of the older generation, including the writer of this book, who are familiar with the writer Hana Ponická knew of Corky as a story book character who one day popped out of a bottle of sour wine and began living his own life. Ponická was a courageous woman who lost her job after signing Charter 77, and subsequent generations grew up without knowing Corky, who never returned to his bottle, but was recycled.

Getting back to the Israeli Corky, David already had a nickname among the locals, who called him Machinist. When the first attacks against Israel took place, the army had Czechoslovakian weaponry, but the operating instructions for the tanks were in Slovak. During a feverish attempt to find a translator, David was discovered. He would climb into a tank and translate everything, giving rise to his nickname.

While in Haifa, Tereza liked to visit a family that made ice cream, and she helped the daughters sell it. Standing behind the counter and serving up the cold little mounds gave her great satisfaction, and she ate enough ice cream to last her a year.

The local people reminded her of her mother and father in that they also did not force their daughters to be overly religious. When she joined them in going to the synagogue, she stopped in front of the gate and looked around.

"Why are you looking around?"

"To see if anyone is observing me. In Bratislava I try to get in as quickly as possible. Not just me, all of us."

"Are you ashamed of being Jewish?"

"No, but State Security..."

"What's that?"

"The Secret Police. There's a window opposite the synagogue where they secretly film everyone who enters, you see?"

"What for?"

Tereza threw up her hands. How can you explain the unexplainable?

"No idea. Let's go."

They went up to the balcony reserved for women and girls, and Tereza found a place with a view similar to that at home. She closed her eyes as the cantor's singing transported her thousands of kilometers away...

She was standing in the synagogue in Bratislava, resting her left shoulder against the wall as she shifted her weight from one foot to the other in boredom. As usual, when the ceremony took too long, she had slipped into the garden to socialize with her girlfriends. The parents let them leave rather than putting up with their disruption. Many parents never taught their children Hebrew, wishing to protect them. They were supposed to blend in with rest of the population, but that was impossible; they felt increasingly set apart and learned to be free in the small space exclusive to them.

The courtyard of the synagogue on Heyduk Street was surrounded by a tall fence and seemed created for quiet meetings. Even the birds in the trees seemed to sing sweetly about it. Here, in Haifa, so incredibly far away, the courtyard in Bratislava seemed dearer to Tereza than ever. Many friendships and even marriages had been born there, including Tereza's, although she didn't know that yet.

This was where she had met Milan, and she was thinking about him again. She knew that he and his family had driven to Yugoslavia in their new Škoda 1000 MB. She smiled at the thought of the car's trunk packed with the canned food and camping stove that Czechoslovakian tourists always took along when visiting a foreign country. She imagined Milan in the back seat, surrounded by sleeping bags and holding a thermos of coffee in his hand. Now he's probably breathing the same salty air as I am, Tereza thought.

She happily anticipated reuniting with him in Bratislava after their vacations.

Little Motor

Alexander didn't let his colleagues know about his little railway, which was remarkable, given that visitors came to the apartment up to five times per week. His car made him exotic enough, and each additional eccentricity would make him more vulnerable.

There was miniature countryside with artificial trees (you could distinguish coniferous from deciduous trees, and there were also birch trees) on a hilly terrain, with paved roads and white milestones with black stripes guiding cars to a gas station, in front of which a miniature Wartburg (of East German origin, as were all the little trains, houses, and people) was gassing up. It all betrayed the owner's desire to create his own universe and suggested an intriguing question: "Comrade Engineer, is our beautiful world not good enough for you?"

Or to put it differently: "Why don't you like our socialist reality?" Should he answer that his world was actually a miniature socialist paradise, another question might follow: "Are you suggesting that we're too small to survive? Your parents weren't Party members, were they? We know that they were landowners, Comrade Engineer, and that your grandfather was an exploiter. And now you're a leading employee in a key factory that supplies the entire socialist camp with medical instruments?"

It would be safer to pretend to engage in hobbies better tolerated by the authorities: making wooden objects with a coping saw, gardening, making honey from dandelions, or lying under a car that was constantly broken down. But Alex was a sociable person. He liked having people over and also liked to visit them. All of their guests would end up in their living room, where the modern cave dweller fixed his gaze not on a fire, but on the screen of a black-and-white Orava television.

Each guest had to try the White Venus or Cloister Red for routine visits, or for deluxe visits a sparkling wine from Sered' that unenlightened people (including this writer) called champagne for decades. Next came open-face sandwiches with potato salad, mayonnaise, boiled eggs and ham, and sweet and savory baked goods. Like many other women, Anna expressed love especially by baking.

They lived in a two-and-a-half room apartment rented from the state. It was made of honest whitewashed brick, and all of the rooms had hardwood floors. The half room was actually a child's room, a bit larger than the old-fashioned servants' quarters, but working people no longer exploited servants. And why should they? Women continued to do all the drudgery right into the third millennium. Petra lived in the room only when she left her sublet on the weekends. Her room included a narrow couch and a little desk with a shelf; there was no space for a wardrobe.

Our tour ends in the main bedroom, which is where Alex, that cruiser of married life, hid his miniature railway under their joined beds.

Nobody had an inkling of his passion until a female guest became unwell—she was pregnant—and the hosts had her lie on their eiderdown. She didn't notice the electrical cables running under the bed until she ended her ten-minute rest by stepping on a switch and was startled by the gentle noise under her feet.

Since Alex's only child was a girl, he was obliged to tell the truth: This thing on the floor that buzzed, glowed, rattled, hummed, scraped, gleamed, and trembled was his secret child.

"The gauge is HO."

That was all he said. When the visitors left, he added, "Did she have to step right on the switch?"

"But she was green, didn't you notice? She was sick."

"Did you vacuum before they came?"

"Well, we aren't going to breathe dust just for your sake!"

It was her fault! His wife's! The tip of the vacuum cleaner had bumped the switch (which he had so carefully hidden) under the bed. Slamming the door behind him, Alex went out in an old flannel shirt (without buttons, to keep from scratching the paint) to polish his Felicia, though it was already quite shiny. He knew what would follow.

The very next day a joke circulated around Sanola that Alex kept a little train under his bed for him and his wife to strengthen the sacrament of marriage, and which sped up or slowed down according to their sexual tempo. "And at the end, it toots when it leaves the tunnel!"

The train revelation soured Alex on his hometown. The mountains, meadows, and sidewalks were tolerable, but he cared less for the people who walked along them. Stará Ruda had officially become a town in 1962, but in terms of the relationships among its residents, it remained at the village level. Everyone knew everyone else and could see into each other's bedrooms as well.

Now he sat at the kitchen table, slowly removing screws from the locomotive, which fit into his palm like a dead sparrow. He carefully removed the plastic chassis with its smokestack and checked the tiny motor, where he found one of the contacts torn off.

With the push of a button, Alex's soldering iron lit up. He dipped the red-hot wire in rosin and then touched it against the tin. The smell of burned rosin reminded him of the forest, and the liquid tin evoked a raindrop. He blew gently on the new contact. He placed the skeletal locomotive on the rails and switched on the electricity. The little bird leaped from his hand and began whirring as its motor revved ...

The motor of Czechoslovakia was also running full throttle and the country progressed by leaps and bounds. Once-closed windows were opening, the abundance of fresh air intoxicated people. Purposeful reforms launched by those in power were taking place, introducing an explosive palette of colors after decades of grey, intimidating the Communists in the state structure with their boldness.

The social reforms started with politicians at the top, but this story views them from below, from the point of view of the pawns on a chessboard. In 1968 the people of Czechoslovakia lived by politics as seldom before or after. They lived with the hopes they had sincerely invested in one political party. There were no others. The Communists were so unbelievably popular that people trusted their every word and were ready to sacrifice themselves as never before. The names of politicians were heard not only in the press, radio, and television, but also in daily conversations in shops, at bus stops, in factories, around the dinner table, in the park, everywhere.

Writing a story about these years means mentioning those names. If you mention D, you also have to mention C and E, and of course, H. But because fiction involves the art of selection, here is my selection: I leave out the names that electrified our mothers and fathers and that buzzed around our ears as children until we waved them away. They initiated great historical events, but my concern is the history of the little people. The politicians pushed the car of history into motion from above, but it careened down the hill, taking with it many of those who climbed on along the way. History has not bothered to remember those trusting and nameless people who were crushed under the wheels of history, their bloodied corpses hurled into the bushes alongside the tracks.

Therefore, no politicians will be named here. They don't deserve it.

Heart

Jozef was broadcasting on the *Good Morning* program. While Edith Piaf finished her song, regretting nothing, but absolutely nothing, he managed to smoke another cigarette by the open window. Dawn was breaking and the silhouette of Bratislava Castle was emerging. The ruins below the castle looked like a film set through which blue and white police cars and the morning's first early pedestrians were passing. It was time.

He sat down in his armchair just as the sound technician cued him with his hand. A red light turned on and his voice flew into thousands of homes whose occupants were just waking up.

"Good morning, dear listeners: I cannot resist repeating something that surprised all of us yesterday and filled us with joy as the first news of the day. Yesterday, on July 9, 1968, in Bratislava Clinic Number 2, led by Professor Karol Šiška, the first heart transplant in the socialist bloc was performed. The team of surgeons was led by Doctor Ladislav Kužela, who spoke with our colleague."

Jozef looked at the technician. The recorded tape started to roll and the studio was filled with the voice of the doctor.

"The operation was very demanding from the point of view of the surgical procedure, but also due to the available equipment. We used a special pump made by a specialist from the Sanola Company in Stará Ruda. The pump diverted blood from the heart while we worked on it. The blood was cooled in order to lower the risk of damaging the organism, and at the same time, it had to be oxygenated in place of the non-functioning lungs. The oxygenated blood was returned to the patient's body. The donor's heart was ready to be used, resting in a special ice solution. Several surgical groups had to work simultaneously: one took out the heart of the donor and another, our group, had to transplant it."

"Comrade Doctor, could you explain to our listeners how it is possible to replace a complex organ like the heart?"

"We used the method successfully tried out by Professor Barnard in Cape Town. As you know, he was the first to transplant a human heart. The main thing is, we're only exchanging the heart muscle and attaching the donor's heart to the vasculature of the recipient. We have to work very fast to prevent irreversible damage to the donor organ and the body of the recipient."

"What did you do after attaching the heart?"

"We started warming the patient, using the same instrument we used to cool the blood. When we reached the desired temperature, we used electroshock to revive the new heart. It was very rewarding for all of us to observe the heart starting to pump and how it was beating."

"The public watched your excellent effort. How do you feel about being the first in the socialist camp to achieve this?"

"The first person in the world to receive a transplanted heart, Louis Washkansky, lived for eighteen days. We face dozens of questions about how to help the body accept a new organ. The body is defending itself against an invader and produces antibodies to get rid of it. We have to prevent this in the future. Technically our operation was a success. We transplanted a new heart that began to beat, but it lasted only five hours. Nevertheless, it's a giant step for our socialist healthcare."

"Comrade Doctor, I thank you for this conversation."

Jozef cued the technician and approached the microphone.

"Dear listeners, to make your way to work more pleasant, I will now play this song by Marta Kubišová."

The technician was ready and the dark-haired beauty began singing her hit song "Lamp." Jozef turned his head in what he thought must be the direction of Clinic Number 2, only a few hundred meters away. A workday was beginning behind its raw brick walls. Other patients were being prepped for their operations and metal oxygen bottles were banging as doctors finished their morning coffee. Maybe the cold body of Charlotte Horvath from Bratislava still rested there: the first to die with an alien heart in her chest.

Is five hours of life too little or too much? Was it worth it? It was obviously the patient's last chance, and she agreed to everything as she was sentenced to death. There was always the possibility that she would last a day, a week, or a month, as was seen in Cape Town...

Jozef was already thinking about his own problems. The day before he had broadcast a story about parents offering bribes to get their children accepted into medical school. A radio executive became really upset about that story, possibly after a phone call from outside. Jozef had heard rumors that he could expect to be released from his broadcasting duties until further notice and that today's *Good Morning* broadcast would be his last for a long time. He didn't yet know that he would only be banned for a month and a half, and that the decision would be spontaneously reversed by an event that would turn this small state upside down, along with the lives of millions of its inhabitants.

Our first patient lived five hours after her operation. In 1968, all of Czechoslovakia tried to exchange its old heart for a new one. It lived for three hundred days.

Lake

Petra lay on the beach, the gravel etching patterns on her skin. Rudník Lake was not created by Mother Nature, but by employees of Sanola National Enterprises, who built a dam and cleaned up what became the bottom of the lake. The stream gradually filled the valley, and only a small artificial island remained above the water as a natural destination for swimming competitions and quick sex. Petra still vaguely remembered her mother and father returning from the brigade on the bed of the truck like a battle unit, singing of happiness. Instead of weapons, they carried shovels and rakes.

The mother of her youth wore a scarf on her head like all women did, whether in the city or in a village, whether office workers or factory workers protecting themselves from scalping by a spinning lathe. The scarf was the icon of the farmer's wife, the symbol of the proletariat, and the elegant accessory of an urban lady.

Petra couldn't remember her father dressed in anything but a suit and tie. Unlike his colleagues Alex wore his executive uniform in a becoming manner. It was impossible for her to imagine her father as a man in a truck bed dressed like everyone else and singing with them about the youth of Communist leader Gottwald and about ordering the wind to blow and the rain to fall. It would have been even more incredible if he hadn't joined a brigade, but she had never seen him in overalls. Even when he had to crawl under his car he would wear an older pair of dress pants. Who knows how it was in those days?

Lying on her belly, Petra squinted at the beach around her. The heat hummed and energy rose from the water as insects flew everywhere, drawn by the sun. The lakeshore was filled with vacationing children. The little ones were having fun riding a partially submerged carousel, while the older ones glided back and forth on metal swings and the eldest kids pulled their way along ropes that connect the shore to a metallic tripod anchored in the lake. It looked like a giant spider, with the Sanola trademark replacing its head.

Foreign tourists usually flocked to Stará Ruda's top summer attraction, but this year they stayed away. Who would have guessed that the Soviet Union's Sputnik Tourist Agency would cancel all trips to Czechoslovakia? Foreign countries were warning their citizens against visiting and the French, Spaniards, English, and West Germans were fleeing, emptying the Carlsbad and Piešťany spas within hours. The noose of friendly armies was tightening around the country in a way that didn't seem friendly at all.

It started in June with military maneuvers in Poland and East Germany. Then the exercise moved into Czechoslovakia under the codename Šumava. This latter maneuver was supposed to be the Trojan horse to get the Soviet armies in with no resistance. They did come and carry out exercises in the borderlands, but the government managed to negotiate their departure, leaving the country paradoxically again empty as a garage.

All of this was endlessly discussed in the papers and on radio and television. People also discussed it in daily conversation, but life went on. A military attack was simply unimaginable. It hung over them like a cloud in the sky and wound through their minds like an echo, impossible to dismiss. The stress of waiting was balanced by the everyday portion of hope, which grew day after day.

Petra found it impossible to relax. She couldn't stop thinking about her recent discussion with the head doctor. She had been accepted as a junior consulting doctor in the hospital's internal medicine department and was supposed to start the following week. The hospital was in Trenčin, which meant a daily commute of at least an hour in each direction.

They offered the possibility of a hostel, but the prospect of a common shower and cooking on an electric plate reminded her of the student dormitory she'd escaped.

The distance from home was the only drawback her future presented. She was looking forward to the hospital. She couldn't wait to see her patients and release the pressure of all the knowledge she had accumulated, while at the same time she was beginning to realize with horror that this knowledge might not last.

The knowledge she had gained was starting to slowly disappear, so as she sunbathed she tested her knowledge. For a week now, she had been following the alphabet, asking herself a question on a subject starting with each letter in turn, and forcing herself to answer right away. She was silent, but her lips moved, and she was unaware of how strange she looked.

Upon reaching CH: Chondrocyte, she had suddenly found herself unable to recall its histological picture, and ice-cold sweat drenched her. From then on, she brought her textbook to the beach. All her life she had lacked confidence, afraid that she would fail as a doctor. She realized that as a beginner she had the right to make mistakes, but she was also aware that a doctor could make a mistake only once.

She studied every day until sunset and was one of the last to leave the beach. In the meantime, her parents tried to find housing for her. Alex, the realist, began working all of his contacts and started applying for a coop apartment in Trenčin.

Anna, on the other hand, planned to repaint the room the "little one" occupied and equip it with more functional furniture. It's hard to know if life exists after life, but work after work was the engine of

Czechoslovakia's grey economy. Anna went to a local cabinetmaker with an Austrian furniture catalogue that had been passed from family to family like a forbidden publication. It gave people hope with its visions of a beautiful and practical life—the possibility of being someone who put things away in a pine dresser or hid their bedding in a bin with wheels.

Imagining her daughter's beautiful new room was only the first step. She was also preparing a speech to persuade her husband to let their daughter use their bedroom while they slept in the living room. Alex's railway stood in the way of this courageous plan, but Anna suddenly felt equal to any challenge. She sensed her daughter's insecurity and wanted a few more years with her before she embarked on her independent life.

Alexander, next to her, was in a deep sleep. When he turned on the bed, the trains beneath him rattled gently. Life was good. Anna fell asleep as happy as she could be. It was the night of August 20th in the year 1968.

Tanks

The weather had been exceptionally sultry for quite a long time. The apartment building on Kmeť' Square absorbed the sun's rays during the day in order to release them on its inhabitants after sunset. Just as the heat always failed in wintertime, the concrete walls could be relied on to overheat every summer. In a country where air conditioning was not yet a standard feature, no one expected otherwise.

What no one expected was the column of trucks, armored vehicles, and tanks advancing down the square. The roar of transport helicopters filled the air, and gigantic Antonov transport planes were landing one after another. With the windows of every Bratislava home thrown open against the heat, many people immediately knew what made headlines a few hours later all over the world. The occupation of Czechoslovakia had begun.

Jozef was running at the time. He had no idea who was chasing him, but he ran as if his life depended on it. But his legs refused to obey him, as if gravity had increased tenfold. He was sweating. The shadow of his pursuer drew closer. Suddenly it caught up with him and with its ghostly paw grabbed him and placed him under a bell made of shiny metal. Jozef crouched, barely fitting under it. In the middle was a steel axis with two balancing balls that suddenly began to rotate, hitting the bell. In a millisecond he understood three things: he was inside a gigantic bicycle bell, he had to crouch to avoid being crushed by the balancing balls, and nothing would really happen, because he was dreaming…

"That idiot will wake the boy!"

The telephone was ringing. He angrily snatched up the receiver. It must be the porter from the radio station, who liked to drink all night and then ring up the announcers to tell them not to be late for their morning broadcast. He always called too early, so all of them had to clear their heads with strong coffee.

But this time it was their neighbor.

"Mr. Rola, the Russians are here," she said.

"I beg your pardon?"

"The Russians are here!"

She hung up. Jozef stood with the receiver in his hand. The bicycle bell was still echoing in his mind as he became aware of a constant hum from the city center. As he went to the window, Erika, still in her housecoat, embraced him and burst out crying.

"What's going to happen to us?"

"I have to get to the radio station."

A man on a bicycle speeds through Bratislava at night, pushing through the stuffy air that envelops his body and dries his sweat. The man is not crying. The man is very, very angry. He is offended. He is thoroughly humiliated. He gulps. Gnats strike his face from time to time. The man passes a column of trucks, where the tired faces of soldiers look out at him. As a schoolboy, he had seen a huge poster on the wall of his classroom with dozens of figures dressed in national costumes—they were "the brotherly nations of the Soviet Union." Now this poster comes alive among the figures sitting in the trucks. Wide faces, Asian features, slanted eyes, prominent cheekbones, blond hair under military hats. None of them smile at the man, and he tries not to look at them. People dressed in pajamas look into the street from open windows and gesture threateningly at the tanks. The man knows he's experiencing history. He knows that his wife and son and his country are butter and history is the knife. And he also knows that somebody is spreading them on bread and is getting ready to take a bite this very second.

The man wants nothing more than to live a boring life, but in the land of his birth it is not possible. So he pushes hard enough on his pedals to break his personal record, though nobody will know. Upon reaching the radio building, he leans his bicycle against the wall without bothering to lock it with the chain as he normally does. When he leaves, the bicycle will still be there, surrounded by tanks and hundreds of people. In another time, it would have been stolen, but in the days that follow crime all but disappears in Czechoslovakia as the underworld voluntarily limits its activities so as not to increase the chaos that seeks to envelop the country with its prickly cloak.

"I'll show those Russians!" the radio porter threatened, no longer trying to hide the red currant wine that filled his mineral water bottle. He obsessively cleaned his service pistol, even sacrificing his shirt to polish the barrel in preparation for action.

"We won't let them get away with it!"

Even if the army didn't act, he would! A magazine lay on the table, along with a spring and a few parts. The pistol was turning into a pile of shiny parts that his hands would turn into a weapon again.

Jozef ran into his office. It was his first day back at work after his suspension. He knew his country was balancing on the point of a needle, but he naïvely believed, like millions of others, that the world would not allow anything to happen.

But the world did allow it. The Russians were not prepared to watch a courageous state try to squirm out of the socialist camp they had managed to create after the war. The Hungarians had tried it twelve years ago, and now it was the turn of the Czechs and Slovaks.

"What are we going to broadcast?"

"We're taking over the Prague broadcast. They turned off their broadcasting and only their local cable radio works."

Jozef held a statement by the top representatives of Slovakia, which had just been phoned in. He passed his eyes over it a few times to avoid a misreading, although at this moment, listeners dying for information would excuse him anything. He read the first declaration at four thirty in the morning, and then after a musical interlude he read another more substantial one. Finally, the words that move people to this day, including the author of this book, materialized from the ether:

"To all the people of the Czechoslovak Socialist Republic! Yesterday, on August 20, 1968, at twenty-three hundred hours, the armies of the Soviet Union, the Polish People's Republic, the German Democratic Republic, the Hungarian People's Republic, and the Bulgarian People's Republic crossed the border of the Czechoslovak Socialist Republic. This happened without the knowledge of the President of the Republic, the Chairman of the National Assembly, the Prime Minister, or the First Secretary of the Central Committee of the Communist Party of Czechoslovakia. We are asking all people to keep the peace and not to resist the advancing armies. That is why our Army, Security Forces, and People's Militias have been ordered not to defend our country. The leadership of the Central Committee of the Communist Party considers this act as a violation of all principles governing the relations of the socialist countries, as well as the norms of international law."

And so on. The sky was getting brighter and the streets were filling with people. Rather than go to work, they stood on the sidewalks and talked to the soldiers. But it was a monologue. The soldiers seemed surprised at how well we spoke Russian. What a good province! They had no idea that Russian was the only compulsory foreign language taught in all of our schools—not out of an ardent love for the nation of

Chekhov and Tolstoy, but because of the decision of politicians. Some clever pedagogues managed to see to it that decadent French or English was taught to a minimal number of children.

There was no discussion; the officers wouldn't allow it. When anyone in the crowd touched the tanks, soldiers fired warning shots into the air. The mob retreated gently after the shots, but then returned, not to fight, but to shout the most popular Russian word of the day: WHY?

Shortly before eight that morning, Soviet soldiers entered the radio building. One of them, holding a Kalashnikov machine gun, pushed Jozef away from the microphone. It was impossible to broadcast anyway. The soldiers shot the cables, and Bratislava Radio was dead. The tread of military boots echoed throughout the building as people were expelled from their offices. The smoke of burning cables hung in the hallways.

Looking out the window, Jozef noticed technicians taking equipment out of the building so they could continue broadcasting. This day gave birth to thousands of anonymous heroes; if their identities were revealed, the consequences would be fatal. Jozef had no idea that in a moment he would become one of them.

People filled the streets like a human river. Motors rumbled as some tanks remained stationary while others started up and belched black exhaust. Turning on its axis, a tank raised sparks on the paving stones. Lovely young girls in miniskirts looked disdainfully at soldiers who did not yet realize that they were engaged in lawlessness, but who understood very well that if beauties despised them, something must have really gone wrong.

Some people stood along the walls of buildings while others carried the Czechoslovak flag and sang the national anthem. All that gratitude for the blood Russians had spilled in the fight for Bratislava in 1945 turned into crystal-clear hatred in a twinkling. This would not be forgotten for generations.

It was a hot day, and people dressed in light summer clothing were rushing to the university, where the occupying army had shot a young girl. The captain of a Danube trawler fell elsewhere. Improvised altars made of bricks appeared on the pavement wherever drying blood was found. Pedestrians stood around with somber faces or crowded around the radio building with the castle silhouetted in the background. Among many speakers the famous actor Záborský began reciting, and people who had previously underestimated poetry finally understood what it was all about. The crowd was electrified as a century-old poem raised goosebumps.

Some stood and cried, some clenched their hands into fists, some painted on the wall "Lenin, wake up! Brezhnev has lost his mind!," and others quickly bought up everything that might come in handy. The stores quickly emptied, but there were still a few more products to put in the basket. People needed supplies. Who knew if this would result in war?

Everyone on the streets, near the trucks, in the stores, on the sidewalks, lining up for gas fell silent when the clock struck twelve: to start fighting? No. To start sounding their car horns and sirens and ringing bells. This was the signal for the national strike that interrupted the motors and the shooting of the invaders for a moment.

We shouted and felt better, and Bratislava churches rang their bells, all those sounds joining in the kind of cacophonic accord that had become common in what was imprecisely referred to as serious music in those times. The protest had a musical quality because we are a people of musical gestures.

We are a nation sentenced to tenderness. Such a nation is easy to occupy.

"My little one, thank God!"

"Don't cry Anna, I beg of you..."

"I've been trying to get through by phone since morning, Erika! I hope you're being careful! Don't go out! We're watching a TV channel from Vienna and they're showing fighting going on in Bratislava!"

"Anna, please, there's no fighting, or at least I don't know of any, and everyone has been told not to resist."

"There were airplanes flying here all night long. They say there are paratroopers in the hills where they have a broadcast antenna."

"Luckily you're far away from Bratislava."

"They said some children were shot dead. Is little Peter all right?"

"I didn't take him to kindergarten. We're reading fairy tales to him. What's Alex doing?"

"They've been in a meeting all day. Sanola has called a holiday, but everyone came to work. I've never seen anything like it. By the way, I was listening to Jozef, but they turned him off."

"What is Lajo saying?"

"He disappeared."

"Typical."

"Don't say that, Erika. He's our brother."

"I feel sorry for him. If he's the kind of Communist he pretends to be, he should feel really bad."

"I'm sure he does. He can't have wanted this."

"And who did? Did you? Did I?"

"Erika, for heaven's sake..."

"I'm sorry, Annie, my nerves are shot, don't be angry with me. No, Peter, I'm not crying... I'm sorry, I have to go."

"Kiss him for me."

"I will. See you."

"And you and Jozef mustn't play heroes, little one! You have a child."

"Don't call me little one. You're only one year older."

"As you please. Take care of yourselves!"

It took Jozef half an hour to get away from the Radio Building. He would meet in the evening with his colleagues and they would try to broadcast from a different location. The soldiers had already occupied several studios but others had less visible antennas, and only the people working there knew about them. Jozef pushed his pedals and thought about what he would pack for himself.

Just as he approached his building, a greasy truck equipped with a crane stopped near its entrance. The driver cheerfully waved as Jozef's mother stepped out from the other side of the cabin.

"For heaven's sakes, how did you get here?"

"Our young friend Štefan is smart!"

His mother smiled at the lanky man in overalls, whom Jozef recognized as his schoolmate.

"The road was full of tanks, but I told them I had to move the trucks that were stuck because of the tanks, so they let me go."

Jozef's mother gave him bags filled with homemade sausage and bacon. He would need them so he would have the strength to continue broadcasting. And he would continue telling the truth, because he was the son who gave up the ministry because he didn't want to lie. She gave him a hug and climbed back into the cabin of the truck, and Štefan pulled out in the direction of Modra before Jozef could ask them in for coffee.

He stood there holding the bags, the aroma of smoked meat tickling his nose. Now he could leave in peace. He had no idea if the food supply would collapse or if bread would disappear. He didn't know if jet bombers would return to the city. Like everyone else in Czechoslovakia he knew nothing at that moment. Anything was possible, including civil war, blood and murder—even this surreal visit from his mother and the greasy driver. He looked at the bags in his hands. He wasn't dreaming.

The noisy truck disappeared in the distance. Sometimes an angel appears in gorgeous feathers and sometimes simply in a Praga crane truck.

Lime

Stará Ruda was boiling. It had always been a sleepy little town but it came alive after this August night. There was no place on the map of Czechoslovakia where the invasion did not bring out the best in people. The importance of the capital cities of Prague and Bratislava is undeniable; that is where most of the victims perished.

The politicians urged people to weigh their actions. The radio and special edition newspapers cautioned people not to respond to provocation. People listened and kept their cool. They didn't build barricades or mix Molotov cocktails. Instead, they wrote.

Petra was among the first to take a pail of water and lime and write slogans on the walls. Just two hours earlier her tearful mother had shaken her awake and given her food she had prepared for herself. Anna didn't feel like eating and probably preferred to be careful with food, like all the other women lining up in front of the grocery store. While they badmouthed the store manager, who had locked herself in her office and was reluctant to open the store for fear that it might be plundered, the men went on strike.

Sanola National Enterprises put all its staff on furlough. All employees had to take a vacation at the same time whether they wanted to or not. This made this strike such a curiosity: they had to pretend they were working despite their vacation. At six o'clock sharp they opened the gate and found the manager of the company readying the courtyard for a speech.

When he noticed the kind of crowd that usually only appeared for May Day celebrations, he collapsed. The music was missing, and there were no flags or signs carried by cheerful people who would typically skip the event to go for a drink or to shop for oranges and other goods that were available only on rare occasions like this. The manager was not a bad man but he was a weakling. If athletes dope themselves with hormones, his dope was his working-class origin.

He would mention over and over in his speeches how he had been apprenticed as a lathe operator at a stock-holding company, known then as Mayer and Son and run by the former owners of Sanola. He could talk about the exploitation of the workers, but he didn't mention the fact that it was Mayer who had sent him to the Bratislava branch to learn his trade. He was reliable in following orders from above and had no personal opinions about anything. When he saw the crowd that day in August, the absurdity of the moment lay open before him like a dissected cow with its innards spilling out. They managed to grab him before he hurt himself too much.

The crowd below was noisy. They liked the old man. He wasn't evil; he could tell funny jokes. He took an interest in his employees and even helped a few of them find housing or get their child into an exclusive school. While they carried him to a small conference room, the man who really managed the Sanola Company appeared on the balcony. It was Alexander.

"Here's what I propose: the government needs our support. We have to let them know that we, as one of the largest companies in Czechoslovakia, stand by them. We don't want to fight. We don't produce weapons: we make medical equipment. We won't be provoked.

We'll immediately sign a proclamation protesting the military invasion of our country. We're a sovereign state and we consider the foreign troops occupiers of our state. We have to be united. We have to show the world that we reject this reprehensible act and stand behind the duly elected representatives of our country!"

Alex had never experienced such stormy applause. He immediately dictated the proclamation to his secretary. The manager had locked himself in his office and ignored any knocking on his door, so Alex read the proclamation to him through the door. The old man was no doubt curing himself with plum brandy of the best quality. His muffled reply was deemed agreement. We should add in defense of the old man that he didn't subsequently qualify this murmur as dissent in order to vindicate himself in the eyes of those who, six months later, sent him into early retirement.

Within ten minutes, the proclamation was copied and the people in the courtyard began to sign it. The town was divided into three groups: one signed the petition, the second lined up at the stores, and the third painted signs on the sidewalks, walls, and fences.

Petra's signs were distinct from others because of the calligraphy she had learned from her mother. For Anna, penmanship was everything.

"The way you write is the way you live. Your writing shows more about you than you think. Don't just scribble. With beautiful writing you'll have a better chance of getting a good job."

Oh, dear Anna, and all the other mothers who sometimes say such odd things! Perhaps during the time of Emperor Franz Joseph calligraphy did open the way for a government position, but it was an anachronism in the era of rock-and-roll and transistor radios. But we don't argue with people we love, and that's why Petra adopted the old-fashioned script that Anna used for her accounting forms. As she painted an exclamation mark on the last fence, she unwittingly looked into the garden behind it.

A familiar face was looking at her from the window of a house. It was her Uncle Lajo. He was not on greeting terms with her family and in fact ignored them. Petra knew that he had never moved a finger when her aunt Erika was expelled from school. He had also written to Anna's superiors saying that she was too unreliable to be a payroll accountant and to know how much money every comrade made.

Nobody knew how Anna kept her job: was it her husband's position, her reliability, or the laxness of the period before that August night? Or was it the fact that everyone, from the simplest people to his superiors, knew that her brother was an idiot?

Her uncle disappeared from the window and Petra returned to her work. She had never managed to say hello to him in spite of deciding long ago that she would greet him ostentatiously at every opportunity as her Gandhi-like response to his stupidity. She thought no more about him or why he was there when he lived elsewhere, and instead joined others in turning traffic signs in the opposite direction.

New signs quickly appeared: *Moscow 2,000 km*, while other signs were simply torn down. She had one in her hands and ran down the road with it, but then hid in the woods, stopping to catch her breath. She knew it was pointless. Why did she tear it off?

It was a *No Stopping* sign. She carefully laid it by the sign that a short time ago had showed the name of the town, and then walked home along the side of the road. Nobody knows if it was because of her work, but it is a fact that not a single tank stopped in the town of Stará Ruda.

Lajo stood motionless in the room, trembling at having been found out. He lit another cigarette, feeling like his chest was about to explode. What had compelled him to stand at the window? He blew smoke into the curtains, formerly white but now permanently yellow. He had been cheating on his wife for quite a few years, but she silently suffered through it since she was afraid of him. The August invasion gave him a legitimate excuse to disappear; he told her secretly that the Party was going underground and had given him a special assignment. His wife believed him, because it never occurred to her that he would be able to lie about a situation that shook every family in the country. She even embraced him so tightly and lovingly that he was moved for a moment, but then he quickly patted her shoulder.

"There, there..."

And that was why Lajo, a swine hardened by the school of hard knocks, could have uninterrupted sex with his girlfriend, a secretary from the tire service, during the invasion. And then just when he went to air out the smoke-filled room in her house, Petra's head appeared above the fence, causing him to utter a juicy curse.

We'll let him spend a few pages in fear that his sister's child might betray everything, even though we already know that Petra cared so little about him that she had no intention of telling anyone that she'd seen him.

He was worried less about the discovery of his love relationship than about the discovery of his secret hideaway.

Lajo always tried to combine business with pleasure. When he and his girlfriend weren't in bed they would sit in front of the television and watch the Viennese TV news. She would go out to shop and cook and he would plan the right moment to emerge in public.

The District Committee had lost a few people like him. When he found out that they were considered possible victims of the invasion who had been kidnapped by the Soviet Secret Police, he always smiled gleefully, even though the idea of a Siberian prison was not pleasant. He knew he would make the right choice when the time came. He didn't feel threatened. He didn't shout like Alex or write anything on the sidewalks like the stupid students. He wouldn't lie down in front of the tanks like hysterical youths. But he would light up a cigarette. He would have a smoke break. He would wait.

Then he would join the victors.

Pears

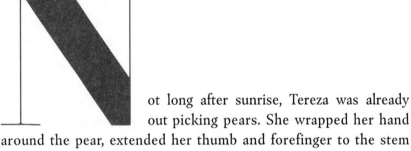ot long after sunrise, Tereza was already out picking pears. She wrapped her hand around the pear, extended her thumb and forefinger to the stem and gently broke it free from the branch. The pears had to be put in the basket with their stems still attached, or they would go bad sooner.

She loved this fruit, its taste and aroma. Kibbutz Masaryk had hundreds of pear trees, and she gazed at them as she rested against the trunk. After five weeks here, Mňačko's children were reaching the end of their stay. While resisting more than others, Tereza had finally yielded to environmental pressure and had started dressing like everyone else in shorts, a stretched-out t-shirt, and a hat. A week ago she had put away the earrings worn in protest against the kibbutz uniform. She was playing a game in which she became an incognito observer who had penetrated this unknown territory to get to know it better before accepting it. For that reason, she didn't want to stick out. Next to her worked Alena, her cabin roommate, and another couple was nearby.

Tereza yawned, still unaccustomed to getting up early. Alena was also not an early riser, and her eyes were swollen from interrupted sleep. They looked at each other and burst out laughing.

"Well, the Israelis won't get much fruit today."

Only a few pears lay at the bottom of their basket. As someone approached on the path from the main building the girls began moving faster. It was Corky, alias Machinist. They waved at him.

"Ahoy!"

Corky answered when he reached them. "Hi, Russian children."

Alena didn't understand at first, but Tereza blanched immediately. This was no joke, and Corky wasn't smiling as he watched them through narrowed eyes. He had never looked so serious.

"All the radio stations are broadcasting it. The Russians are in Czechoslovakia."

Alena screamed and slowly collapsed under the pear tree, her hands shaking. Sitting on the ground, Alena began eating dirt before Tereza could stop her. Grabbing fistfuls of clay, she shoved them into her mouth, smearing dirt all over her face and mingling her tears with dust. Tereza to this day doesn't know where she found the strength, but she went to her friend and picked her up, then cleaned her face with a corner of her t-shirt and, with Corky helping from the other side, half-carried Alena back to the main building.

The usually orderly construction site was filled with noise as students helplessly milled about, some cursing, some threatening and others crying. The older settlers had already heard the news and were taking a break from their work. Tereza ran to her cabin and took the transistor radio out of her suitcase. Everyone gathered around her, but all she heard was static.

They ran to the showers and placed the radio on the water pipes, and Doris, the little radio high above their heads, became their only source of news. From fragments of sentences they learned no more than what they'd heard before, and what was repeated on stations throughout the world: that five armies had occupied Czechoslovakia, and that it was an invasion of socialist states against another socialist state; that it was probably the greatest treachery possible, when brothers attack their brother; that the streets were filled with unrest; that one could hear shots and even machine gun rounds; that Prague and Bratislava were filled with tanks and that people had been killed. They listened to the news again and again because it was so incredible that their hearts refused to accept it, even though their minds believed it.

"Is Bratislava burning? Are they bombing it? Is our house still standing? Are our relatives still alive?" Nobody knew.

Soon cars began arriving at the kibbutz—they were reporters, radio and television journalists. Standing before the cameras, their first time appearing in major newspapers, the young kibbutzim found it hard to express their feelings about this stunning turn of events. The journalists asked them the details of something thousands of kilometers away that they knew nothing about. They could only repeat that they were shocked and horrified, and they protested this barbaric act.

They had arrived here as Mňačko's children, cheerful and carefree students, only a month ago, and now on a single summer's day they had suddenly matured.

The brigade finished before its due date, and they all had to decide what to do next. Some wanted to get back to Czechoslovakia right away, and others wanted to go somewhere else in Europe, but the majority stayed in Israel. Those who packed their bags and flew home said their goodbyes with the feeling that they would never see each other again. Those who stayed received a typewriter from Mňačko's wife. Tereza and a few other students formulated their group's point of view and sent it to the newspapers. Tereza started pecking at the keys like a bird, but by the end she was tapping like a machine gun. As her typewriting skills improved, her position on the occupation hardened.

She wasn't ready to return home, but she had to do something; she had to make a living somehow. Israel offered them education and financial support so they could continue their university studies. The Czechoslovak university students were a boon for the country. They would receive a modest living allowance of 170 Israeli pounds per month. Transportation and housing were free.

Not everyone was happy with this. The older settlers from the kibbutz didn't agree with the allowance. They hadn't received anything from the government when they arrived in Israel after 1948, and they'd had to build their farms with their own hands, literally from nothing.

The money would not get them far, but fortunately all of the Czechoslovak students had a major resource that was of no interest to the banks, but that would help them survive: their youth.

Tereza continued to room with Alena. They were both lost and had no idea what to do next. Finally, with great difficulty, submerged in the noise and whistles of mysterious frequencies, Tereza managed to reach her parents in Bratislava by telephone.

"Hello, Papa, it's me..."

"My little kitten!"

"Please, don't cry."

"I'm not. How are you?"

"I'm going to school here, they're taking care of us. And how are you doing?"

"It's uncertain here... very uncertain... I'll write to you, okay?"

Tereza, schooled by years of living in Czechoslovakia, understood that not only her father was listening to their conversation, and that is why they started corresponding by mail. Ferdinand knew that a postcard was less suspicious than a sealed letter, even though anyone could read it. Most letters would not be delivered anyway; each would be opened, and in each would be found more than people actually wrote.

But who would suspect a postcard? That's why Ferdinand wrote them in his own secret language.

It would make me very happy if you came home. But you're an adult and must make your own decision. We received an announcement of your expulsion from the university here. The Kitten should go to

Vienna to see Kalish. Marcus could visit her there. Kitten's mother says that she can come back here if she wants to. Nothing happens to returnees. So many have returned. Write to us if you want us to send you something. See you at Kalish, if not elsewhere.

Kitten was Tereza. Marcus was her father's nickname at home. Kalish was a Turkish businessman in Vienna who passed messages for people. Tereza had been expelled from her studies in Bratislava and if she returned, she would be on the list of undesirables. Mother had enquired about that, and Ferdinand communicated this in their secret language on other postcards.

She didn't have the courage to write that she wasn't coming back. She was afraid to return to a city filled with negative energy, even though people there loved her above all else. The only solution was Kalish. That was where Kitten could meet Marcus and they could tell each other everything. There are things you can't write down on paper. Very well. She would travel to Vienna and find Kalish.

Before that, however, she had to attend a funeral.

At the very beginning—when they had been at the kibbutz for only a couple of days—Alena told Tereza about an event from her childhood. As a little girl she had woken up and found nobody at home. She was terribly scared, having no idea that her mother had gone out to do some shopping. She walked around the apartment looking for her mother. Then she opened a window, and the view so engaged her that she forgot how afraid she was. She sat on the windowsill on the second floor swinging her legs and enjoying it very much. People in the street stopped and pointed at her. Alena waved at them and smiled.

Her mother was still out shopping, but her father, a teacher in a nearby school, came home unexpectedly. He had put his books away in the staff room and asked to be excused for the rest of the day. He couldn't explain why, but he sensed something, and when he approached his building he understood. He ran to the second floor and opened the door as quietly as he could, not wanting to startle her. Inch by inch he moved towards her, trying not to make the wooden floor creak as little Alena sat in the window, the wind playing in her hair. Finally he reached her, and with lightning speed he took her into his arms and pulled her into the room. Then both he and his frightened daughter broke down in tears.

This is what Tereza was thinking about, standing above the grave in a borrowed dress. No one had a black dress; why would anyone take a black dress on vacation? Nobody expected that one of them would die. So she had borrowed a dress from one of the Israeli girls.

Something had happened to Alena. She found it more and more difficult to make sense of things. She didn't know whether to stay or return to Bratislava. She started to go to school in Haifa like Tereza, but one morning before class, she sat on the windowsill of an empty fifth floor lecture hall. And no one was there to silently embrace her.

That day Tereza walked by the pear orchard for the last time without even looking at it. She headed for the airport and bought a ticket to Vienna. For the next forty years she avoided eating pears. She couldn't even stand their scent.

Radio

Erika hadn't seen Jozef for several days. He didn't show up at home, nor did he phone her. She knew why. Men wearing summer jackets had been dropping by, and she sensed who they were. Her family's history was interspersed with visits from the secret police.

They must have been Slovaks since they were able to find her apartment. The street signs had recently disappeared, so the occupiers would have difficulty orienting themselves. But the locals could still find their way.

The men enquired about Jozef, and when she told them that he hadn't been home for a long time they were polite enough to remain outside. It even seemed that they were uncomfortable with their assignment and were only performing their duty.

The country was in a hopeless situation, but the resistance was alive. People joined together and helped each other. This was not the acquiescent Czechoslovakia of a year later, when yesterday's rabble-rousers recanted their opinions and those who called the occupation by its real name were expelled from their schools or places of work.

As soon as the State Security officers left, Erika went to talk to her husband. She turned on the cable radio, and after another announcer finished his broadcast, she heard his voice:

"You are listening to the free broadcast of Czechoslovak Radio."

"Hello, my dear."

"We warn all our listeners not to listen to the collaborationist Radio Vltava, set up by the occupying army for the purpose of disinformation."

"A couple of men, you know who, were here to see you."

"And don't listen to radio station Užhorod that broadcasts in poor Slovak."

"Your son is asking about you."

"Moscow's *Pravda* is reporting that our population cordially welcomed the army that came to free them from the counter-revolution. Use all means to inform foreign countries of the real situation! Take pictures of the soldiers, record people in the streets, and make movies if you have an amateur camera. Many foreign television crews and foreigners are in the cities. Send this material out of the country so the world finds out about the injustice inflicted on our peaceful country."

"Take care of yourself."

Every journalist dreams of capturing extraordinary events. One of the great arts of newsgathering is to disregard danger and inform the public. The golden period of Czechoslovak Radio started immediately after it was silenced. The illegal broadcasts started with cable radio in the first few hours. Cable, using wire, was harder to silence because it was not broadcast through the airwaves. Technically speaking, it was easier; it could be done through any telephone. Initially it was done from the Ministry of Agriculture.

Jozef knew that technicians were using lines beginning with the number two. The army, the government, and all health institutions used these lines, and that was why they didn't come under suspicion. Who would look for an illegal broadcaster there? Even when discovered, cable broadcasts continued; after all, the telephone lines of the police could not be disconnected.

Jozef and his colleagues had to move to a new location every day. They broadcasted from Koliba Hill above the city, or from a riverboat. They called themselves Radio Station Dunaj. Editors monitored the situation in the streets or supplied news covered in the foreign press. Pages would be quickly typed and delivered to the announcers by motorbike, bicycle, or even ambulance.

Caution was essential. The majority of the State Security apparatus served the occupiers. Even the country's leadership was divided. Some politicians sharply protested while others met secretly with Russian generals at the airports. The radio station's leadership was sending messages to the underground broadcasters to return to the fold, but no one did; they knew very well that they would be exposed and locked up.

Not every editor was prepared to take the risk. Some went to stay with relatives and others hid in their vacation homes. No one involved in the illegal broadcasts was a Party member. After the initial frantic resistance, the situation stabilized and the official broadcasts resumed, they were called back to work. The people who invited them back were the kind who were waiting to see how the situation developed. Jozef returned to work but he didn't trust them and they didn't trust him.

The difference between the Communists and the non-Communists was widening again. Not that true reconciliation was ever possible between victims and the victimizer, a criminal party capable of sending tens of thousands of people to prisons and uranium mines for political reasons. However, even strong resisters of communism had supported the Communists in 1968, when it seemed that the new leadership sincerely regretted the crimes committed by their predecessors in the 1950s and that the present government was really trying to improve the situation.

The first weeks of the occupation, however, made it clear to both former and future victims that nothing was going to change. The once and future criminals began preparing their revenge. Compared to the brutality of tanks or the hangings that had taken place fifteen years earlier it was a velvet revenge; people would simply be vetted, and those who passed would stay while those who failed would have to go.

No, they would not go to prison. Professors would simply become manual laborers, medical doctors would work with concrete, engineers would become stokers, poets would work as gardeners, and writers would become night watchmen. Nobody would be hanged but tens of thousands of people would lose their professions and their dignity. Humiliation, though bloodless, is still humiliation, and the nation that loses its brightest minds is doomed to stagnation.

As a trained actor, Jozef felt natural in front of a camera. Sitting by the microphone and reading the news he was playing himself. For the last hour an American film crew had been shooting a documentary that they claimed would archive the events of 1968. Through a complicated conspiracy they had managed to find the temporary location of the underground Radio Station Dunaj. Jozef learned that Erika and his son were safe and staying with Erika's mother in Modra. He talked to the Americans in his broken German and a radio crewmember spoke some English, so the Americans got a lot of information from them.

But to Erika's great surprise, while watching a Viennese TV channel a month later she saw her husband in an American documentary called *Seven Days to Remember*. She burst out crying. Jozef was easily recognizable, chain-smoking and gesticulating wildly. The atmosphere in the illegal studio seemed hectic, and would have been even more so had the staff known they would soon appear on television. Nobody knows whether it was the stupidity of the film crew or their absolute incomprehension of the conditions in socialist countries. Taking democracy for granted since birth, the Americans had no idea that they could actually hurt the people they were filming. It is certain that they didn't want to do that, but they did so nonetheless.

The next day, everyone at the radio station avoided Jozef. They hated the people of Radio Station Dunaj because of their courage. To salve their own guilt, they dropped remarks about the unprofessional conduct shown in the amateurish documentary. The fact that their own courage consisted of watching Viennese television safe at home while their colleagues were risking their necks was simply ignored.

Jozef's superior, a Communist, was a decent person. He advised Jozef that in his precarious position, the best way to avoid catastrophe would be to join the Communist Party. Jozef, as so many times before, made the right choice.

"You know I can't do that. I understand you're trying to help me, but I will not join the Party."

"I expected that. But then..."

"I understand. And I thank you."

Tereza's parents were in a double bind. While worried about their daughter in distant Israel, they also had to watch out for her brother. Janko, like many boys from his class, never missed an opportunity to write slogans on Bratislava's walls. He had never lied to his mother until now, but this was a matter of being a man, and how could mothers understand that? For the first time he disobeyed his mother's curfew.

Maria was unaware of it until her agitated neighbor stopped her on the staircase.

"I saw your boy. He was throwing tomatoes at the tanks."

Maria broke out laughing at the ridiculous notion. "Ferdinand would do that? Are you kidding me?"

"Janko."

Maria clutched the railing to keep from crumpling onto the old wooden stairs, which creaked beneath her. People were dying out there, and her child was provoking soldiers who were so worked up that they opened fire before anything actually happened. Her face pale, Maria thanked her neighbor, who squeezed her hand compassionately.

She had to do everything on her own. Ferdinand spent all day at the railway station trying to ensure the provisioning of the capital city.

In the evening, they wrote postcards to Tereza, spending hours composing a few lines that contained as much information as possible. Ferdinand took them to the post office having no idea if they would ever reach their destination. But they had received information that their daughter was alive and planning to come to Vienna.

Janko came home, but Maria said nothing; she just fried schnitzels, his favorite dish. Then they looked through the world atlas. She had decided not to argue with him. He asked where exactly his sister was, so Maria showed him where Haifa was on the map. Then she embraced him tightly.

"I would die if something happened to you in the streets!"

Janko, as an adolescent boy, usually tried to avoid his mother's tenderness, but at this moment he understood and hugged her back. After he fell asleep, Maria went down to the cellar, and next to a pile of coal she found bottles filled with benzene cleaner.

He must have spent all of his pocket money on it. There were at least twenty bottles in that deadly arsenal. Each bottle was stopped with a bandage. A Molotov cocktail was a primitive weapon, but a terrible one against the tanks and for those who threw it. Soldiers trapped in a flaming tank didn't take time to hunt down the culprit; they shot indiscriminately at anyone nearby. Maria poured the benzene into the canal, then smashed the bottles in the courtyard and dropped the broken glass into the garbage. From then on, she never let Janko out of her sight. Ferdinand had to do all the shopping.

Only when the armies began slowly withdrawing from the city did she go out into the streets with her son. Bratislava looked like a military front had passed through it. The walls of buildings were scarred with bullet holes, roads were scraped by tank tracks, and almost all of the houses defaced by protest signs were now covered with white paint. People's faces were no longer enthusiastic, but tired and resigned. On every corner they met men with brushes.

The truth was being painted over.

Little Suitcase

The sun was setting over Stará Ruda. It looked very poetic, but these days few could enjoy it. The sun slowly followed a downward path to drop behind what had once been the Jewish cemetery, now a jungle of weeds and broken grave-stones. No one was there to remember the old dead. The new living had enough problems of their own and didn't think about the fact that tomorrow they might be the new dead. They lived only for tomorrow. And suddenly it was dark.

Only the kitchen window was lit in Alex's home. Petra was asleep in her little room, while Anna sat with an unfinished cup of tea in front of her and her husband mechanically stirred a cup of coffee that had been warm an hour ago. It was half past two in the morning.

"You should go to bed."

"I'm afraid for her."

"You would be even more afraid if she stayed here."

"How will she manage?"

"Anna, please! She's an adult! A medical doctor! And Hansi and Resi are looking forward to seeing her."

"Still..."

"It's only temporary, until things calm down here."

"I don't know what will happen..."

"Neither do I. That's why we need to get her out of here."

"Did you talk to her?"

"Not yet. Let's go to bed. At least for a while."

"You know I won't sleep."

"Try."

Alex's alarm clock went off at six. Standing on a plate, it rang quite desperately. Groggily, he switched it off and went to his daughter's room. He shook Petra's leg but there was no response. He had to tickle her to wake her up, a method that had worked since childhood.

"What is it?"

"You have to leave, my dear. Take the smallest suitcase so you don't look too conspicuous."

"What?"

"You have to pack your things. Your train will leave soon. You're going to Vienna. The smallest suitcase."

"On a trip? Is that a good idea?"

"It's not a trip."

Alex left her to get dressed and walked to the kitchen for a glass of water. They followed the popular practice in Czechoslovakia of using old mustard jars as drinking glasses that they called "Russian crystal." Anna entered the kitchen as he was about to take a sip.

Alex dropped his glass. Anna was grey. A few hours ago, her hair had been a dark chestnut color, but it had turned white overnight. She looked at her husband in surprise. He pointed at her, his hand trembling.

"Your hair..."

Anna patted it without interest.

"I will never see her again."

Alex wanted to embrace her; he wanted to shout that it wasn't true, that it was only for a while, that this was a big misunderstanding and would end well, but he simply sat down and looked at his wife in silence. He knew she was right and that they would never see their daughter again.

Petra sat weeping in the Felicia. She was more shocked at her mother's appearance than at suddenly leaving home. Burned into her retina like a sunspot, her mother's white hair didn't disappear even when she closed her eyes.

She tried to catch her train but it never came. Alex waited with her, but they gave up after an hour. Many people managed to spot them. Even though she was only carrying a small suitcase, Stará Ruda would be filled with rumors that the technical manager's daughter was emigrating. They went home, and Alex decided to try the highway.

He put up the roof of the convertible, since they would be meeting columns of military trucks and tanks. The drive to Bratislava that normally took two and a half hours stretched to five as they followed the armed columns. The soldiers eyed Petra with weary eyes. She tried to make herself inconspicuous, small and tiny, the tiniest in the world, but still she caught the attention of some soldiers.

Those were not the eyes of conquerors. But if not them, then who? And why?

"Resi and Hansi are great, you'll see."

"I don't want to go there."

"They've invited you so many times and you've always wanted to go."

"That was before those fellows showed up."

"Petra, I beg of you. It's only for a while... you can see what's going on here."

"I want to stay here with you."

"We'll come and visit you."

"Then why don't we all go together?"

"I can't leave the factory, the people... you're young."

"Is it because I'm young, or because you're worried about the factory?"

"Please, don't make it even harder. The borders are open. We can see each other any time."

The border in those days was really a promenade, as one politician would soon comment. And then he closed it. But for the time being, people could leave and come back to Czechoslovakia. Alex had arranged for a permit to Austria as a gift for Petra when she graduated from medical school, but the long-planned trip suddenly turned into an escape for which she did not need a permit. After the invasion the government opened the border and allowed citizens who felt endangered to leave. Some days there were so many people leaving that the normally uncompromising border guards, who used to shoot anyone who attempted to cross the border, let people go even if they didn't have papers. If there was no passport to stamp they would stamp a hand. Many people left without documents, and someone even crossed the border using a public transport pass.

After the long, exhausting trip to Bratislava Alex said good-bye to his daughter at the central station. Neither of them cried; they postponed that for later.

"Call us every day."

"Come."

"Call from Hansi's right away."

Petra barely made it into the corridor. She suddenly appreciated the small suitcase. Whole families were packed into the train. The children were looking forward to an adventure but the eyes of their parents betrayed fear. She opened the window and waved at her father. She was certain they would see each other again. No, she was not being naïve. She understood that they wanted to spare her from what was coming, but she believed it would come later, after they managed to get out as well.

The train pulled out of the station, and the few dozen kilometers to Vienna dragged on for hours as the train stopped several times. Once everyone had to get out while soldiers with machine guns checked all the compartments. No one knew if they were looking for somebody or were afraid of a bomb attack. Then everyone got back on the train and the cars jostled against each other and creaked into motion. It was stuffy and hot inside the train compartment, and the window seat that she'd taken by luck became priceless as a slight draft helped her survive. And then there were Silvia and Rudo.

Both had just graduated from the College of Fine Arts; they were eighteen and unmarried and the whole world was opening before them. They had no children and no ties, except for their parents, of course, who wished them luck. This couple belonged to a large group of people for whom the August invasion presented an opportunity to leave a country that offered them very little for the future, even without the threat of tanks. They were leaving with light hearts, everything they owned packed into two canvas backpacks.

As they began conversing with Petra their calm optimism slowly washed over her. They couldn't understand what she was afraid of. She was a young medical doctor with a diploma in her pocket, educated in a field that was in demand everywhere in the world. Petra began looking at her situation from a different angle. It was not an excellent situation, no, and she wasn't about to become a carefree butterfly, but she understood that the cards dealt to her were not bad at all.

Her relatives were waiting for her in Vienna. She had a place to stay and wait and think about her future, and then she would decide what to do next. But she was sure that whatever she attempted would be done along with her parents.

In the meantime Alex was returning home. He always loved to drive, and in particular felt pleasure when driving his Felicia, but today he drove very slowly. By the time he reached home it was dark. In the

meantime Anna was in line at the butcher shop. It was Friday and people were expecting to get meat. Meat was available in Stará Ruda only
once a week, but the people lining up didn't know that it wouldn't come
today. The line in the store was like a snake with a head, body, and tail.
In a country where people had to line up for everything, this form of
killing time had a long tradition. Those at the tail of the line were apathetic, having almost no chance of getting anything. People in the body
of the snake, filled with justified hope, were the most disciplined and
served as guard dogs to prevent others from jumping the line. If anyone
so much as stepped across a line or, heaven help us, checked what was
behind the counter, the guard dog would bark and the rumbling of the
mob would send the daring malefactor back to his place.

The snake's head was the most poisonous, consisting of the
long-distance runners who spent long hours waiting in front of the
locked doors of the butcher shop. They knew they had a real chance to
buy pork and beef, but usually preferred chicken. Roast chicken was
the quintessence of Sunday dinner in Stará Ruda, and the icon of local
well-being.

What kind of life would it be if we were deprived of that miserable
chicken on Sunday?

Suddenly the door opened and the snake moved into the store.
The counters were almost empty: nothing had arrived. The head was
confused and began to get mad. What's this supposed to mean? Why
are the hooks empty? They saw the meat truck leave! Who was the
butcher hiding stuff for? They knew him well; he always put something
aside for his friends, but he had never failed to put at least something
out for others as well! How disrespectful!

Anna stood at the tail of the snake, oblivious to everything and not
even reacting to the shouting inside the shop when a quarrel began
over the hard salami. Nothing bothered her. Facing things like this
throughout our lives, day after day, we become desensitized. These
people had been ready to put their lives on the line yesterday; today
they would sacrifice it for salami.

Anna didn't notice the head of the snake stop jerking, but sensed the pause. Her daughter was now heading far off to a place that was unreachable, not because of the distance in kilometers, but because of the barbed wire. Anna caught some whispering.

"Tell me, please, who is that... white lady?"

Many people knew Anna the way we know the accountants who process our salaries. All of them spent time with her at least once, bringing in a certificate showing that their son or daughter was studying, or to maintain their children's allowance, or to present medical documentation. Hundreds of people knew Anna, but nobody recognized the woman with the white hair. When they realized who it was, they were in shock.

They paid for their shopping and shyly walked past her as if afraid to say hello. This woman had experienced something that might happen to them as well. Occasionally someone wished her good day, and she acknowledged it with a nod. When the tail of the snake approached the counter, the butcher, struck by her appearance, offered her a slice of beef tenderloin that he had put aside for someone else, and no one objected. Anna thanked him and left, the whispers following her.

From then on, nobody called her anything but White Lady.

Lice

Hansi and Resi were waiting for Petra when she got off the train in Vienna. The platform was filled with white signs with names, but only one box of cookies bearing the sign: PETRA STARÁ RUDA.

They kissed her with some hesitation, having last seen her when she was only ten years old. Hansi and Resi were almost seventy, but looked fifty. Well kept and well dressed, they radiated wellbeing like a hundred-mark banknote. Their faces showed the superiority that our exhausted retirees quickly lose while struggling to maintain the last vestiges of human dignity—if they have even achieved it in a country that sentences them to abject poverty.

Resi's hair was dyed red, and Hansi wore the dark suit in which he, until recently, had chauffeured the Austrian Chancellor, his erect stance betraying his years in the Wehrmacht. He extended his hand to her and mumbled something in Viennese German. With an uncertain smile Petra replied: *"Küss die Hände!"* That was all the German she had. She knew English and a bit of French, but would not get far with those two even in *Hochdeutsch*.

She could not ignore the uneasiness she read in their eyes. She had gotten off the train as an elegant young lady wearing an outfit personally tailored for her graduation, her hair styled in the latest fashion and huge sunglasses covering her teary eyes. They were expecting a starving wretch in a twice-altered coat, and her elegance disappointed them. It would have been easier for them to do a good deed had she been poorer. They were ready for charity work, but needed a bit more inspiration.

They had many questions about her father, to whom they were related very distantly but in a way that was unclear to Petra, in spite of all the times Alex had named the uncles, aunts, and grandmothers that were connected to them like poles to a telephone hub. They proceeded to Hansi's beloved Mercedes, an old model from 1958, polished and well maintained.

After an hour of careful driving, Hansi gallantly carried her suitcase from the car while she helped Resi up the stairs to their huge Art Nouveau apartment on the corner of Mariahilfer Strasse. They showed her the room where she would sleep. Even though it originally belonged to the servant girl, it was still three times larger than the one she had in Stará Ruda. She had not yet managed to unpack when Resi tactfully asked her how long she expected to stay. Petra had no idea.

In the meantime, Hansi was discreetly removing a tiny carton resting in the middle of her bed. It was lice powder, which the couple had now magnanimously concluded might not be needed. As soon as Hansi put the disinfectant into his pocket, he smilingly demonstrated the newest accomplishment of civilization: a window blind. You pulled it down and the room was dark, pulled it up and you had sunlight in your room. Pure genius and yet so simple! Surely they didn't have such things yet in Czechoslovakia! Then they showed her the bathroom and toilet. The girl from the Eastern Bloc reacted to all of it with a stony face.

Resi started to talk in a general way and Petra remained silent. She was trying to make some sense of what she was hearing; sometimes she was not sure she understood, but other times, unfortunately, she knew all too well. Resi's monologue was mixed with Slovak words, since she'd been born in Czechoslovakia when the country was still part of the Austro-Hungarian Empire. She was fifteen when she came to Vienna to work as a servant and stayed there.

"You know, *meine Liebe*, we're poor people and we don't know what will happen. Today, the Russians are in your country, but tomorrow they may be here. Yesterday somebody planted a bomb in an Israeli airplane. The streets are filled with refugees from your country and we're glad to help you—we Austrians are Christians, it's our duty and that is why you're here, *liebe* Petra. We hope you'll enjoy your time with us; we'll give you what we can, though we don't have much. We live modestly, and that's why you shouldn't turn on the hot water; I will take care of that when you want it. Just let me know. We bathe every Friday and will be glad to help you. But you also have to think about your future. You're a doctor, and we respect doctors, but there are so many doctors in Vienna that some end up sweeping the sidewalks, so I'm not sure you can get a position in Vienna, but maybe in Graz, or the Alps. They said you like to ski and I was thinking that maybe Tirol would be good for you; there are so many sick people there! That's a paradise for doctors. They catch cold so easily there as they run around in those leather shorts. You would think it would make them healthier, but it doesn't. And it's not good for the ovaries, either. Little Petra, I no longer have my ovaries and half of my stomach is also gone: the doctors cut out everything they could, and now I am a cripple and happy to be alive. We will help you, Hansi and I, but we don't have as much energy as we once had. We're here today, but tomorrow, well, you know what I mean... Look around Vienna, visit St. Stephen's Cathedral, and by the way, we'll take you to Wienerwald for grilled chicken. After all, to come to Vienna and not taste the grilled chicken at Wienerwald means you weren't in Vienna at all! So, have some fun here, my unhappy girl: I don't envy you for what you'll have to do, but you're young and strong. By the way, you could help me. I have three shirts that I just washed. Could you iron them for me? I'm no longer able to do it – look, my joints are so swollen! What do you think it is? Look at these pills. I'm supposed to take them;

they cost twelve schillings. Is that fair? All our lives Hansi and I slaved for Austria and now I have to pay twelve schillings if I don't want my joints to hurt. They swell so frightfully that sometimes I can't even wipe my bottom – you must pardon me, my dear Petra, when I say that, but you're a doctor, and doctors have to listen to everything patients complain about. Yes, we're the patients, and in spite of that, we'll help you get a start so you can go find your happiness and not be held back by sick people like us who would only be a burden to you. The iron is in the cupboard. Here's the plug. We don't have an ironing board. I used the table while I could; now a *Frau* comes to iron for me, but she's expensive. Imagine, she asked me for twenty schillings an hour! For heaven's sake, how terrible is that? Some kind of dirty Pole or something. You want to do a bit of good for them and give them work and they splash vitriol on your face. Don't cry, my little one, your parents will call, don't worry, but don't make a call from our phone, we only use it when we need a doctor. If you need to, go and call from the post office; it's much cheaper there. You can't imagine how much they charge for a minute when you phone from your home. They would rip our skin off if we didn't watch out. You can also iron these lacy tablecloths. I haven't put them out for twenty years, so you'll have to air them out, or better yet wash them first before you iron them. Hansi bought me a washing machine. It's a terribly new machine—look at those buttons, like a rocket ship. We call it Apollo. It washes all by itself. You won't be slaving away here, my *Liebling*."

And so Petra became a servant on Mariahilfer Strasse, just as Resi had once done for a storeowner called Cermacek. True, Resi and Hansi called her "our dear guest," but Resi found new tasks for her to do every day. After she finished ironing countless baskets of white wash, she washed other items. She took down the curtains and soaked them. She beat the carpets, and scrubbed the hardwood floor with a wire brush and then treated it with yellow polish. Then she washed all the pots and pans and cleaned the water stains from the water basins.

With Hansi's help, she moved the old furniture away from the wall where spiders had lived since the era of Chancellor Dollfuss.

She was not a princess. She was used to work. While in her Bratislava sublet she had helped Tereza's mother when she was tired of studying. It was a form of relaxation for her.

As a reward, they took her once to the giant Ferris wheel at Prater. Only Petra went up; they stayed down, saying they were afraid of vertigo, but Petra knew they were saving their schillings. Hansi read ads in the newspaper every day and weekly supermarket flyers for better prices in various parts of Vienna. They bought the cheapest cuts of ham and fatty salami, as well as long wieners and thick sausages that turned Petra's stomach. She ate mostly bread and marmalade and drank milk, which fortunately was excellent. They also went out for grilled chicken, and Hansi, with unusual generosity, would order a Coke for her. It reminded him of the first time he drank it in the prisoners of war camp, when the American Red Cross showed up. Petra preferred to see St. Stephen's Cathedral on her own, although the pair informed her that they had donated money to pay for a ceramic roof tile during a fundraising drive to repair the cathedral's roof after it was destroyed in a fire during the war.

She called home daily from the post office. Even though she didn't speak of her disappointment, Alex could tell that his child was unhappy. The only thing she let him know was that she couldn't stay in Vienna very long. And then Alex told her about Tereza.

"Imagine, she's coming to Vienna."

"Tereza? Oh my God, that's wonderful! When?"

"Nobody knows. I gave her parents your address, just in case, so she can find you."

"I'm so looking forward to seeing her. When are you coming?"

"They say the border will be closed soon."

"Dad!"

"Don't worry, I won't leave you alone."

Alex worried about her a lot. The Austrian address was the only way he could have helped her. He was heart-stricken at the thought of having sent her abroad, and even the pleasure of knowing she had been spared the horrible situation his family had recently encountered was only a minor consolation.

He was being called in daily to answer before all kinds of commissions, partly because of the strike that he was said to have organized, but mainly because of the factory. He was still the only man who could keep production going at Sanola so he couldn't be replaced, at least for now; that would endanger deliveries to dozens of foreign countries, which paid in dollars for medical instruments. That money could put a smile even on the faces of Communist politicians. The Republic needed strategic raw materials that could only be bought with dollars. Without Sanola there would be no dollars, and without Alex there would be no Sanola.

No matter how you cut it, without Alex the Republic would be on its knees.

But without Alex there would be no Petra, either. He knew she wouldn't last much longer in Austria without him. And then he remembered his sister in Ottawa. She had left before the war and married in Canada. Her husband ran a successful business trading in rare metals. He had died a few years ago, Alex recalled from the announcement that had arrived in a torn envelope. The security police read everything. He had saved his correspondence with his sister even though it was mainly limited to Christmas and Easter cards.

Suddenly, an idea occurred to Alex: Petra could go to Canada! She had to get as far from her homeland as possible. Europe was like an infected gall bladder. It would be better to leave a territory that could be totally occupied by Russian tanks in just a couple of days.

Certain that his home and office phones were tapped, he arranged a business trip to Hungary. After a meeting during which his Hungarian engineers would express shame for their part in the invasion and occupation, they would all get drunk on cherry brandy, and Alex would go to the local post office to place a call to Ottawa.

Chestnuts

The first cold days had arrived when Tereza rang the bell in Mariahilfer Strasse. Petra opened the door and found her in the same summer dress that she'd worn when she arrived in Israel. She hadn't packed anything warmer, expecting to be home after the summer vacation. Without a word the girls embraced each other. Petrified Hansi and shocked Resi were looking at Tereza's suitcases, which didn't bode anything good.

"This is my friend from Bratislava. I stayed in her house for two years."

"Na ja. Gut."

"Could she sleep here?"

This question gave Resi something like a kidney seizure, and Hansi had to help her to her room. Petra followed them inside and closed the door. Resi was lying on her bed with her pillow covering her head, though she could still see out from under it. She forgot to sigh, as upset as she was by the decisiveness of this girl from Czechoslovakia.

With lightning speed Petra calculated all the work she had done for them and how much they would have had to pay "that dirty Polish woman," and it was quite a sum. While she was very grateful to them, she said, and she would never forget them, she had hardly been simply resting there. On the contrary, she filled her days by helping the old people, and did it gladly, but if they were Christians they should not deny shelter to a homeless girl.

Standing in the hallway, Tereza felt bad, especially after her disappointment that morning. She had rushed straight from the train station to Mexikoplatz, to the store owned by the Turkish businessman Kalish. During the five minutes she spent there at least ten people showed up, five of them from Czechoslovakia.

Kalish had never heard of her father. Either his message hadn't gotten through or it was lost among the others. Kalish sold everything possible. His shop was filled with carpets, water pipes, and carved tables, and next to the digital watches and fountain pens that revealed a naked woman when turned upside down was a table where people could leave letters. The mustachioed merchant allowed Tereza to search in the letter pile, but she found nothing relating to her. Only Mariahilfer Strasse remained, but bad luck found her there as well.

Just at that moment the bedroom door opened and a joyful Petra waved her in. Resi and Hansi had agreed to three nights, but certainly not more, and it would be necessary to register with the police, as they were not a night shelter. But they agreed to three nights.

When they found out Tereza was Jewish it was Hansi who for a change had a fit and fainted. Petra let him smell some dubious-looking drops he had bought from a Chinese store, and Hansi opened his eyes. Immediately he and Resi became martyrs. They had helped Petra so much and had sacrificed so that she could stay there, and now they were getting absolutely no gratitude from her. Instead, she had disappointed them by bringing a dangerous foreigner to their home, imperiling their lives and Petra's as well. Hadn't she heard about the Palestinian attacks against Israelis in Vienna? They agreed to one night.

The girls refused dinner and locked themselves in Petra's room. It was dark outside and a cold wind was blowing.

"You can only imagine how embarrassed I am."

"Say nothing more about it."

"I stayed so long at your place..."

"It's not your fault. It's not your apartment."

"Where will you go?"

"To Kalish's store. When my father said to go to Kalish, it must be Kalish."

"How was Israel?"

They talked all night long because they couldn't sleep; the bed was so narrow that either one or the other was in danger of falling off.

"Do you want to go back?"

"Where?"

"To Haifa."

"I don't know."

"Sometimes I feel like just going to the station and buying a ticket back to Bratislava."

"Me, too, Petra."

Vienna in those days could be called Little Czechoslovakia. The Czech and Slovak languages were heard more than German. Austria was sympathetic to the plight of the refugees. Offices lengthened their workdays, charities worked right in the streets, and most of the population joined the surge of aid. But there was an undercurrent of fear, especially among older Austrians.

Who are these people? What do they want? How long will they stay? Will they endanger us? The citizens of Czechoslovakia accepted their help with thanks; it seemed a matter of course to people who were fleeing hell. It helped in the first few days to get over the shock and away from the tanks. But the refugees had short memories. Unfortunately, forty years later, the people of the Czech Republic and Slovakia, now living in a democracy, have not been eager to help new refugees from the Third World for whom our land is a refuge as Austria once was for them.

Tereza considered herself a transient. After leaving Petra, she spent her days walking back and forth between the railway station and Kalish's store. She didn't find her father or his message anywhere. She checked her suitcase into the baggage room, and the railway washroom became her bathroom, waiting room and living room. Soon she had spent all her money and had nothing to eat. The chestnut seller, an elderly invalid missing a leg, agreed to save all his burned chestnuts for her. He left her a lot of burned chestnuts, but added in some good ones, too.

A burned chestnut tasted like charcoal. So what?, she said to herself, at least I'll have a healthy stomach. She ate so much coal that she felt like a locomotive. That was how her chestnut days started.

During the day, on the way to Kalish's, she would run through the market, where peddlers gave her spoiled fruit. She would cut the good parts off of half-rotten bananas. At the used clothing market she bought a warm coat. An arbiter of elegance, she would never have worn it in Bratislava, but here it was easy to decide between charm and pneumonia—she would sacrifice the charm. She had nowhere to sleep and she couldn't ask Petra again, since Hansi and Resi wouldn't let her in. The waiting room was locked at night, and for the first time in her life she slept under a bridge. Luckily, Vienna has many of them.

It was not so terrible. She would wrap herself in her new coat and lie down on the dry grass. Behind her was a concrete support and in front of her was the lazy Danube River. She would not allow herself to think for a second how dangerous her situation was. She was a traveler: she had overcome the desert and the trial of fire and had to get lucky. Simply had to. And she did.

The next morning she headed to Kalish's store, thinking about breakfast on the way: would it be coal or a banana? Vienna, the city of grilled chicken, tortured her with its refined aromas, and ethnic restaurants produced their own bursts of perfume: her nose captured explosions of Indian, Chinese, and Thai scents She walked around them with her eyes closed as the windows tempted her with sharp yellow sauces, white coconut milk, and red meatballs.

Again there was no message at Kalish's store. She sat down on the bench and placed her coat, wrapped in colorful paper, next to her. With that package she looked like a young lady returning from shopping. Then she noticed a small figure at the end of the street walking toward her with a gait that she would recognize among thousands of others. Despite the multitude of pedestrians in the morning rush she was certain it was he. Father was coming.

With his head bent down Ferdinand didn't see her at first. She didn't yet know that he was short of breath and hiding it from the gaze of others. He walked slowly, a packed net bag hanging from each hand. They say that light is faster than sound. Wrong. He heard his daughter first.

"Daddy!"

"Kitten!"

He didn't know how to embrace her. Finally he set his bags on the bench and took his child into his arms.

"Mama has sent you some food and *sholet*, too. And she also packed your warm coat. Why are you wearing so little? You'll catch cold! How is Petra? Are you staying with her?"

Tereza told him everything. Not a muscle in Ferdinand's face moved, and then he took his daughter by the elbow.

"Come."

He picked up the net bags and they left. The coat in the colorful paper remained on the bench.

"Was that yours?"

"I'll leave it for someone else."

Tereza put on her elegant Bratislava coat and they went to a restaurant. Ferdinand couldn't wait until he finished his soup to ask, "Are you coming back, Kitten?"

"Tell me—what should I do?"

"You know how much mother and I both love you and want to have you with us in Bratislava, but..."

"What do your friends say? They've always had good sense."

"They're afraid that... I don't know. I don't know what's going to happen. I want you at home, but I'm also afraid that something will happen to you."

"How is Janko doing?"

Instead of an answer, her father took out a folded sheet of paper. Tereza opened it and her eyes filled with tears. Janko had drawn their house and added an arrow to the windows on the second floor: HERE WE ARE!

After that he remained quiet until she finished her food. She could see clearly that her father had to force himself not to ask her to come home. She felt that he strongly desired her return but at the same time didn't want to influence her free decision. By the time they finished their coffee her father understood that his daughter would not be returning to Czechoslovakia.

He was ready for that. While at the Vienna train station he had talked to Austrian railway employees who told him where the refugee hostels were located. After lunch they began checking them out, one after another.

Tereza noticed right away that her father was having breathing difficulties and was trying to cover it up. He hadn't been in perfect health when she left for Israel, but now he looked much worse. She was beginning to worry about him. They stopped at shop windows where he pretended to be interested in the goods behind the glass, but in fact he was trying to catch his breath. His face was pale and drawn. He'd aged terribly in the months since they'd seen each other.

He was no longer angry about about her being expelled from the university for not returning. She even missed her summer practicum in the Slovak Archives, having chosen the trip with Mňačko's children instead... But all of that was in the distant past, pardoned and washed away by the events that had turned their lives upside down.

In the first hostels Ferdinand experienced a shock. He saw long corridors with open doors leading to small rooms, where entire families were crammed onto narrow bunk beds.

"Father, what's wrong with you?"

"Nothing, I just... Oh, nothing."

Ferdinand had to lean against a wall, and then she took him to the shared bathroom. Women were washing bedding in the washbasins. Ferdinand washed his face, excused himself for disturbing them and left. He didn't tell his daughter that the hostel reminded him of the camp where most of his family had perished during the war.

His mind told him that these people had come here voluntarily and that they were being helped, that nobody was imprisoning them here and that they could leave at any time. Also, while the beds were made of iron and came from the army surplus, they were clean. The walls were painted and there were no wooden beds—Ferdinand saw all of that with his brain, but his heart felt how much it all resembled that time when his uncles and aunts were transported from their country in cattle cars...

He understood that he was being unfair to the Austrians, who were coping with an influx of refugees, but he was a Jew—which meant he had antennae that his daughter would inherit from him, and her daughter from her, so that they could—sooner than others—feel that something was off.

Tereza took her father by the arm and they went outside, where Ferdinand sat on a bench and took a nitroglycerin tablet.

"When did you start taking those?"

"About a year ago, Kitten. Your mother doesn't know about it. Don't tell her."

Her father tried to joke the way he did at home, like when he wouldn't reveal where Maria hid the chocolate until after the children had eaten dinner. A spasm of pain crossed his face. Then the pill slowly melting under his tongue brought his smile back, and the fresh air helped, too. He jumped to his feet like a young man.

"Come, let's find someplace decent!"

On their fourth try they found a place with fewer people than elsewhere. While Tereza had to share her room with four women, she had her own cupboard and bed and a roof over her head. She walked her father back to the station. They were still talking when the train began to move. Ferdinand stood at the open window, waving.

"My father told me that a good Jew always has to prepare two things: a packed suitcase, and a passport in his hand! We'll send you food packages. Your mother knows a bus driver. We'll call each other. You can come home any time. We'll be waiting for you. Make your own decision. You can do it, Kitten. You can!"

The train chugged off, turning this way and that, until Tereza was left by herself. She returned to the hostel but was unable to think in all the noise. During dinner in a Jewish dining hall she met a boy who was serving food. He was from Bratislava, and they had seen each other fleetingly in the local dining hall back home. She sensed that he liked her. He invited her to a Bee Gees concert at the Wiener Stadthalle. It was her first rock concert, something she'd never expected to experience in her lifetime. So this was freedom! The band sounded great, but she couldn't relax. Freedom didn't taste the way she'd thought it would. She was experiencing something completely new and different but she wasn't enjoying any of it. She had made a decision out of necessity, and it was a choice that was more forced than free. Then the young man began pressing himself on her. Without even waiting for the Bee Gees to finish, she fought her way out through the crowds of shouting people.

Her parents never made another train trip to see her, since the border was sealed tight the next day. She went to the bus station to ask about the driver, but it was pointless. No parcel arrived.

Tape

The Secret Police were again looking for Jozef in the Radio Building. He knew they were after him, but he also knew they had a lot of work. The list of people they were looking for was enormous, and every day some of those they could not find would be moved from the "Unable to Contact" column to the "Emigrated" column.

His superior greeted him, face pale.

"Jozef, they just left. I haven't told you anything and I haven't seen you." He shook his hand. "Good luck."

Jozef had just come back from recording the famous speech in which a politician talked about the border being a promenade. There was no need to wait any longer and no reason to keep up false hope. A failed pastor and actor, as the people responsible for arresting him called him, he had one last opportunity to leave Czechoslovakia or he could put on a prison uniform and let his family be persecuted.

When he arrived home, Erika was whistling in the kitchen, a sign that she was in an excellent mood. She had just finished marinating the rabbit and had managed to get fabulous bacon at the market. Peter was

watching with interest as she sliced it into tiny white cubes. Jozef
stood for a moment in the hallway, summoning the courage for what
he had to say. Then he entered.

"We have to leave."

"Leave? And go where?"

"To Austria. They wanted to arrest me today."

"But I'm frying the crackling!"

Erika spoke like a practical woman. They had to leave now, while
she was frying the crackling and marinating the rabbit? Where would
they go? Dinner was almost ready! Not for her, but for them! But she
didn't say what was going through her mind, knowing that her husband was right. They had to leave.

"Luckily I have a full tank of gas. Pack warm clothes for the winter."

"That doesn't sound temporary, does it?"

"Austrian Radio will help us. They're employing our people and
will get us work and housing."

Peter followed their conversation attentively.

"Mum, where are we going?"

Erika started to say "on a vacation," but her voice broke. She
embraced the boy, but he shouted joyfully. Vacation! He had to pack
his little cars.

During his last trip to the Radio Building Jozef returned his reporter's
tape recorder. He wouldn't let them make a thief out of him. He went
to see their neighbor in the building, the one who had called them that
August night and told them about the Soviet invasion. He left all his
receipts with her, showing that he had paid off his television and the
fridge. There was nothing left to say.

His biggest regret was that he couldn't say goodbye to his mother.
She told him that police from Modra were even looking for him in their
vineyard. He was in a terrible predicament, having to leave without

kissing the person who had sacrificed so much for him. So he called Erika's sister.

Anna answered after a long pause. Her voice had changed. It sounded tired, as if coming from a deep well.

"Hello? Is that you, Anna?"

"Jozef? Where are you calling from?"

"From a phone booth. How are you?"

"Well, you know. Petra left."

"I know... please don't cry. Everything will be fine. I have very little time... I wanted to hear your voice."

"I'm happy you called."

"I have a favor to ask of you. Could you visit my mother, now and again, when you're in the area? She has no phone, as you know. Tell her I love her very much."

"I will, don't worry."

"Say hello to Alex."

"I wish you the best of luck."

Jozef put down the receiver. The silence interrupted by electrical frequencies in the phone spoke more eloquently than dozens of words. He could be silent and yet he'd said everything.

Captain Poliačik, a quiet forty-year-old man, was in the Passport Office. He gave Jozef and his family permits to go to Austria without asking any questions. His department had been doing this all summer long without stopping anyone. Anyone who wanted to leave could get out. Jozef thanked him and left the office.

That day Captain Poliačik gave out several other travel permits. At the end of the day he wrote one for himself and his wife and children. Then he wrote a letter to his superior that would arrive by mail two days after he left the country.

"As a Communist Party member I should stay, but as the father of a family I cannot."

The white Škoda MB, packed with pullovers, coats, and winter boots, crossed the border at seven thirty in the evening. There was a comforter on the seat, and their cutlery was wrapped in a tablecloth. In the trunk were the fresh cracklings and the marinated rabbit.

Officially Jozef was on a work assignment, but the customs officers were not surprised by anything. Hundreds of cars were leaving the republic loaded like his. But the days of tolerance were coming to a close. The next day the state would decide to strictly control the border, and the fact that this was even announced was considered a special favor. The government was quick to forget the leniency of yesterday.

When the red and white barrier lowered behind them, Jozef stopped the car and got out. He opened the engine compartment to check the oil, but Erika knew he was looking at the silhouette of the vineyards above Bratislava. None of them had an inkling that it would be twenty-one years before they returned to their former homeland.

Peter was the most content of them all. He looked at the barrier separating them from Czechoslovakia and then turned in his seat and said, "Now the Russians can't get us."

The people at Austrian Radio and Television behaved very humanely, accepting Jozef as a colleague in need of help. They arranged housing for his family, gave him tickets to the station's dining hall, and financial support in the sum of 5,000 schillings. Then they started looking for work on his behalf.

Even so, Jozef slept very poorly during his first night. He remembered that his program, *Watch Out for the Turn*, was supposed to be broadcast the very next day at noon. The entire show was on tape, and suddenly he, the perfectionist, realized that he had left it locked in his desk in the editorial room. How would they find it? Would they even remember it? He would put his colleagues in a terrible bind and endanger the broadcasting of Czechoslovak Radio!

A cold sweat covered his brow when he quietly got up very early, started his car, and returned to Bratislava. His papers were still valid for one last day. He was among the first to arrive at the Radio Building.

When a colleague saw him, he almost collapsed. They'd all presumed that he'd gone abroad, and there he was giving them a tape.

"This is *Watch Out for the Turn.*"

"You're insane, Jozef. You'll get arrested. Where's your wife?"

"In Vienna, with our little boy. I am going back to them."

"Go, for heaven's sake!"

The man who risked arrest for an automotive radio program must have been protected by a higher power. He got into his car and for the last time crossed the Czechoslovak border, which turned into an impenetrable fortress that night at midnight.

Sewer

Lajo surfaced like flotsam carried through the sewer. Using his good Russian, he went to see the nearby command of the occupation forces. Actually it wasn't clear where he was and how he had managed to get there, but when he returned three hours later he looked very somber. At the District Office of the Communist Party he made it clear that he had been assigned exceptional tasks, and that was soon confirmed by a telephone call in Russian.

He'd resurfaced at the right time, before everything was won. The supporters of the Prague Spring were still quite strong, and their liquidation by the Moscow Winter group was still a work in progress. One could even speak of risk. Not great risk, as the chance of a reversal in the situation was minimal, but that slight risk gave Lajo an advantage and strengthened his position on the side of the victors.

He deserved some credit, after all. He wasn't just hiding somewhere, waiting to see how it all played out, at least not for very long; he'd grabbed the rudder and turned around! The brunette from the tire service was beginning to bore him. She constantly nagged him about getting a divorce and marrying her, and that was certainly not in his plans for the moment, or ever. Fully stoked and pumped with adrenaline from sex with his mistress and his oratorical performances in the factories, he, a public figure, decided to take on a small private mission.

He visited Alex in his office. Sanola was the right place for them to talk. A café would give the impression of a family debate, and visiting him at home meant seeing Anna. He wasn't in contact with his sisters, but he'd found out about Erika leaving through a reprimand from his superiors: "Lajo, your family is emigrating and you're just standing there watching like an idiot."

Alex was checking his production statistics. Production of dental equipment had gone up, and more had just been ordered by Egypt. The departure of his daughter had disturbed the fragile balance between him and the state in a direction that he felt was moving unstoppably to his disadvantage. The warning signs of his fall remained minimal, however; he was still the only person who could keep the factory going as it began to rebound from the summer interruption. He was checking the numbers, but Ottawa began to emerge before his eyes.

His sister was initially surprised by his telephone call, but then she was pleased. She had no children and would welcome Petra into her home. Alex began thinking of how to arrange that. First he gathered together all the postcards that Mariška had ever sent them, the Christmas ones showing Ottawa under snow and the Easter ones showing it filled with tulips. He looked at them for hours, analyzing every point and trying to memorize the appearance of the city, guessing what it would really look like when his daughter got to see it.

While his eyes were looking at numbers and his soul was in Canada, Lajo strode into his office, chased by the secretary, who was trying in vain to prevent this unexpected invasion. She looked at her boss and he just shrugged his shoulders. Time had taught them how to tolerate rudeness.

"Hello. I have to talk with you." Lajo turned to the secretary with a stern expression. "As a Communist talking to a Communist."

The secretary quietly backed away.

"Take a seat."

Lajo remained standing. He paced around the room on the Bulgarian carpet, gesticulating with his hands under the silent gaze of the President's portrait. In the glass showcase were dusty syringes with matte glass cylinders, and next to them needles of various sizes arranged in a fan. Then came the scalpels and surgical scissors, ending with laparotomy hooks that reflected the autumnal sun beaming through the windows. The bottom shelf of the showcase ended the Sanola exhibition with a hydrometer, a gas meter, and a milk meter.

Behind Alex was a photo of Christiaan Barnard shaking his hand in Workshop Number Four. Both of them were smiling, and the world-renowned surgeon from Cape Town looked like he was having an indescribably amazing time touring the greasy factory. Lajo zeroed in on a framed family photograph placed on the desk. His eyebrows knit into a frown as he looked at Petra standing between her father and mother, immortalized by the self-timer of the Flexaret camera. Then he said, with conviction through his teeth: "Nice."

He shifted his upper body closer to Alex above the desk. "Good job!"

Alex stood up, and for a few seconds they looked each other in the eye. Then Lajo started in, "That you shit on your family doesn't surprise me. You're shitting on me, as well, on my position. You're damaging me. You never liked me, but what I don't understand is why you're now shitting on your own child as well. You want her to have a rotten life? But I know who's behind it. It's my sisters. They're always whispering behind my back. They've always had secrets! You wouldn't believe how secretive they are! Erika took off with her pastor, and now even your daughter is gone. How does that make me look? Do you realize how that makes me look?"

"You look well, Ladislav."

"Just keep on joking, you'll stop soon enough. I look like an idiot who has no idea how to keep his own family in order. It's from watching television. I just don't understand it. We're surrounded by mountains here, but everybody is watching Viennese television. It makes you stupid. But what you're seeing isn't real; what they broadcast is all a show. There is no Vienna, at least not the one they're showing you. The place is racked with unemployment. Beggars fill the streets. Barefoot slum children are begging everywhere.

"I've never seen that in Vienna."

"Because you haven't been everywhere. They make the tourists go where they want them to go. When they show those gleaming streets, I have to laugh! It's not real! Where would they get shops like that? After the war we had to send them three wagons of potatoes so they wouldn't drop dead! Now they've built a Propaganda Strasse in their studio and put some fake gold in the shop windows, rubber salamis, children's watches, and they pay whores to walk back and forth in front of the cameras. Those are capitalist tricks but they don't fool me! They have special transmitters from the American Army that can reach all the way up here over the mountains."

Lajo paused, breathing heavily.

"I'm wasting my breath. But I'm not a swine. I want to help you. Wake up while you still have time."

He turned and left without saying goodbye.

Alex never found out whether his brother-in-law had coordinated his visit with what followed, or if Lajo, like all careerists, was simply superbly attuned to the theme hanging in the air. Less than two hours later he received a phone call.

"Comrade Technical Deputy, please come to see me."

Alex walked past the secretary. "I'm going to see the old man."

He'd brought along the correspondence with Egypt, expecting to be praised for the great success they'd achieved in Cairo. But the old man looked worried, and instead of being in his office, he was sitting in the outer room where his visitors usually waited for him. Alex realized that the manager was a visitor now and that he only had a few days left.

"He wants to talk to you." The manager pointed his head towards his own office. Alex entered. Inside sat a forty-year old man wearing a modern leather jacket and elegant loafers. He seemed quite sophisticated. Alex felt he must have seen him somewhere before.

"Please, sit down."

The man offered him the sofa while he remained seated behind the director's desk. In the middle of the room was a giant model of a syringe made of polished bronze, with the needle pointing proudly towards the ceiling. After several visitors had criticized the work of the famous sculptor as looking as if it wanted to pierce the portrait of the President of the Republic, it had been turned to point at the window.

The man smiled and Alex froze. Now he remembered. This man had spent three full days with Alex after he'd taken a trip to San Francisco. He was interested in whom Alex had met, what they talked about and what the others were doing... The man was particularly interested in his description of a Dixieland band full of elderly African Americans. They played fantastic music and radiated the kind of peace that he yearned for now. The man had mentioned the songs they'd played and what drinks Alex had ordered with the friends at his table. They'd clearly had their own man in the club.

"Where is your daughter, Comrade Director?"

"She went to Vienna, Comrade Major."

"How do you know my rank? The last time we saw each other I was only a Captain."

"I still have friends."

"Your friends won't be in their high positions much longer. You still have a chance. It doesn't look good when the daughter of a man like you leaves. Especially when you took her to the train station yourself."

"She's young and has her life ahead of her."

"A medical doctor? We'll give you another chance, Comrade Director. You'll get a visa to go to Austria. We know that Petra lives there. In Mariahilfer Strasse, right? We know much more. So tell me: will you try to persuade her to come back? Our leadership has decided to offer this chance to many of those who have made mistakes. You're among those they trust. Don't spoil it. Do you realize how many are coming back? After all, the situation at home is normalizing now. What is waiting for the traitors abroad? Engineers are cleaning toilets and doctors are washing dishes. It's undignified, don't you think? Our Party can pardon those who were misled by propaganda, but it won't last long."

"Will you invalidate the warrant for my daughter's arrest?"

"I'll tear it in pieces in front of your eyes if we make a deal. If she doesn't return within a week, she'll be sentenced in absentia to three years in prison for illegally leaving the Republic. It's a serious offer, Comrade Director. You'll get a visa. Your wife, of course, will stay here. She'll be waiting for you and will not move, I can guarantee that. Go and behave like a Communist."

Alex stumbled out of the office white as chalk. The old man said nothing.

Alex had no idea if they were playing games with him or testing his reliability, or whether this was indeed a serious offer. Did they know anything about Ottawa? They couldn't tap every telephone in Hungary! What if they arrested him at the border or followed him?

Dozens of agents had left with the refugees. Alex didn't take the threat lightly; he never underestimated State Security. They really were professional, and those who thought they were idiots (as in jokes about policemen) were mistaken. Maybe they even spread those jokes about the police so people would be less careful.

Alex had been afraid all his life. He was afraid because of the information they had about him and how they could use it against him and his child. He was afraid. Fear, cold and clammy, had probably been part of him since birth.

But while he was young, he'd had no fear... how and why? He didn't have it while he was single. When he got married and Petra was born, he was trapped. He was in a position to be blackmailed because of his love for his family. The challenge issued to him barely five minutes ago paralyzed him like poison.

After he came home from work he took Anna for a walk. It was windy and getting dark. Anna wore a scarf, and he had to hold his hat on his head with one hand. They walked down their favorite path above Stará Ruda, looking out on the two church steeples, the cemetery, and the factory chimneys. When they were certain that nobody could hear them, they started talking quietly, the wind cutting through their words as they left their mouths.

They took turns bending their heads and speaking clearly and slowly into each other's ears.

"Tell me, what should I do? I'm going crazy over this."

"Go and see Petra."

"What about you? They won't let you see her."

"I'll join you later. I'm sure they'll let me go."

"But that could take years. Do you know how many cases like this there are?"

"Better that I should be alone than our daughter. I know all about this place, but she knows nothing about the world over there. It's a new world for her."

"Oh my God, I don't know. I don't like this. What should I do?"

There were only two possibilities, and both were bad. Alex had to either leave Petra alone, or leave Anna alone. And he had to make a decision, because the game was already on. The next day he really did get permission to travel to Vienna.

The dice were thrown, flying through the air and falling on his head.

Parcel

Meeting his daughter exhausted Ferdinand's last bit of strength. As soon as the Vienna train station disappeared from view, he went to the washroom, as pungent and filthy as all train washrooms around the world, and tucked another nitroglycerin pill under his tongue. He was ashamed of his weakness. A railway man through and through, he felt that people would recognize him the moment he boarded a train. And also that nobody had the right to know his problems.

While the train heading for Vienna had been packed with passengers, it was returning to Bratislava half-full. Sitting down in a compartment, he immediately understood that he had joined a broken hearts club. Around him sat mostly older people, teary-eyed women and pale men, the mothers and fathers of children left on the platform in Vienna. No words were needed. Each of them was experiencing a loss so fresh that none could bare to talk of it.

Ferdinand closed his eyes. He thought of Tereza: how she was always at the top of her class, how she excelled in everything. She had won a competition without telling him, and one day, with an innocent expression on her face, she turned on the television and her parents saw her moderating a program called *Swallow*. There she was on the screen, holding a microphone as naturally as if she were born for it. He remembered how she liked to sit by her open window and listen to the organ, how she played Trouble with her brother Janko and always let him win, and how she would help her mother with everything except ironing...

Ferdinand felt as if someone had placed a hot iron on his chest. He couldn't breathe, and the searing pain beneath his rib cage pushed him back against his seat, shooting down into his left hand and causing spasms in his little finger.

"Is anything wrong? Are you in pain? Oh my God, call a doctor!"

When the train arrived at the station, the conductor called an ambulance, which immediately took Ferdinand to the hospital in Mickiewicz Street. Maria and Janko arrived less than twenty minutes later. Ferdinand managed to tell Maria about the parcels for Tereza before he lost consciousness. Doctor Glauber, who knew their family, could do nothing for him. It was a myocardial infarction, and Ferdinand died an hour later.

Tereza would not find out until a week later. She was unable to phone home: Every time she tried, she heard a click followed by a busy tone. And so she lived in blissful ignorance while waiting for the bus and promenading through Vienna. At least she could be with Petra.

Petra invited her to Café Sacher, one of the pillars of the monarchy. As good tourists, they ordered the famous "Sachertorte," named after the great owner and inventor of the fabulous cake smothered with apricot jam and paved over with a thick carpet of chocolate. Tereza was at first unwilling to enter this luxurious place for fear that her host would impoverish herself.

"Don't worry, I have enough. Hansi and Resi paid me. My father is supposed to come tomorrow and they're behaving like they never have before. They've finally given their slave some coins."

"Have they grown a conscience?"

"I don't know if that word exists in the Austrian dialect."

"Are you still cleaning and ironing?"

"I've done everything. I've even scrubbed their wallpaper and repainted their washroom."

Petra was enjoying being able to go out with her friend at least for a moment. Hansi and Resi kept her quite isolated from everything. She really did spend most of her time cleaning, but at least that kept her from thinking about herself. She wasn't meeting fellow refugees or going to the cafés they would go to. She basically avoided them. Even while still at home she'd had few friends. A medical student is always studying and has no time for relationships of any kind. On top of that, she felt undeservedly lucky. No matter how impossible Hansi and Resi were, she still had room and board with them, together with privacy. She didn't have to sleep in a crowded hostel or shower in a bathroom where everyone could see her.

"My parents haven't contacted me. I can't reach them."

"Don't worry, Tereza. I'm sure everything is fine."

"Are you looking forward to seeing your father?"

"I'm a bit afraid. He sounded so mysterious."

"Only a madman would say anything on the phone."

"I saw the actor Werich here."

"Ján Werich?"

"Yes."

"The actor?"

"He was smoking a cigar and walking along Mariahilfer Strasse. More people were greeting him here than in Prague."

"If even he has decided to emigrate, there will be no more fun back home."

"You think there still is some?"

Waiting at the bus terminal proved pointless. Tereza watched for every bus from Slovakia, looking for her parcel or for anyone she might know. But fewer and fewer people were arriving from Slovakia, and she didn't know any of them. It was as if her luck had abandoned her. She was known for unexpected coincidences and was always running into acquaintances. Now there was nobody.

Despite the family tragedy, Maria hadn't forgotten about Tereza. She prepared a parcel filled with canned goods and warm clothing and begged the bus driver to take it with him. He didn't want to do it; each trip was closely watched, and he risked his job or even worse. But he knew about Ferdinand's death and agreed to help. Even so, the parcel for Tereza did not get far.

Everyone had to get out of the bus at the border, bringing their belongings with them and standing behind them on the sidewalk. Only one parcel was left on the bus. Nobody claimed it. The soldiers were tense, having experienced a bomb attack recently with a similar parcel. With the machine gun aimed at him, the driver was ordered to take the parcel aside, far from the bus. Then they shot it to pieces.

By the time Tereza was finally able to reach home by phone, her father was already buried. Maria tried to console her by telling her that she wouldn't have been allowed to cross the border at any rate, and if she had succeeded, she would have been arrested and sentenced unconditionally to three years in jail. Everything was conspiring against her. Vienna became instantly hateful to her. The Art Nouveau boulevards and monumental palaces and statues seemed to threaten her. She had to get away as soon as possible.

She had put aside money for airfare and had preferred to forego eating rather than spend it. The next evening she flew to Tel Aviv.

Battery

The most beautiful Czechoslovak car drove its last few kilometers on the badly neglected paved road. Unfortunately the road was a Czechoslovak one; like the bread, milk, and air, even a paved road indicated its country of origin. Ours are full of cracks and poorly mended potholes. There's no mistaking the groaning shock absorbers and body jolts: we're in our homeland!

The driver steered his Felicia carefully to avoid road damage. It looked like he was waiting to be noticed as usual, but this time he actually wanted to be invisible. Gone were the times when people waved at him; now everyone had turned inward and preferred not to look at their surroundings. The slow driving was not caused by the state of the road but rather by the state of mind of the driver.

Anyone looking at his face would have seen a small drop glistening in the corner of his eye. Of course, the roof of the Felicia was down, and it could have been the cold wind that brought tears to his eyes.

Anna had persuaded him that he had to go and that she would stay there alone. That was her decision. That diminutive White Lady was stronger than she looked. Now Alex was sitting in his car with an apple cake, undergarments, and medical books. He'd also brought along a photo album from their family vacations.

There they were at Lake Balaton, Petra with her flat chest covered by her first swimsuit, which she'd argued for even though her mother tried to persuade her that a six-year-old girl didn't need upper body covering.

There they were in Vrátna Valley, Petra brandishing an ornamental walking stick made of lacquered wood and looking forward to potato gnocchi with sheep's milk cheese at a nearby mountain chalet. After drinking sheep's whey she spent most of the next three days on the toilet. From then on she called vacation "toilet time."

There they were in front of their building in Stará Ruda. Later, in Ottawa, this photo would move them because of its spontaneous quality. They didn't pose to give an impression of family happiness or a vacation idyll. They simply stood in front of their apartment building, breathing hard after a long walk, and everything seemed simple and natural.

Alex joined a line of waiting cars. The regional bus pulled up next to him. Passengers climbed out, carrying their luggage. Border guards and Russian soldiers were everywhere.

Alex handed his passport and permit to a woman in a green uniform who checked him out with professional skepticism. She perused the small piece of paper for ages, checking out the stamps. A Russian officer watched them from the door of a recently slapped-together wooden barrack. Just as the woman was handing Alex his passport, the officer came up and whispered something in her ear.

Alex broke out in a cold sweat. This was the end. He would never see Petra again. This was only a trap after all, and he, a trusting idiot, had fallen for it!

Alex got out of his car as the officer's gaze drilled into his back. He opened the trunk. It must be obvious to them that I'm trying to escape, he thought feverishly. He was bringing so many things! And he'd stuffed some dollars under the seat!

"Not there, Comrade driver, open the front."

The customs officer was not interested in the trunk so Alex opened the hood and stepped aside. Why were they torturing him? The Russian officer perked up and smiled. With a grunt of admiration, he bent down to examine the Felicia's engine. Alex was so tense that he didn't immediately realize that the God of Automobiles had sent him a car enthusiast.

Under the sympathetic gaze of the customs officer, the Russian admired Czechoslovak technology. This restored Alex's self-confidence, and with a voice trained in presenting medical instruments, he addressed the man who was practically licking the engine. In decent Russian, he informed the enthusiast that the 50 HP engine had a volume of 1800 cc and could reach a maximum speed of 128 km per hour. The soldier nodded his head with respect and pointed: "What a small battery!"

Alex agreed, thinking: Yes, we like everything small and human-sized, that fits in your hand. Only in your country is everything big.

"You can go!"

The last bit of tension had left Alex; he smiled politely at both officials, closed his hood and crossed the border. After a few short formalities on the Austrian side, he parked his car behind the customs house and just sat there, his hands shaking as he gasped for air. The fatefulness of his act overwhelmed him. He was saving his daughter and sacrificing his wife.

He believed it was only temporary. He would get his wife across the border to join them. He would make a big stink, petition all the offices and embassies! His country would be so ashamed that they would reconsider whether it was worthwhile separating families. The joy of seeing Petra again suppressed all negative thoughts, including the one that a man of his intelligence had to acknowledge: it was naïve to think that his country would not punish two successful escapes. He hadn't gone quietly, he'd banged the door behind him. And that was unforgivable.

Hansi and Resi took pains to prepare an excellent beef stew. Resi went out that morning to buy a nice piece of lean beef, and while Petra assisted her with the cooking, she complained nonstop about the frightfully high prices and the cheekiness of the butchers for asking so much. She was in a good mood at finally being freed of this stone weighing down her neck.

Right after welcoming Alex she handed him a big envelope with a significant look on her face. Foreign stamps covered the envelope. It was a letter from his sister in Ottawa containing all the necessary forms and a letter of invitation in which Maria Emma Duvier certified that she would sponsor her relatives from Czechoslovakia.

Petra could not get enough of her father. She constantly sat next to him and even followed him as he moved around the apartment and looked out on Mariahilfer Strasse from various windows. She felt like a little girl inseparable from her parents. Even so, apart from a few polite phrases, they didn't really talk in the apartment. They needed privacy for what they wanted to say to each other. Finally Vienna's most famous street swallowed them in its careless bustle.

"Mom can't stay there!"

"She won't. But she has to for now. It's her decision, Petra."

"I'd rather go back!"

"Then your mother's sacrifice would be senseless. If you return, they'll blackmail you for the rest of your life for leaving the country without permission and for getting your arrest warrant annulled—if they annulled it at all, because you can't believe them. Even if they did, they could reinstate it against you at any time! And against me as well, because I helped you! Things would be even worse. Petra, I promise that the first thing I'll deal with is getting your mother to join us."

On the same day that Anna accompanied her husband to the garage, watched him back out with his Felicia, and then turned around and walked away with unusual slowness, the post woman brought a package to her door. When she unwrapped it, she found the keys to Erika's apartment with a quickly scribbled note saying they were leaving. Erika apologized for leaving her alone in the care of Alex. She offered her anything that she wanted from the apartment, but urged her to go quickly before it was sealed off.

The property of a person who emigrated became the property of the state. Vacancies were rising in buildings throughout Czechoslovakia. Neighbors would be awakened in the middle of the night by noise in the empty apartments above, but nobody called the police. They knew it wasn't thieves, but rather relatives trying to take away a few useful things while they could.

After the summer vacation children found themselves in half-empty classrooms. In some locations, several classes were combined into one because there were so few pupils. The number of sealed apartments grew, gardens became overgrown with weeds, and apples dropped and rotted in the grass. Kindness and humanity disappeared and remained missing for the next twenty years.

Anna traveled to Bratislava, knowing what she would do. In Erika's living room hung a pastel picture of a village. Behind it was a pointy hill—it was too pointy, like a sharpened pencil, and the church steeple below it was crooked. The picture also lacked the proper perspective, and the untrained hand of the artist was evident, but it radiated love for the country. Erika had painted it right after she graduated, and it represented the world as she wished to see it, but which unfortunately never existed.

Anna carefully wrapped the picture in a newspaper and locked the apartment. The journey back by train lasted forever, but she had plenty of time. All of her duties had suddenly ceased. She had nobody to clean up after, to cook for or to argue with. The world stopped turning.

Alex likewise lost a piece of his life. He not only lost Anna but also had to say good-bye to Felicia. He'd known this moment would come. He had wanted to leave the country in full glory with his Felicia, and Anna didn't oppose it. He tried to tell her that he needed it to take things to their daughter, but Anna didn't even protest. He continued entangling himself in illogical constructions until she cut through his chatter with a kiss.

In the end he told her not to think he wanted to drive a car that she couldn't stand, but the truth was that he wanted to drive the car one last time: the car that she couldn't stand. He couldn't leave it at home; it would be confiscated. But what would he do with it in Austria? At first he thought of parking it in a side street and sending the keys back to Czechoslovakia so somebody could come and get it. But who? Anna? Lajo? One of his friends from Sanola? Nobody would risk taking a car whose owner had committed a crime.

He would rather give it to Hansi. Hansi wasn't very happy about it—he'd have to register the car, give it an overhaul, and who knows if he could even learn how to drive a car of the Eastern European type, he said, decisively refusing the offer. Alex was as furious as the father of a rejected bride. For heaven's sake, a vehicle of the Eastern European type? He would rather sell it to a used car dealer.

When he arrived at the used car lot, he became almost petrified. The courtyard was full of old Škodas, Octavias, Spartaks, MBs, Trabants, and even one Felicia, although in much worse condition than his. The owner spoke decent Czech.

"Vienna is filled with them, filled with them, my dear sir. How much do you think people would pay for it? You should pay me for taking it!"

When the offended Alex silently started his car, the man blocked his way and offered him some money. Alex didn't try to bargain; they'd need all the money they could get. Although he was a top specialist at home, his salary wasn't high. In those days people of his standing had no foreign bank accounts. Even if such an account could be arranged, there would be nothing to deposit in it.

Alex came from the generation that hadn't yet learned to steal. Alex didn't steal, and neither did the general manager of Sanola. And strangely enough, neither did the people in the government. It was not a den of corruption the way it is now. But officials broke the Ten Commandments in a different manner. They were drunk with power, an aphrodisiac that ruined their characters, and they would put their friends in prison if they felt endangered. This was the consumption of unlimited power under relatively modest conditions. Today we cannot comprehend whether it was worth it.

Map

Financial aid from Austrian Radio helped Jozef survive the first few weeks. Every day he ate with his family in the company cafeteria, where they would meet some of their friends. Their conversations had two themes: what was new at home, and who was traveling and where.

Cases varied. Some people left to save themselves from imprisonment, but others used the exodus to solve their personal problems. Once the family ate lunch next to a man who had left his wife at home, just taking off without saying a word. Their marriage wasn't working, and here was a chance to leave. He'd decided to start a new life far away, in South America. He finished his schnitzel with potato salad and drank his coffee, and they never saw him again.

Conflicting news reports came from Bratislava, some hopeful and others just the opposite. There was less good news as time passed. Returning home was not a certainty. Everyone was trying to find a country to settle in. Nobody planned to stay in Vienna. Although thousands of people migrated there from Czechoslovakia, Vienna was only a transfer station. Jozef was lucky; Radio Free Europe offered him a position with a two-room apartment in Munich and a salary of 2,100 *Deutschemarks* per month. But Erika opposed it.

"You know, I don't mind the German language, I mind the Germans. When I went to Germany for a practicum I met a lot of former SS men. I cannot live there. But it's not only the Germans. I don't want to stay in Europe, period. Let's get out of here. Let's go overseas. Europe is full of spies."

From time to time they heard about the deaths of people who had left Czechoslovakia. There were suspicious car crashes and unexpected heart attacks. It wasn't that Vienna had fewer car accidents than Bratislava, or that a tense period didn't provoke heart attacks more than a calm period, but it still seemed just too much. People reacted to each death in an exceptionally sensitive manner as refugees were mowed down. People whispered that State Security had infiltrated the refugees and was recruiting informants, and that those who refused had to die.

"Europe is out!"

Jozef had to admit that Erika was right. He rejected the Munich offer with regret and went back to square one. He was tremendously disenchanted with the behavior of some of the radio people he knew from Bratislava. While the border stood open, they registered with Austrian Radio as refugees and received financial aid, then suddenly sold their cafeteria tickets and returned home with a few schillings. One had to get away from people like that.

"You're right. Let's leave Europe."

The Office of Catholic Charities had a giant map of the world hanging on the wall showing all the states that welcomed refugees. Every day, the refugees would gather in front of it, pointing and whispering to each other. It was a sad lesson in geography, showing something that had ended, but it was also filled with the hope of new experiences.

After persuading Peter that Trinidad, Easter Island, and Madagascar were not the best places to emigrate, they settled on three real possibilities:

Australia, Canada, and the United States. Now it was a matter of seeing who gave them visas first.

Australia was quickly eliminated. When they visited the Australian embassy in Vienna, they found it a big mess. The embassy was being painted and cartons were piled everywhere, spattered with white paint and trampled by dozens of shoes. Painters on ladders and other workers got in the way of irritated officials. Erika and Jozef turned around and left. Sometimes a painter's brush is enough to change one's fate. For years after that they met people who remembered how the refurbishment of the Australian embassy made them choose another country.

They liked Canada, which had adopted an accelerated program for refugees. They had no idea that famous compatriots, the Czech Tomas Bata and the Slovak Stephen Roman, who were successful businessmen in Canada, had spoken on their behalf. Canada still had a great deal of unpopulated territory that it wanted settled. The government was equally interested in acquiring educated people, and most of the refugees were doctors, professors, or university students. That's why many chose Canada. When Jozef went to the Canadian embassy, he learned there was no demand for pastors at the moment among the small Slovak community.

Jozef's late uncle had been a Lutheran minister in Pittsburgh. In letters to Jozef's father he had written about the many Slovaks, referred to as "bread immigrants," who had settled in the United States during the years of the Great Depression. They made a decision: they would go to the United States. Even the accelerated program would require three months for their visas to come through, but at least it gave them certainty and a goal.

One day, while Erika was hanging laundry and Jozef was playing with Peter, a name was repeated over the speaker of the hostel.

"Jozef, they're calling you."

He began paying closer attention.

"Me? Who would be calling me?"

But she was right. The loudspeaker repeated his name along with a German word that he understood: telephone. He quickly ran to the porter, who handed him the receiver through a small window. What he heard on the phone he refused to repeat to Erika.

"Your brother called."

"Lajo?"

"He was terribly vulgar to the point where I can't repeat it. He said you endangered his family and that they would suffer for your escape."

"How did he find us?"

Jozef shrugged. Nobody gave out the names of refugees. They changed hostels that same day. Lajo used to go out drinking every day with the Secret Police. What if he was able to harm them even in Vienna? They feared for their safety until their departure.

The staff of hostels and government departments always treated them well, but ordinary people on the street were not as nice. They were afraid of the crime and disorder refugees brought. Shop clerks looked at them with even more distrust, following them as they wandered among the counters and searching their shopping bags for stolen goods. And many refugees did steal, because they lacked money, or because they could not help themselves when for the first time in their lives they held in their hands the kind of merchandise that was never available in their country. And it smelled so nice!

Stores in Czechoslovakia smelled of disinfectant. Here one smelled fine perfume. Everything smelled of it, from ironware to fluffy pullovers. The bright colors tormented hungry eyes. Even simple things were packaged so nicely that you wanted to buy them. Reach out your hand!, the merchandise seemed to say. Take me!

Czechoslovak citizens would experience this embarrassment again twenty years later, with the fall of the Iron Curtain. Again the Austrian sales staff would suspect them, even as they welcomed them into their stores. But there would be a slight difference: the uninformed Czechoslovaks of 1989 would buy all the second-rate and out-of-date goods, as a result of which they would be welcomed with a hearty *Grüss Gott!*

But for now it was the number 1968 being written on frosty windows. The temperature had dropped sharply and people walked around in scarves and hats. Jozef looked like an obvious foreigner in his fur hat with earflaps, but he could tolerate the mean looks. There are stupid people in every country, and where he came from they even reached the level of executive power. They would just have to find a way to put up with it until they took off. Three months to go. Almost one hundred days!

With the help of a distant relative, Jozef found a job in the U.S. that could be called, tongue-in-cheek, assistant to the secretary; he would fetch the mail, pick up parcels, and make copies all day.

In the meantime, Erika tried to keep the household in order. She bought cheap meat at the *Naschmarkt* and was happy to be able to cook something for her boys. When she found out a month later that they were actually eating horse stew, they became vegetarians for a while, eating only vegetable soup and potatoes prepared a thousand and one ways. They also drank hundreds of gallons of tea.

But the hard work paid off. A Lutheran minister cannot arrive in America in worn-out jeans.

Each religion had its own organization in Vienna. Catholics had Caritas, Jews had HIAS, and Protestants had the World Council of Churches. Only Communists had nothing. It's true that they did not belong to an actual church, but they were not far from it; their faith merely had other symbols and ideas.

Emigrating Communists were easy to spot because they kept their own people at arm's length. Alex was so busy handling his emigration that he had no time to feel ashamed. We know he was a Communist in name only, but in Vienna he heard so many insults against the Communists that he preferred to keep his background secret.

He immediately submitted an application to the Red Cross for his wife to be allowed to leave Czechoslovakia. An identical application was submitted to the Czechoslovak Embassy. Nobody would speak to him there, so he requested acknowledgement of his application; the stamp they resentfully banged on his receipt was the only response he got from the officials. He bought English and French textbooks for Petra and they began studying together. She had learned both languages in secondary school, but had largely forgotten them during her university years.

Alex knew some English. Although he had spent only eleven days in total abroad and could only communicate with partners in the technical departments who were tactful enough not to correct his accent and poor vocabulary, he was certain that he had mastered the language of Shakespeare. He soon found out that there were two kinds of English: his, and the kind that was spoken by the rest of the world.

"I'll never learn this." Satisfied that he had learned enough, he switched to French and began reading a conversation on page three: "Je swee Alexaaandr."

"Dad: not 'je swee,' but 'je suis.'"

"Je swee."

"Je suis."

"I'm only Alex, you'll have to excuse me."

Petra laughed.

"You certainly are."

Snow

History surprised Milan on a Yugoslav beach. He and his parents didn't hesitate for long. They dealt with the formalities, and after boarding a ship for Haifa along with their car, they ate the last of their Czechoslovak canned food. At the port, Milan tossed the cans into a wire basket in what seemed a symbolic parting. They never considered returning to a country full of Russian soldiers. They were Jews and had roots as well as relatives in Israel, and if it was possible to speak of optimism in their situation, they believed they had been given a new chance.

Their Škoda MB, the jewel of the Czechoslovak car industry and once a valuable piece of property, lost its value the moment it touched Israeli soil. Milan had thought they had brought something of value with them, but one look at Haifa's roads and modern cars brought him back to harsh reality. While the Škoda rusted quietly in the port, his parents moved in with their relatives, and Milan set off for Kibbutz Masaryk.

Tereza was no longer there; she had flown to Vienna. Everyone said it was just for a short time, however, so Milan decided to wait.

He registered for Ulpan, the language school for foreigners. Knowing Hebrew was important; without it he had no chance. He hadn't even been there three days when Tereza walked into the classroom. She knew most of the faces when the teacher introduced her, but one was a big surprise.

Milan waited for the break, when everybody went out to the courtyard, and then he embraced her. She embraced him back, and from that moment on, they knew they belonged together.

"I came because of you. I want to be with you."

"Are you serious?"

"I want to marry you... if you want to."

No, no, it didn't happen that fast. Tereza would certainly object to my description, but fiction speeds time along. And their time had been set long ago, when they met for the first time in the courtyard of the synagogue on Heyduk Street and Milan's father said, "May I introduce you to my son?"

Milan's father was a dentist. After returning from the concentration camp, he didn't want to stay in Bátorove Kosihy, the village from which he'd been sent to the transport, so he resumed his post-war practice in Šamorín. Milan remembered the modeling wax used by dentists and how his father modeled the ships and airplanes he liked to play with as a child.

His father's fingers were nimble and quick. A dentist is a bit of an artist, too, even if he doesn't feel like one. What are dentures, if not small sculptures? Even the author of these lines once studied stomatology for two semesters and had to cut models of teeth from chalk. The pieces of art that we use for eating are no less precious than the art we look at; it's only that one stays in our mouth while the other hangs in galleries.

Her experience in Czechoslovakia had made Tereza dubious of any kind of patriotism; Communist ideologues had misused it so much that it had become unpalatable for young people. But in Israel people saw things differently. For example, their teacher in Ulpan didn't want to go on vacation to Spain where she had relatives, because she didn't want to leave her country for even one day; what would the country do without her? She meant it. Amused at first, Tereza then began to regret that she could be proud of Czechoslovakia sometimes, but not all the time. Unfortunately, she had felt that way all her life.

Only letters from her mother reminded her of her homeland. They came every week and she tried to answer them, but sometimes her letters didn't arrive for a long time. Sometimes a letter would be lost, especially if it contained photographs. Smiling faces on a street in Tel Aviv displeased somebody. But maybe she was only imagining it. She would then try to repeat what she'd written before in her next letter, but she hadn't kept a copy, and apart from practical information, she couldn't replicate her original tone; repetition weakens love, like a kiss that is not spontaneous, but forced.

"Yesterday I washed the window in your room and cleaned the curtains; they're already hung. Otherwise, I'm not doing much cleaning. In autumn I dusted everything in your room and covered the armchairs and couch. No one has slept there, everything is clean. Your beautiful room misses you. The radio, record player, and telephone are silent, and I keep buying things for you, like pillows and shams. Janko bought a black candlestick with a red candle for your birthday and I'm not supposed to tell you this, but how can he give it to you if you're not coming back? It's such a pity that a clever girl like you, who has almost finished university here, has to look for support and work over there. It was a big deal, getting accepted by the university, and you had everything and now you have nothing. You should come back and take a break from that heat; it's not good for you. I'd better not show anyone that picture of you in the miniskirt. By the way, it's lovely, and both you and Milan are smiling nicely, but that skirt.... I know it's the fashion, but think about it—people can see your stomach! You know I love you more than anyone in the world, I'm your mother and want nothing but the best for you, but think about it. There's an opportunity to exchange our apartment for one with two bedrooms and central heating. But you have to tell me what you think about this idea, because if you want to come back, you'll need your room. I'm waiting for your decision, realizing that it's not an easy one to make."

Reading her mother's letter tore her to pieces, but her brother's letter brought her back.

"Hi, Terry. There is big news in Bratislava. They opened a gigantic new department store called Prior. I've been there twice. There are even escalators and elevators with thick shock absorbers, but I like the escalators best. You can buy almost anything at Prior, especially nice pullovers and musical instruments. On the floor with the instruments you can hear strange sounds. Last week I was sick. The doctor smiled and told me I had stomach poisoning and put me on a strict diet. I spent three days in bed, and even though I've been fine for a few days, Mom won't let me eat meat with sauerkraut. I can only watch sadly while she eats it with a big spoon."

Tereza spent her winter holiday with Milan and other friends. They rented a jeep and drove into the mountains. It was quite an expedition; after an hour of hiking up Hermon Mountain in the Golan Heights, they saw snow in Israel for the first time. They had a snow fight on the sea of rocks until a military patrol showed up.

"Are you crazy? You're in Lebanon! This is the border!"

They had crossed the border in the middle of their snowball fight and had to turn back right away. Luckily the soldiers were Israelis, otherwise they might have been shot or at least arrested.

Tereza carried some snow with her. It disappeared into a puddle in her hands, but she remembered its cold feeling for many weeks.

Airplane

They hadn't yet managed to get Anna out, but Alex wasn't giving up. Their date of departure was approaching and they could wait no longer. The Red Cross employee advised them to fly since the greater the distance between them, the better the argument for reunifying the family. Petra felt helpless. Her mother was as inaccessible to them right across the border in Bratislava as if they were across the ocean in Canada. The distance was not measured in meters but in the legal clauses of a divided world.

Everything was mitigated by the fact that they were flying to a country that had decided to accept them. They talked on the phone with Mariška and she told them that the Canadian government had organized a free six-month language class for all refugees (not necessary for Alex, of course), an allowance for the household (his aunt had refused it, because her late husband would turn in his grave), as well as clothing and shoes (the latter donated by Bata Shoes). The flight to Canada was a gift from the prime minister.

Jozef, on the other hand, didn't get anything for free. The World Council of Churches paid their airfare to New York, but it would have to be repaid to a post office box in New York. They would receive no help in the United States: no money or language courses. They had to take care of everything by themselves. The Americans would just shake their hands and say: "Welcome!"

Even knowing that Jozef was grateful. He felt that he, an ordinary person, was for the first time in his life playing chess with himself, and that whatever move he made, good or bad, would depend solely on him. He would not be able to blame anyone else.

Alex and Petra's last supper with Hansi and Resi could be considered surprisingly pleasant. The old couple could relax, since in twelve hours they would be free of the problem brought on by their magnanimous invitation three months ago. Resi had even begun to feel that Petra had worked too hard as her guest, and she asked Petra to join her in the pantry, a conspiratorial look on her face.

Resi kept her jewelry in a carton of dried mushrooms that she had gathered with Hansi a long time ago. The fungal smell of this biological cover provided natural protection for the treasure hidden inside the damp-stained Camel cigarette carton. They had found a space for it in the pantry after nearly throwing it away with the garbage where they used to keep it while on vacation, not trusting the banks. Petra unwittingly covered her nose, but Resi didn't notice. Her face turned tender as she gazed at the rows of gold coins arranged on velvet. She picked out the smallest one, featuring the face of the assassinated President Kennedy, the martyr of that time. With a reverent expression, as if about to sacrifice her own liver, she handed the coin to Petra.

"It's for you, to remember Aunt Resi."

Overcoming her distaste, Petra kissed her.

Jozef was able to see his mother after all, although only from a distance. The same tall man, Štefan, drove her, but this time in an old Wartburg.

They strolled along the Devin embankment, carefully watched by border guards. Quite a few people watched from the opposite shore. People were still allowed to stand along the Dunaj below the ruins of Devin Castle, and from there, divided by the border, they could see their loved ones on the other side of the river.

Brothers came to look at their sisters. Fathers looked at mothers, parents looked at their children, and children looked at their parents. They were not far from each other, separated only by the river Morava as it flowed lazily to join the more impetuous Danube.

In a coppice on the Austrian side, Jozef stood with Erika and Peter. An Austrian soldier smoked within eyesight, as did the soldier on the Czechoslovak side, except the Austrian smoked a Marlboro while his opponent smoked a Mars. There was another little detail to consider. If Jozef jumped in the river and tried to swim across, the Austrian soldier would jump in to save him from drowning, while the Czechoslovak soldier would send him to the bottom with a single burst from his machine gun. None of this tells us anything about the character of these armed youths, except that they had different commands to obey.

"Which one is Granny, Daddy?"

"The one in a kerchief."

"The old one?"

"What a way to talk about your granny, Peter!"

"I want to go to her."

"Don't move, or you'll fall into the water!"

"Granny, Granny!"

"Be quiet, dear, I beg you, be quiet, or we'll have to leave."

"Mummy, is Granny laughing or crying?"

Petra lay in bed, unable to sleep. She hadn't helped anyone since finishing her medical studies. By now she should have been working in the internal medicine ward of Trenčin Hospital for three months already. She felt she had forgotten everything. She had been looking forward to working in the hospital. Although shy, she could always talk to patients straight from her heart. When it concerned people she didn't know she was empathetic, curious, and the first to ask questions. Her communication gifts would have eased her first years of practice.

Now she was flying to a country where she hardly knew the language and where she would have to overcome communication problems even before professional problems. Her greatest fear was that she wouldn't understand what her foreign patients were saying to her. Finally she fell asleep before daybreak, dreaming of the pale faces of sick people emphatically speaking to her in a language she didn't understand.

Jozef's family had to spend the night before their departure in a hotel provided by the airline. They were flying to New York with the Israeli airline El Al, which had been the victim of a terrorist attack at Athens Airport less than two months before. Whether it was for this reason or immigration rules, the family had to change their accommodation, and Peter was delighted. They found themselves in a much more luxurious room than their previous one, and the little boy liked the gilded door handles so much that he opened and closed them a hundred times an hour.

Erika smiled, happy that her son was in such a good mood and unaware of the poorly-masked tension between his parents. Jozef read the letter of recommendation and the Bishop's invitation for the umpteenth time. The Zion Synod needed a Slovak pastor because previous pastors had spoken very poor Slovak.

At least he had some certainty to start with. However small, it was still there.

At Vienna's Schwechat Airport, two airplanes prepared for takeoff just a few minutes apart. They slowly moved in tandem with others, waiting for the tower to give them permission for takeoff. In one plane sat Erika and her family. It was a regular flight to New York with tourists, businessmen, a black family and nuns on board. The flight attendant offered them menthol gum to help with ear pressure and Peter hungrily grabbed three pieces. The attendant smiled and a moment later returned with some crayons and a coloring book of airplanes. Peter thanked her.

As the airplane lifted off the runway, Erika felt her heart tear. She looked out the window and saw her heart rolling on the skid-marked runway. As she looked, it continued to roll. She grabbed Jozef's shoulder.

"I was just remembering your radio program about the heart transplant, do you remember it?"

"Why do you ask?"

"They're taking out our hearts and giving us new ones."

"Erika, please..."

"That woman lived for five hours!"

"Don't worry, we'll manage."

Meanwhile, Alex and Petra sat in a Boeing that the Canadian government had sent for the refugees. The plane was packed, and they saw the familiar faces of people they'd met around the big map. Petra would remember the smell of this airplane forever: leatherette, plastic, baby milk and children's sweaty heads, hastily stubbed out cigarettes and perfume that couldn't cover fear.

A flight attendant came down the aisle with her serving cart.

"Whiskey? Beer? Wine? Cognac? Juice?"

Initially surprised that nobody ordered anything, she finally worked it out and announced to the whole plane, "It's free!"

The passengers came alive, and the attendant gave them the biggest smile possible. As she gestured towards the drinks cart, Alex turned to Petra. "Can you imagine? It's free."

Once the news spread throughout the plane, the flight attendant poured drinks non-stop. Everyone started drinking, and Alex joined in as well.

It was the saddest party he ever remembered joining. Some people sang and some laughed, but with nervousness and tears in their eyes. They all drank while wondering what was in store for them in Canada. Strangers assured each other that it couldn't be worse than being back home in a country occupied by tanks, and they almost believed it, thanks to the ocean of alcohol only slightly smaller than the ocean they flew above. People are such strange optimists.

When the New York-bound flight reached cruising altitude and frost started painting the windows, Erika turned to her husband.

"Jozef, you're a pastor, say something."

Jozef bowed his head.

"Lord God, we thank you for not abandoning us."

That was all. Then they kept silent for a long time. Now that fifty years have passed since that moment, Jozef knows he should have said more. For example: "Dear God, we thank you for two things: that you have not abandoned us and that you have not told us what awaits us."

The Others

Anna started cleaning. She washed the white front door and the linoleum in the hallway. She cleaned the Bulgarian runner that Alex had brought back from one of his business trips. She scoured the bathroom with powder and cleaned the grouting with chlorine bleach. She emptied all the kitchen cupboards and washed them with soapy water. She placed clean paper on the top of the cabinets, which no one could see but where dust constantly settled. She vacuumed the rooms and polished the Golden Susan collection—every family's cult glassware. She washed and ironed all the bed linen. The duvets would be cleaned as soon as she saw the mobile cleaners, a service provided in this region from time immemorial by a Roma family.

This was only a fraction of the work she did in the apartment, and it took her less than a week. Afterwards everything was spick and span, and as we know, nothing beats spick and span but the beautiful future of Communism, so finally Anna stopped. She had decided not to give in to despondency, but knew only one remedy against it: work. But before she could think of the next thing to clean, Sanola

was nice enough to enable her to forget about work in a very inten-
sive manner.

Once Alex's emigration was confirmed, even the few people who
had still stopped by to say hello no longer greeted her. When she lined
up in a store or came to pick up medicine at the pharmacy, everybody
went silent. The White Lady was the spirit of winter 1968: silent, invisible, and discouraging to others. Her former colleagues from the accounting office would cross the road when they saw her. Since there were no
wide boulevards in Stará Ruda, only narrow streets, even the opposite
walkway was unacceptably close, so people would duck into a doorway
or into a store where they had nothing to buy. Some even turned around
and walked away. Why did her former colleagues act this way? Because
less than a week after Alex's escape, Anna was transferred elsewhere.

She was no longer allowed to work with sensitive data, such as
salaries. She was no longer allowed to go to the bank in an armored car
to fetch the salary money. She would no longer sit next to the two half-
drunk guards who liked to fence with their fully loaded Scorpion sub-
machine guns, even though nobody ever attempted to steal Sanola
workers' salaries. Anna was no longer worthy of such responsibility.
She calmly accepted her transfer to manual labor that required less
than half an hour of training.

"You put this thing here...push it...do it twice...then move it with a
hook and put a new one there."

This is the literal transcription of the specialized instructions for
the new worker in Workshop Number Three, also known as the Water
Meter Painting Shop. Anna learned fast; it wasn't complicated. She put
the thing there, pushed it twice, moved it with a hook and put a new
one there. Her moves became mechanical, and the regular whistle of
the spray gun was calming. She wore a respirator on her face, and a
strand of white hair would escape from her headscarf after a moment.

When the siren sounded, she would turn off the compressor, put
her work clothes into a locker. and go home. She didn't eat in the factory
cafeteria, first of all because they cooked inedible substances called pea

mash with wiener or bread pudding with stewed fruit. She also didn't feel like socializing with anyone. She felt bad that she compelled people to embarrass themselves by pretending they were interested in something that happened to be on the other side of the universe.

In a cafeteria it was impossible to escape meeting someone in the critically tight space around a table. If she sat down first, no one would join her, but if she joined someone else, that person would feel obliged to bolt down his or her food, or even dump the uneaten portions rather than speak to her. But no, I have to correct this; they still had enough pride not to get up but would go red in the face and mumble something with their mouths full that might have been "Good day," or "What rain we had last night," but you also couldn't rule out "Locomotive Kladno will drop out of the League."

No, nobody needed this, least of all Anna. That's why she preferred to cook at home and watch for spring to arrive. But the expression "watch" is not really fitting in this case; it had been removed from her vocabulary. She was merely waiting. That January, as snow covered the ground, she cleaned her whole apartment and even the entrance to the building. When spring came, she would work the narrow band of soil between the building and the walkway and plant it with flowers. For now, she made black tea and read the card from Ottawa for a thousandth time.

"Warmest greetings! We think about you all the time. We both have our own rooms; Mariška is taking good care of us. Petra has started studying for the licensure exam, since her diploma isn't valid here. I walk a lot in town and I miss you. See you soon! Alex and Petra."

As it had always been with postcards from Mariška, this one showed Ottawa in the season coordinated with the time it was posted. It was not of the downtown area, but of a snowy park with a residential neighborhood in the background. It was not until a week later that Anna noticed something else on the postcard. An arrow, gently etched on the postcard with the point of a needle, pointed to a house. Were they perhaps living there? Anna memorized those few points of color: a bit of brown and grey, with a red roof and a white window—or was that the door?

Brown, grey, dark red, and white: from then on, they became the most important colors in her life.

Maria was cooking two portions more than she needed for every lunch and dinner. At first she thought she was simply unable to adjust after cooking for four as long as she could remember. Eventually she had to admit that she was consciously cooking a portion for Ferdinand and one for Tereza, at least symbolically.

And she put out cutlery and a plate for each of them. She knew they would never be a complete family again, but she still believed, every evening in fact, that she would hear the sound of keys in the lock, and that Tereza would walk in. Every time she wrote a letter, she would remind Tereza to eat regularly and never scrimp on food, because the most expensive meal would be the one she didn't eat, which would be reflected in her health... Whenever she heard noise in the stairwell she would turn towards the door. It didn't happen often, as only two families lived on their floor, but her hope made noise on that wooden staircase day after day.

While she couldn't see her daughter, she tried at least to make her happy by sending parcels—one day a kerchief, another time warm slippers, sometimes a skirt. And to her friends in Israel she sent a cut crystal vase. Czechoslovakia was the country of crystal and china. Before it had exported machines, and now fragile glass. Above all it exported machine guns, but that was not mentioned aloud. All the armies of the Third World appreciated them, including the future incubators of terrorism for whom we trained soldiers and instructors in killing. The glass, despite its fragility, was above all. It was immortal. It became a payment of gratitude; if they gave you service, you gave them crystal.

That's why Maria joined the endless lines of people waiting in front of Bratislava's stores. Permanent scarcity forced people to think about where to shop rather than meditate on politics. It would take some time before a wave of goods rolled over the store shelves of Czechoslovakia like a gentle tide with the local mutation of well-being. And many would say it was not that bad here, and that it could have been much worse.

The snaking lines of Bratislava differed from those of Stará Ruda in length and width. If the Stará Ruda line could be called a blind worm (I don't like to say a grass snake, and even less a viper, since the waiting people were guilty of nothing, but only victims), in Bratislava it was not an animate creature, but a force of nature. Slovakia's largest department store had opened here not long ago. Thousands of hopeful people lined up in front of it every day. The line was reminiscent of a river and even flowed in the same direction as the Danube. Every fifteen minutes the door would open and allow thirty lucky people in.

Janko was waiting with his mother, not caring that it might take hours for them to get in. He patiently waited and listened to his transistor radio. He was well provisioned with chocolate wafers and yellow lemonade, and his spiritual needs were satisfied by a popular magazine and, above all, his objective. In the music department he would check out the guitars. The rock-and-roll wave was dominating Bratislava clubs and Janko had just reached the age where the music of British rock bands (among which he could not yet differentiate) caused a vertigo not unlike falling in love. He and a couple of other guys from Panenská Street would start a rock band! They would become wildly popular and would be invited to perform at the school dance in the gym! Janko would sing and play guitar!

This great plan had a few drawbacks. Janko didn't have a guitar and he didn't know how to play one. In addition the guys from his street preferred exploring the ruins of Bratislava Castle to practicing rock music in the bathroom. Also, they had no idea that they were about to become members of a rock band. But Janko was thinking in a systematic manner. He had 170 crowns, which he'd saved up, in his pocket. He would look into the prices and buy the cheapest instrument, secretly hoping for a subsidy from his mother. From then on, nothing would stand in the way of the rock-and-roll revolution at Panenská Street 23.

Once upon a time there was a vineyard. The vineyard was sleeping. The roots of the grapevine were sleeping. The animals in the forest were sleeping and even the fields covered by a blanket of snow were sleeping. But Granny wasn't sleeping. She couldn't with her suffering forcing her eyes open, so she decided to go to the vineyard in the evening. Grandpa, her husband, was lying in his bed with a book covering his face. No, he wasn't reading, he was snoring. Granny slipped on her felt boots and out she went. The snow crunched under her feet, and the moon shone on her footprints, white on white. Everything was in its place: the vineyard, the moon, and the sky, as was the bench her son had built last summer. It had been a month since she'd seen him, and she hadn't really seen him then.

She was standing along the Devin, and three figures were waving at her from the other shore. It could have been anyone, but she had sensed that it was her son, his wife, and their son. Having left her glasses at home she could only guess, but she had guessed right. The organ of guessing is to be found in the transverse-axial muscles of the heart. Its precise location has never been determined, even by the famous Jan Evangelista Purkyně, who knew a lot about the heart. But Granny also knew a lot about the heart—enough to receive its message that her son would write to her today. Or tomorrow. Or the day after tomorrow.

Let us be more precise. It wasn't that her son didn't write, but that the letters didn't reach her. If letters don't arrive, it doesn't mean that no one is writing. Letters by airmail on a very light paper, white as snow, in envelopes marked Par avion, began to fall like a curtain in a winter fairy tale. Once upon a time there was Czechoslovakia, and in it a vineyard, and in the vineyard an old lady, and in her was a heart and in her heart was something that knew how to wait. And in that country, wrapped in red fabric, there were many hearts like that, and all those hearts were waiting, waiting, until they died.

America

When Jozef finally heard the longed-for "Welcome to New York!," he had many documents to sign; for example, declaring that he would join the army to defend the United States if drafted. Jozef signed it, but he was shaking inside. He had fled from a country occupied by tanks, and now he was promising to throw himself under a tank if asked to? Where had he brought his child?

America was like a naked high-tension wire. It was the beginning of 1969, the height of the Vietnam War, and the army was drafting more and more conscripts to be sent straight to the Vietnam meat grinder after training. Resistance was growing among young people who were unwilling to die in a jungle that meant nothing to them. University students were rebelling, there was a shooting at a university campus, and the number of war dead and wounded was rising. Jozef felt bad. You could not escape from the world.

They stayed only a few days in New York. Little Peter was sad that he had no toys and friends. Erika worried about whether it had been a good idea to flee from Europe. An icy wind blew, discouraging walks outside. Of this immense city with a population as great as all of Czechoslovakia, they saw only a few streets through the windows of taxicabs. That was why they looked forward to their redemption on Saturday: they'd received airline tickets to Pittsburgh, where there was need for a Slovak Lutheran minister.

After flying through a snowstorm, they deplaned with great relief at Pittsburgh Airport. The Bishop was waiting for them in the arrival hall, but instead of taking them to a taxi, he led them to another departure hall for another flight. There had been a change of plans; Jozef would not be staying in Pittsburgh but would fly to Milwaukee, where he would await further orders.

The Bishop talked and talked, and Jozef was speechless, his one certainty disappearing like a fistful of snow. He had no work, no accommodation, nothing; not even a Bishop, or at least not one who would look him in the eye. They were all very hungry, and the Bishop, feeling sorry for the boy, bought him an ice cream cone. At least Peter enjoyed a wintry dinner.

Jozef couldn't understand what had happened. Why had they suddenly rejected him? He had no inkling how fate had toyed with him. The Bishop had received information that Jozef was a problematic person who had rejected his ordination at home. At any rate, this was the first time he'd seen a young pastor from Eastern Europe, and it scared him. The man had long hair! Might he be a covert Communist? How had he gotten to the United States when it was impossible to get out of Czechoslovakia? Weren't the borders surrounded by electrified barbed wire? Who had given this hippie permission for an overseas trip? Might he have been sent by the Communists to infiltrate their church?

And so Jozef Rola, who had refused ordination because he didn't want to inform on his people, was now suspected of something that he'd fought against all his life. But we shouldn't be surprised by the Bishop's behavior. He acted clumsily, like all inhabitants of democratic states, like the American film crew, and like every foreigner who asked us the same question that we couldn't explain: why did we vote for the

Communists while we were cursing them? Since each side was coded with a different system of knowledge they could never understand us, just as we couldn't understand Western leftists or young Parisian Maoists. Our experience made it impossible for us to sympathize with café revolutionaries. If their previous generation had had their shops suddenly seized, or had been thrown out of their apartments, or if their fathers had been arrested and forced to work in a uranium mine, they might have caught on.

And so the Bishop of the Zion Synod, the only one who could help him, sent Jozef away. It was six in the evening when they took off, with empty stomachs, on the evening flight to Milwaukee.

Erika thought it couldn't possibly be worse than the flight from Vienna, but it was. She had left her heart on the concrete runway in Vienna, but now she lost her eyes, crying so hard and long that her tear ducts went on strike. She sat there and silently moaned, her tear-less eyes red and swollen.

And then, at cruising altitude, high enough for angels to find agree-able, one appeared. Wearing the uniform of a young flight attendant, she tried to find out why the lady in seat 16A was crying. The angel couldn't understand the language of the lady, who like her husband and son could not speak English. From their mouths came a language familiar to the angel, but where had she heard it? Yes! It was the captain of the plane who occasionally spoke it. So the angel went to the cock-pit and brought out the captain.

An invisible network of communicating vessels connects the world. Something bad happening somewhere is balanced out by some-thing good happening somewhere else, establishing equilibrium. The problem arises when these places are thousands of kilometers apart, and the victim of evil finds herself lacking the help she needs. Good tends to somehow arise spontaneously, usually where nobody needs it. In this case, however, it worked at the right place at the right time.

It was an incredible coincidence; the captain of the evening flight had a Slovak mother. If Warhol could, why not the captain? Although he was born in America and could barely speak his mother's tongue, he understood what had happened from Erika's sobbing and Jozef's gestures. The pilot was from Milwaukee, and Erika's cousin lived there. They'd never met her and didn't know where she lived; they only knew her name. They told it to the captain, and he wrote it down and returned to the cockpit. From there he connected with the tower, and the people there found out everything they needed in half an hour. Since he had to focus on flying the plane, the pilot let them know through the flight attendant that Mrs. Darina would be waiting for them at the airport. She had been getting ready to go to the theater, but they'd managed to reach her by phone just before she left.

I'm writing a documentary novel, and I've changed the names of my characters, but the name Darina is real. The fact that she appeared and what she did may look like a sentimental invention by the author, but that's really how it happened. Communicating vessels. Everyone should experience it once in a lifetime. I hope that all of us have a similar opportunity awaiting us.

Darina was a leftist. She voted for the Democratic Party and worked as an accountant for a union. Her son was a Marxist and had no idea what it meant to come from a totalitarian country. Jozef didn't try to explain much; it would have been pointless and impolite to their hosts, and he didn't have a sufficient command of English in any case. Darina, who was born to Slovak parents in America, was fluent in the dialect of Modra, and they could communicate with her very well. However, three days later she left on a trip to Quebec that she'd planned weeks before. They stayed alone with her son and his wife, neither of whom spoke Slovak.

Their conversations began to resemble Ionesco plays. The first evening after Darinka's departure they sat together in the living room and tried to explain what had happened with their hands and feet and by drawing in the margins of newspapers. Darinka's son and his wife knew about the invasion of Czechoslovakia, but the news had been overtaken by the student rebellion in France. It was still something happening far away in Europe. A far more painful theme was the war in Vietnam, and here they were in agreement: no one liked the war. Having exhausted political themes during the first evening, they switched to the language of looks and smiles.

Jozef immediately began looking for work. He shoveled snow for a few dollars, working in his best suit to distinguish himself from other unemployed people. He spent hours waiting at the office, which was advantageous, but boring. For a whole day waiting for work, he was paid three dollars, but when he was hired, he made a dollar an hour.

He remembered Darina's advice: "Don't take just anything. You shouldn't always say 'yes.' You can say 'no' as well."

The next day they offered him decent work, but he kept saying "no." I don't want to. No. The man hiring people for construction work was surprised. He tried to explain using his arms and legs, until a "yes" popped out of Jozef like a champagne cork. He came home that evening in a happy mood.

"Erika, I have work for the next two months! We're demolishing a huge building!"

Erika was happy, and conversation was joyful that evening. They all sat in the living room in front of the television set while a bearded man with Tibetan bells on his thumbs appeared on the screen. He stood in the middle of a group of demonstrators and gently rang his bells. Jozef and Erika shouted together: "Ginsberg!"

Their comment impressed their hosts. The poet who had become an icon in Bratislava in 1965 and the King of the May Parade in Prague was visiting Milwaukee. Their hosts showed them a thin booklet with the title *Howl*.

From then on, the bookcase became part of their conversation. Instead of speaking, Jozef stood in front of the shelves, pointing at Darinka's books. When he found a title he knew, he would nod his head.

Steinbeck. Yes.

Hemingway, a respectful nod, accompanied by lifted eyebrows: yes. *Old Man and the Sea.* Clearly, yes.

Ginsberg, as we know, also yes.

Miller. Yes, but...

Look at this: Shakespeare! Jozef had gone to acting school. A nod with a smile. How many times had he played the Gravedigger in *Hamlet*? Seven times? Eight? He took his passport out of his pocket, held it in his hand, fixed his gaze on it and began:

"To be, or not to be, that is the question..."

Quite unconsciously, Jozef now began to resemble his father, who could analyze literature so fabulously while drinking wine. You could find wine here as well, but words failed him, so acting would have to do.

Another volume: *Moby Dick!* A significantly raised forefinger, to which Jozef added: "Hmmm." Darinka's son and his wife nodded their heads. They also liked the crazy Captain Ahab... and so the evening flowed on.

In the morning Jozef started the fabulous job from which he expected so much. They were to demolish a former office building. First they had to remove all the handles from the doors. Then they had to remove washbasins from the walls. This took three days. On the fourth day, the demolition crew drilled holes in the gigantic building and filled them with plastic explosives, and Jozef's vision of two months of work disappeared in a cloud of dust.

A week later the bill for the airline tickets arrived in Darinka's mailbox. Jozef was willing take any job to pay off the debt. In the bitter cold he unloaded raw hides from railway cars. He worked in his dress coat; he didn't have another one and didn't want to freeze. It reeked from then on.

He began learning English in his free time by visiting nuns, who were glad to teach him. After a week, Erika asked about his progress.

"Say something."

"Bird."

He pronounced it beautifully and diligently.

"Biiird."

"Excellent. Try something else."

"Biiird."

"What else can you say?"

"Biiird."

"Is that all?"

"Yes, but can you hear the accent?"

The next day, this man who knew one word of English got a job in an accumulator plant. Every night, when the halls were empty, he and two other cleaners washed the slippery floors. The air was filled with poisonous mercury fumes, but he carried little pieces of paper covered with new words. While sweeping the floor, he learned "Our Father."

"Our Father, who art in Heaven,

Hallowed be thy name,

Thy Kingdom come,

Thy will be done..."

It was three o'clock in the morning. With a wide broom on a long handle, he crossed the empty hall illuminated by small halogen lights.

"On earth as it is in heaven.

Give us this day our daily bread,

And forgive us our trespasses,

As we forgive those who trespass against us."

His fellow workers, two old black men covering the wall with oil paint, looked at this white man as he emptied the garbage cans into plastic bags while reciting the prayer.

"And lead us not into temptation,

But deliver us from evil.

For thine is the kingdom, the power, and the glory,

For ever and ever, Amen."

When he took out the last bag of garbage, his co-workers came over, looking compassionately at him.

"Are you okay?"

Jozef nodded, and in his broken English he told them he was studying for an exam, because he was a pastor. From then on, they called him "Father."

Erika studied English at the university for one term, but they only taught her specialized terminology. They prepared her so well that she could say "scientific-technological progress," but she couldn't ask for a thermometer. When Peter had a fever and she had nothing to measure it with, she put her hand under her armpit in a vain attempt to show the store clerk what she needed. He didn't understand; in America, they took temperatures orally.

When she returned home, Jozef was just waking up from his night shift. Darinka was waiting for them in the kitchen, and they could tell from her expression that something was wrong. They had dinner together and she started asking them about Slovakia, about Jozef's mother, about Jozef's studies and his rejection of ordination, and finally she casually mentioned the name of Erika's brother Lajo. Suddenly, everything fell into place. Lajo had found out where they were staying and had written to his cousin, whom he'd completely ignored up to this point, just so she'd know what snakes she warmed at her bosom. Darinka showed Jozef the letter.

"He's not interested in anything but money. He's a murderer who left his helpless elderly mother behind and ran away to make a career. He's a peerless egoist, and I don't understand how you can help him. You know very well what we leftists are fighting for..."

And so on. Darinka didn't believe the letter; she could see with her own eyes what kind of people Jozef and Erika were. Once they explained how Lajo behaved towards his sisters and who he really was, she considered the matter closed. That day would have passed from their memories if not for the chance mention of a certain word.

"Canasta."

They all knew how to play it. From that moment on, they played every evening when Jozef didn't have to work. The cards broke down all barriers and didn't require a dictionary. Above the table hovered the emotions of the players and the common bond that only card players enjoy. Now they no longer had conversational problems and didn't need to point to the spines of books. They had Canasta.

Jozef soon received an offer to preach for the Lutheran Church Missouri Synod, but he had to pass an oral examination first. He received the questions, but the only textbooks he had were his Bible and prayer book. The nuns helped him out by lending him all the books he needed so he could finally study seriously. He had paid off his flight to America and now made enough for basic housing, so they could finally leave the home of the hospitable Darinka, which was too small for all of them.

They made their move by placing all their luggage in a supermarket shopping cart. Accommodation was not easy to find. Jozef's hair was long because he didn't like to spend money on going to the barber. Many landlords in the city avoided renting to families with children. Finally they found an apartment in a one-story building next to a hippie commune.

The rent cost them all the money they had. Erika was planning how to budget their money when her husband returned, white as chalk.

"I have no money."

"What do you mean you don't have it?"

"The landlord asked for double rent, for the first and the last month. Apparently that's the custom here. Otherwise he won't let us stay."

They didn't have a single dollar left. Peter was hungry and kept asking for dinner. It was Saturday. Having nothing to cook, Erika took him for a walk. An hour later they returned home hungry.

"Mummy, I'm hungry."

She made tea with lots of sugar, and Peter drank it eagerly.

"Mummy, I'm hungry."

It was getting dark. Erika managed to get him asleep by a miracle. She held his hand for a long time, telling him his very favorite fairy tales. As soon as he opened his eyes in the morning, while they were still in bed, they heard his first sentence.

"Mummy, I'm hungry."

They felt desperate, and for a while they lost hope. After all their hardship, they were almost within reach of their goal and suddenly this? Erika was crying and Peter was asking for food. It was maddening.

At that moment they heard someone knocking. At the door stood an elderly woman they'd recently met in church, and who had lived in the neighborhood for thirty years. In her hand was a basket. She said that since the Reverend was new here and surely had nothing to eat, she'd brought a chicken and some vegetables for his Sunday soup. And since he didn't have anything to cook with, she also brought a pot. Refusing an invitation to come in, she handed everything to Erika at the door and left.

It was the best soup of their entire lives. Erika had nothing but salt left, but she immediately put the pot on the stove and began to boil water. Then she added everything to the pot, and they watched it cook in absolute silence.

The hippies in the building welcomed them. While Jozef worked at night and studied during the day (occasionally falling asleep over his books), Erika would go out on walks with her little boy. The long-haired young women often invited her in for coffee. Knowing who she was they didn't offer her marijuana. They were interested in everything, and Erika used gestures to explain who they were and where they came from.

She had never drunk so much coffee before in her life. It was weak, poured from big urns, but when drunk like water it became very strong. She needed this strength to take care of her son and to create meals for three out of almost nothing. She often made risotto with chicken gizzards for supper, since it cost the least. Drinking coffee with the hippies improved her English.

The hippies had a lot of children, and she could never figure out which belonged to whom. They all took care of the children together, so she told herself that they were the children of all of them. Next to Erika lived Marge, who often invited her over. Erika was a bit afraid of Marge and always stayed for only a short while, using Peter as an excuse to leave.

Marge made death masks. She made them perfectly, with real hair and brows, and had a few of them displayed in her apartment. They looked like African totems. They weren't a pleasant sight. Marge tried to talk Erika into letting her make a mask of her face, but she refused; after all, she was still alive. Marge told her it didn't matter: people liked having it done to remember what they looked like when they were younger.

Now, more than fifty years after meeting Marge, Erika doesn't regret her inability to see her former face. She was younger, yes, and definitely prettier, but hers was the face of a person in uncertainty, a person afraid of living forever like a beggar in a house where only voluntary outcasts lived.

When Erika said her good-byes to Darinka, she had to hold back tears. No one in her life had helped her as much as Darinka.

"Please tell me, how can I repay you?"

"Someday help someone else who has problems like you."

Ottawa

Petra could have been born in Buenos Aires.

Czechoslovakia's economic crisis peaked in the 1930s. Thousands of families left the country to look for work abroad. Alex's sisters, sixteen-year-old Anka and eighteen-year-old Mariška, left for the United States. Their parents remained in Stará Ruda.

Alex, too, almost left. But he was only fourteen, and his family decided that he should stay home so his parents would have someone to help them. Alex remembered crying on a haystack. He imagined emigration as a fabulous trip and considered his parents' refusal to let him go as a missed opportunity. One thing was certain now, however: he was not enjoying his forced sojourn in Canada while pushing fifty.

Anka and Mariška each got an emigrant's passport and sailed to Hamburg in 1931. They boarded the transoceanic ship, or as they said, the "shif." When they reached the United States a few weeks later, an unpleasant surprise awaited them. The Immigration Office had put a temporary stop to immigration, and the ship continued on to Argentina, which was willing to take them. The country needed farmers and workers to settle vast territories, and Slovak emigrants who understood farming and could work until they dropped were ideal.

The Catholic Church looked after the sisters, gave them tempo-rary housing and found work for them. They both worked in a shoe factory which was a bit ironic. Their father had been a shoemaker until Bata Shoes arrived and started making cheap shoes in huge quantities, at which point he had to quit his profession. Their father went bank-rupt, and the family hoped their daughters could provide them with income. Ultimately their work skills were not important. In our story, genes played a major role by making Mariška and Anka beautiful.

I will speed it up: they married well. Anka married a construction site manager, who in time became owner of a construction firm. Mariška married a businessman who traded in non-ferrous metals. They pros-pered during the war, but after it ended the country became a hotbed of violence and instability under the Peron government. When Anka's husband came to the site one day to pay his construction workers, two men put a gun to his head, and he had to give them money in exchange for his life. In order to pay the workers he had to sell the construction site. He was broke. Mariška's husband likewise felt uncomfortable in a country where criminals hobnobbed with the president.

Now I will get to the point: both families moved to Canada. Anka's husband failed to thrive in the new environment and died a few years later. However, non-ferrous metals were doing well all over the world, and Mariška's family experienced a post-war boom that eventually allowed her to offer shelter, at the beginning of 1969, to her younger brother and his daughter. And so Alex managed to reach his Argentina after thirty-three years, even though it was a good bit further north.

"Alex, you're a specialist. How do you say it in Slovak?"

"*Odborník.*"

"Look for work and you're sure to find it. Someone with your spe-cialized skills…"

"*Odborník.*"

"As I said, a person like you shouldn't be sitting at home."

He had to put up with conversations like this on a daily basis. He had only two duties: to go to church on Sundays and to look for work. His sister was a strict Catholic and could not believe how her brother could neglect his faith.

"But you were baptized in the church!"

"I don't remember it."

"And you were confirmed! Just before we left!"

"Well, I was."

"Alex, how could you have been a Communist when our grandfather was a sacristan?"

"You'd be surprised what sort of people become Communists."

Mariška couldn't understand this. To join a party for career reasons, that made sense to her, but to stay in a party that had executed so many of its members?

"Weren't you afraid?"

"I beg of you, you can't understand this, so let's not talk about it. You'll just make me angry."

"But tell me, I'm actually interested."

So he started patiently explaining that if he wanted to work as an engineer and get a position that he really wanted and enjoy his work, he had to join "them."

"You mean 'us?'"

"But I wasn't 'them.'"

"But you were a Communist!"

"Good God, I didn't execute anyone!"

"Don't take God's name in vain!"

"I'll have a heart attack, Mariška, if you don't stop!"

It always ended the same way, with Alex slamming the door and going out for a walk, even when it was twenty below. But to keep peace in the family he went to church every Sunday. Mariška and Petra sat in the front pews while he stood near the door. He wouldn't kneel, cross himself, or participate in the ritual of the Mass, but he was there.

His sister was equally insistent when it came to looking for a job. It wasn't a question of money—Mariška was rich and could easily provide for him, but she wanted him to be active. She knew that sitting at home and killing flies might end badly, having keenly observed her sister's husband deal with the bankruptcy of his firm by drinking too much.

For this reason Alex's only free day was Saturday. From Monday to Friday he visited potential employers, and on Sunday he went to church. His greatest joy was watching Petra as she studied. From dawn to dusk she buried herself in her medical books to prepare for the licensure exam.

"Are you looking for work?"

"Yes, Mariška, I am. Every day."

"Get dressed and go out again. You're not going to lounge about here."

So Alex would put on his best suit and go to another company to ask about work. Ottawa was a bilingual city, and everyone spoke the language of Villon and Baudelaire as well as the language of Shakespeare, at least in the companies he visited. He, on the other hand, did not speak either language well enough not to feel embarrassed. He brought his professional biography and a few pages about the production of medical technology, as he was familiar with it from Sanola. Mariška paid for the translation by a specialist, and Alex sent it by mail to dozens of places. He was received everywhere with interest and they heard him out. They read his analysis, and although his linguistic impediment shocked them, the problem lay elsewhere.

What it was really about we'll show through a model discussion of a Czechoslovak specialist looking for work in Canada.

"You have great knowledge in the machinery field, Alexander."

"Thank you."

"Your professional experience is impressive."

"Thank you."

"Your orientation on the current problems relating to the Iron Curtain behind which you lived is surprisingly precise."

"Thank you."

"The solutions to the problems that you've briefly offered are exceptionally progressive."

"Thank you."

"A man like you would be a welcome addition to our firm."

"Thank you."

"Unfortunately, you lack Canadian experience. Don't call us, we'll call you."

Canadian experience was the magic formula that stood between immigrants and a job. You could only gain Canadian experience by working in Canada, but in order to work in Canada you needed Canadian experience. To be more precise, you needed experience in professional work: the kind of highly specialized work at which you excelled back home. You could be the very best, but they would still not employ you.

So you had to find manual labor, and in that way, a specialist with a diploma gained local experience side by side with Canadians, many with no more than a basic education.

Alex didn't give up. He took a shower every morning, put on a clean shirt and his best suit and took the garbage out. He took a walk outside the house and came back. Then he sat in front of the house and watched the clouds. Mariška saw that he was suffering. He had already visited all the firms that had any relation to his field, and they all politely sent him away. She no longer insisted that he continue his search. At least he took the garbage out, did a little grocery shopping and took Mariška's collie for a walk. And he went to church.

Despite what is related here, Canada did a lot for exiled Czechs and Slovaks. Hundreds of engineers and doctors arrived. Their university diplomas were not valid in Canada, however, so they had to take licensure examinations. The textbooks were very expensive, and young doctors had to work during the day on construction sites so they could study at night. Later, when more people came from Czechoslovakia, they were gradually offered professional help as well.

The older immigrants were divided into two groups. One group consisted of those who wanted nothing to do with the new bunch, whom they regarded as uneducated, spoiled by communism and reading strange authors like Havel and Škvorecký. Although they might have graduated from universities, tell me, what kind of schools could they have under the communist regime? Half of the former courses were no longer offered since they were forbidden! The old immigrants looked down on the new generation and their spoken language, which differed from the archaic Slovak or Czech spoken during the great emigration waves of 1936 or 1948. After all, *they'd* had to slave for years in the fields, while these newcomers were given half a year of language courses, money, clothing, and shoes! That was too much!

The other group of older immigrants had no bias and gladly received the new people from the country that had changed in such interesting ways. Although Russian tanks had occupied the country, people coming from there were educated, and these established immigrants were happy to help them. They organized meetings for them: construction people with the local construction people, engineers with engineers, and doctors with doctors.

Out of curiosity, Petra took part in a meeting of young immigrant doctors with Canadian Slovaks who had been practicing for decades. She went with a classmate, but they hadn't talked much while they were in Bratislava and didn't here, either. She only learned that he was washing dishes in a French restaurant.

She also talked to a dentist who had had to organize her final examination herself. She found a patient, paid for her hotel, and in the morning worked on a filling in front of the committee. She was so nervous that her patient swallowed the filling and the examination was over. She had to go back to the drycleaners to work for another three months until she had saved enough for a new examination. They all lived day to day, going to language school and supplementing their income with the modest government assistance.

Petra was not suffering. She had arrived scared by her recent experience with Hansi and Resi, but a miracle happened. Mariška wasn't stingy and gladly bought all her textbooks and didn't expect anything but to see her study. She had never had children so Petra filled that part of her heart. She often came to her room with a cup of tea or an apple. It pleased her to see how Petra studied. When Petra saw the problems others had while she lived in relative luxury, she felt too uncomfortable to get together with other new immigrants.

Why was she so lucky? How did she deserve it? She wasn't exceptional in any way. She wasn't unusually smart or pretty. She had never experienced anything unusual that would be worth sharing with anyone. She hadn't done any great deed that would entitle her to imbibe happiness with gusto. Why she and not others? Was it simply because she had done a horrible thing: leaving her mother alone just to improve her own life?

Night after night Anna appeared in Petra's dreams. She was sitting in some sort of room that didn't look like their small living room in Stará Ruda. This one was much bigger and had many windows. Every time Anna got up to air out the room, there was no countryside outside the windows, but only a brick wall. Then Anna would go back to her seat, and she didn't hear Petra's attempts to talk to her.

Petra saw that her father was suffering. She had finished medical school alone. She had always studied alone and hadn't needed to ask anyone questions about what she was learning. If she had a question, she found the answer in a book. She was used to being solitary among others, whether she was studying among a group of laughing med students in the dormitories or next to Tereza as she gazed out her window on Panenská Street. Now she had to change in order to help Alex.

"Dad, listen. Do you have time?"

"Of course, Petra."

"Could you help me study?"

She handed him her textbooks. In this way Alex found new meaning in life, at least temporarily. When Mariška came in with a glass of milk an hour later, she found father and daughter in the middle of a professional discussion.

"Palpitation."

Petra closes her eyes in concentration.

"A palpitation is an awareness of the beating of the heart, whether it is too slow, too fast, irregular, or at its normal frequency."

Alex smiled and changed textbooks.

"Etiologies?"

"Causes rythmiques, causes non rythmiques?"

"Non rythmiques."

"Context psychiatrique ou psychologique: stress, angoisse, excitation... toxicologique avec l'alcool ou une autre drogue..."

Mariška quietly closed the door.

There were few letters from Anna. When one arrived, it was like a holiday. Petra immediately put her books aside, and Alex quickly finished his lunch so they could lock themselves in a room and read her words. The light airmail envelope with its white, red, and blue border contained almost transparent pages that seemed woven from a spiderweb.

Alex always read the last page first. Before his departure, he and Anna had agreed that if she was writing of her own free will, she would sign as Anka, but if the police were dictating the letter, she would sign as Anna.

No matter what signature she used, they always read the letter breathlessly, Petra anxiously fixing her eyes on her mother's calligraphic writing that she loved so much.

My dear Family!

You have no idea how often I think of you! But I know that you do and that's why I feel bad that we don't see each other. I miss you so much that I've become sick from it. I've begun to cough, Alex. You know there are lung problems in our family and that my father had tuberculosis, but the doctors have told me not to worry. Today they can cure it with antibiotics that are plentiful here. Please come home, as everything has returned to normal and people are coming back from all over. Palko Jurik has returned from Bolivia and is back in school. He had interrupted his engineering studies and has just resumed them again. Alex, people are asking about you. Some are angry about the problems that developed after you abandoned the factory. But Dolhosh told me that you can return and that they won't do anything about it if you come, and you can fully resume your position at work. I'm sure your job there isn't as good as the one you had here. You loved it. And the Head Doctor asked about Petra: why hasn't she started working? Young people get apartments from the state in Trenčín, and Petra would start out with a one-room apartment but wouldn't have to share it with anyone. I miss you, but everything can be resolved! When you return, we'll go back to being a family and everything will be like before! I'm waiting for you! Let me know, call me, or write to me. The formalities can be quickly arranged.

Looking forward to your return, Your Anna.

Anna. Always signed Anna. Alex and Petra could see her bending over the paper and imagined the nearby silhouette of an unknown man as he dictated to her. Anka could not say what she wanted to; only Anna was speaking.

Anna was calling them back to Czechoslovakia, but Anka wanted them to stay in Canada.

Haifa

Tereza seemed possessed by a storm. Something forced her to walk, to move, to never rest. She wasn't happy in Israel. With half of her heart she felt she belonged there, that it was a country that gave her the keys and let her come in.

With the other half, or rather, with her entire second heart—the heart that we see if we turn our playing card upside down and are still ourselves but in mirror image—this other heart told her to leave.

"We're packing!"

"We're packing!"

"We're packing!"

These words could be heard simultaneously on various continents. Each of those involuntarily replanted flowers had to overcome multiple crises since arriving in their new countries, but this one seemed serious. They were tormented by nostalgia for childhood hometowns that they would never see again. They remembered the quiet lanes and gardens they loved so much, their images dimming day by day. Most of all they worried about the loved ones they'd abandoned. Alex suffered in Canada because of Anna, just as Jozef did in the United States because of his parents, and Tereza in Israel because of her mother and brother.

Long after their arrival, after weeks of relief at having a new home, a roof over their heads and even work, when they were no longer desperate, they began looking at their host countries somewhat more critically.

"The salt isn't salty enough!"

"The sugar isn't sweet enough!"

"You can't buy black thread or the right kind of elastic for underpants!"

"They don't let me sit with my child!"

"An impossible country!"

At the same moment all of them, Tereza, Alex, and Jozef—though hundreds of miles apart from each other—began hurriedly packing their suitcases.

"We're packing!"

"We're packing!"

"We're packing!"

Crumpled blouses were mixed with underwear, books with pants. Things came out of their dressers reluctantly; hangers became entangled with shirts as if unwilling to let them go. These scenes always played out between two people as a natural continuation of dialogues that had bubbled like lava between them for weeks.

"I can't take it anymore! I'm going home!"

"Home? Where is that?"

"Our country."

"You'll get three years! Three years in prison! That's your home now!"

"Okay, okay! You don't have to tell me that, I know!"

They kept talking while one packed and the other observed. This was not a solitary act; it always required a partner. A wall is needed for anger to be splashed on like a pail of dirty water. And the partner, the wall, can only watch.

The partners cannot take things out of the suitcase and put them back in the dresser. They have to wait for the right moment when the other person stops. Any careless movement could only intensify the desperation; a sock picked up too quickly would only increase the partner's sense of helplessness.

Petra understood Alex's desperation. Milan sensed Tereza's uncertainty, and Erika felt Jozef's remorse. Luckily, each had the other to set them straight. Petra hugged Alex, Milan kissed Tereza, and Erika squeezed Jozef's hand.

"Are we packing?"

"Are we packing?"

"Are we packing?"

They stood for a while. Then Petra unpacked Alex's suitcase, Erika hung up Jozef's shirts, and Milan folded Tereza's blouses. The state of their souls was best described by the old joke: "Stop the Earth, I want to get off!"

They would experience these small storms again and again. Their helplessness in their new situation would make them rebel again and again. Their environment didn't understand them, was indifferent to them. They hadn't learned to ride a bike here, but they'd probably have to stay here for the rest of their lives. They might want to bid it farewell with a hysterically packed suitcase, but they would welcome it again with their humble unpacking.

After finishing the Ulpan language class, Tereza and Milan began studying at the University of Haifa. Milan chose technology and Tereza sociology. Their insufficient knowledge of the language made their difficult programs of study even harder. Slowly but surely, a storm was brewing inside of them. Milan's parents calmly settled down, which—considering their age—was a surprise. Milan was glad that at least his father and mother were content; he worked as a dentist and she was his assistant.

But the children bet their card, the two-headed heart. Haifa was not an easy place to live in. There was an enormous amount of bureaucracy to deal with, and Russian emigrants, whom they instinctively mistrusted, led many of the administrative positions. But mostly it was the unaccustomed heat and humidity that tormented them. The heat in particular was horrendous. It troubled Tereza more, but Milan also caught himself thinking of cool autumnal rain while wearing a shirt drenched with perspiration. The country simply did not suit them because of its climate. In addition, they came from totalitarian Czechoslovakia, where personal freedom was the most sensitive area that people treasured, despite the times. Here, they had freedom, but not the kind they imagined.

Israel was permanently at war. Military duty was obligatory for women as well as men. Tereza held temporary residency for three years, which meant she didn't have to be drafted and go on regular maneuvers. They were offering her permanent residency and she would have to accept it once she finished school. In that case she would have to put on a uniform.

Milan had no choice; he would soon have to join the army. He knew he could become a good soldier, but something was holding him back. Why escape one kind of brutality only to accept another one? Hell, was there a country in this world where the army didn't treat people like an omelet in a frying pan?

He discussed his departure with his parents, who tried to talk him out of it. Tereza supported him. The older couple had barely had time to rejoice that their son had found a girl he loved and whom they took to their hearts, and now they might lose them? What did they lack? They had everything. Soon they would finish their studies and get good positions. They would build a house. Where did they want to go? How long did they want to keep running?

But the storm was already brewing.

These were happy days on Panenská Street in Bratislava. Still ignorant of their plans, Maria kept reading Tereza's letters over and over again. She could spend hours looking at the small and irregular hand-writing that oscillated on the page like live ladybugs. She was excited that her daughter was studying again and wasn't wasting her talent. Ferdinand would have been happy to know that she was back in school.

In reality, Tereza's letter betrayed more than her mother was able (and yes, willing) to read. The disquiet that had taken hold of her child took over her writing. In addition to detailed descriptions of her lectures, textbooks, lecture halls, and student residence, she mentioned in one sentence that she was considering what to do next. What her mother read was "what next after her studies," while Tereza meant the painful "what next with my life."

Janko was cooling his fingers in the sink, the flowing water soothing the pain in his left hand. He had been practicing chords for hours, and his fingertips responded with blood. Secretly, so his mother couldn't see it, he wiped them with paper napkins and hid in the bathroom. His position as leader of the rock band was threatened. He was not the only one who owned a guitar; the other two also had them, and they knew a few more chords than he did. The leadership of the band was slipping from his hand like its famous name.

"Rockets."

"Are you nuts? Do we want to be named after a Russian rocket?"

"Americans have rockets, too. Like the Apollo."

"That's a good name."

"Are you clueless? There's already an Apollo Beat."

"Where?"

"In the Czech Republic."

"Where are the Czechs and where are we…"

"I don't want to be in a band that has the same name as another band."

"My sis suggested we call it the Singing Diamonds."

"We might as well call ourselves the Marguerites."

"Idiot."

"You're an idiot."

"You can't even play guitar."

"Better than you, Egg."

"Who's an Egg, you kike?"

Janko fought for the first time in his life because someone called him "kike." They sometimes called him that in school, but he never fought. Now it was time. After all, he was a "rocker." While still a little boy he had come home one day with a question.

"Mummy, am I dirty?"

"Why do you ask? You're not dirty."

"In my class they call me dirty kike."

That was replaying in his head as he clenched his small fists and punched Egg in the stomach. The third boy pulled them apart. He was supposed to be the drummer and Janko and Egg were the guitar players. The fight ended all that, and the famous band—"Singing Diamonds," or "Apollo," or whatever it was called—broke up before it even began. Janko was stubborn and wanted to learn to play so well that he would show them. That was why he was cooling his fingertips, full of anger.

Pink water flowed into the sink.

When Tereza and Milan decided to go to London, the storm subsided. They both felt that leaving would solve everything. That was not what Milan's parents thought, and neither did Maria, who also disagreed. But she learned about it only after their arrival in the city by the Thames. For a while they were happy.

"Do you think we'll stay here?"

"I'd better not think about it, I'm just concentrating on our happiness now."

"Good. So am I."

They were twenty-one. They were young and single. They thought with their hearts and London at that time seemed like a good address— except for the fact that Milan was now a fugitive in two countries because of shirking military duty. A warrant for his arrest had been issued not only in Czechoslovakia but also in Israel. There was only one thing to be said about it.

"Soon we'll run out of countries that we don't have to run away from."

"Tereza and Milan—Bonnie and Clyde."

"Soon only the North Pole will be left for us."

"Do you like ice cream?"

"Yes, hazelnut."

"We'll have to get used to it. I'm buying."

Anglos

Jozef passed his examination in August 1969 and on the same day he received a call to become minister of a small church in East Chicago. The congregation had fifty Slovak-speaking and eighty English-speaking members.

The Slovak members had arrived during the first emigration of the 1920s, and now they were grandmothers and grandfathers whose children were employed in the steelworks. Jozef met them for the first time in front of the church, where they sat on benches. He stopped an elderly woman.

"Good day, Sister. Are you Slovaks?"

And the grandmother answered in Slovak.

"No, my son, we're all Anglos."

These people had never learned the language of their new home-land. They didn't need to. They had their own community, their own shops and their own church. After working hard in the steelworks they had no need to converse. The smokestacks that constantly belched thick smoke on the horizon could only confirm that.

The church in East Chicago was poor. Everyone economized wherever they could. Even the former pastor, now retired, would cut the grass and clean around the church, and in the winter he cleared the snow to make some extra money. When they offered this work to Jozef, he refused, although he was penniless. He felt that a minister shouldn't have to do that. He wasn't afraid of work, and few had worked harder in the vineyard than he. But this involved the dignity of his calling, and more importantly, he preferred to visit families and talk to people.

The church organized collections to support the soldiers fighting in Vietnam. When Jozef organized the first one, they collected canned food. His secretary, who had forgotten most of her Slovak, put up an announcement in all seriousness:

"Bring your grub to the church."

Jozef was not amused. He could imagine what he sounded like with his English. He was learning constantly, but it was slow going. Erika followed him like a shadow and translated. Slovakized English was a source of constant amazement to them.

The local people didn't watch television but rather "watchuvali television."

When they drove downtown they "drivovali do downtownu."

He learned how to preach from the American pastors, who gladly helped him because Erika was a great cook. The big hit was a dish she made that combined stewed pork with sauerkraut, known as Szegedin goulash. Erika's hospitality also attracted ordinary people, who helped them out with clothing or toys for their son.

Jozef watched with concern what was happening in America. Vietnam was swallowing more and more soldiers, like a fiery furnace. They were mobilized according to their date of birth. First they selected two months at random; for example, March and August. Later they took draftees from six months of a single year. In the beginning, university students were exempt from service, but that exclusion was later cancelled. Everyone would be drafted without exception.

Once, when a soldier came home to East Chicago on eight days' leave for the birth of his daughter, Jozef baptized them both while the young man held his child. Then the soldier flew back to the jungle, and two days later the news came that he had been killed. So Jozef buried him as well, seeing him lowered into the ground in a steel container that they were not allowed to open.

One could feel uncertainty in the United States, and Jozef and Erika watched this in silent astonishment as Marxism gained followers. There were demonstrations everywhere, even on campuses, including a university in Ohio where students were shot and killed. Young people began avoiding military service and publicly burned their draft cards.

Jozef was occasionally asked to preach in the surrounding districts, which could mean up to five hundred kilometers away. He and his family traveled by bus, and in this way came to know an America they would otherwise never have discovered. This is also how they discovered Slavia, Florida.

A Slovak immigrant named Duda and his family had founded Slavia before the Second World War. They were enterprising people who successfully ran farms and dedicated a piece of land in Florida for a Slovak village. It was gradually settled by retired people, or people who were isolated, immigrants who would spend the rest of their lives there. The village had a seniors' home, a hospital, and even a school. They all lived in simple little wooden houses, and when they died, the houses were sold to others.

They often left behind Slovak books that they'd brought from the old country. After they died the books were donated to the local library. In time, so many books were collected that the library ran out of space. Eventually, as fewer people were able to read Slovak, the solution was to bury these titles in an unknown language in the ground with a bulldozer.

When Jozef learned this by chance, he was horrified. Buried books! When he went to the library and asked about it, he was moved at the sight of shelves filled with tattered volumes, mostly fairy tales but also religious books, novels, and poetry. These books must have meant something to the people who had found space for them in their small suitcases instead of other, more valuable items. And now they would simply be buried?

Jozef took as many books as he could and asked the library to send him the rest. He would give the well-used volumes to anyone who wanted them. He had no illusions about what would happen to the rest of the books after his departure, but it was the best he could do. To this day he owns Hurban's *Olejkár*, a slender volume of crumbling, brownish paper. Every time he looks at it, he recalls that place: Slavia, Florida.

My dear children and my little grandson.

Mother always started her letter this way. As she wrote the letter she spoke aloud for Father to hear. He never corrected her. When he wanted to write something he would, but he nodded with approval and happily agreed with her as she wrote.

Accept from me this heartfelt greeting and loving memory of you. Today I went up to take a look at the vineyard. There were weeds up to my waist and I started to pull them. It took me four days to get rid of them. And then I had to lie down in the terrible 34-degree heat. Passionflowers are rampant. The grape harvest has just started, and with all of the rain we've been having, it will be good. This year is an early harvest. The grapes are already sweet and now it's quite hot. I think about you at night when I can't sleep, and during the day, wherever I am, I see you before my eyes. A man visited us and told me to write to you to say that you can ask for a pardon. I don't know why

they're interested in you. I told him that I don't understand such things
and wonder what they will come up with next. I miss you, and I keep
looking at those pictures when I want to see you.

                        Best wishes to you, with an embrace, Grandma.

That was what Jozef feared the most: that they would not leave his
dear mother alone. They had a thousand ways to make her life more
difficult. He would soon find out how true this was.

Eva was born in East Chicago. They took out a loan for $900 to pay for
the childbirth. Erika stayed in the hospital for only two and a half days;
they couldn't afford to pay for more. She continued to come for check-
ups, and when the doctors found out about their circumstances, they
didn't ask for more money.

Peter looked forward to meeting his sister. The people from the
church organized a collection of baby clothes, bottles, diapers, and a
stroller. Even so Jozef felt he had to move on. He was worried about
the boy's health. Peter was pale and kept coughing, and the doctor recommended a change of environment. The nearby steelworks made
East Chicago an unhealthy place to live.

They had Nansen passports as refugees and were waiting for green
cards. Jozef was extended a call to Masaryktown, Florida. Its name
spoke clearly: everywhere in the United States were communities of
people who had left Czechoslovakia years ago and needed their own
language.

Over the past few months the Slovak population had become
more youthful. The year 1969 saw the largest wave of refugees. As dozens of young people came to East Chicago locals initially regarded
them with skepticism. The newcomers had long hair (meaning that
their hair almost covered their ears), wore fashionable clothing, listened to rock music and spoke what sounded like a pagan language to

the old ladies, for whom time had stopped when they left their homeland. They couldn't understand what had happened to their homeland
over the past thirty years, but everything had changed. It was as if the
world had been combed like a steel brush on a horse's back.

Jozef understood the new people very well and they supported
and helped each other when dealing with officials. Erika took them to
the stores and explained the names of goods and how much they cost.
Most of the newcomers were foundry engineers and their families,
attracted by jobs in the smelter. To this day Jozef and Erika remember
New Year's Eve 1969: their farewell party.

Not long before, Jozef had been invited to Toronto where there
was a small church with good prospects. More and more Slovaks were
moving to Toronto; it was a fast-growing city where he would have
plenty of work. The decision took little deliberation. Their next address
would be in Canada.

The local people were reluctant to say goodbye, having become
attached to Jozef, but their new friends, themselves uncertain how
long they would stay, understood everything. Certainty was as distant
as the mystical year 2000.

Some of the new arrivals brought a recipe book for cocktails, along
with bottles of liquor and ingredients, and they mixed drinks depend-
ing on how much they liked the pictures of the cocktails in the book.

"This one looks good."

"Look at this color."

"Do we have the ingredients?"

"Let's make something yellow."

They weren't drinking piña coladas or daiquiris, but rather page 24
and page 36. The first year of emigration was ending: a year filled with
stress and fear of what the future would bring. Far in the distance the
sun was rising. Out of relief, sadness, nostalgia, anxiety, and the stupid
beauty of life, they got terribly drunk.

Because of pages 24, 36, 41, 59, and especially 73.

Bamboo

The Vietnam War could be heard all the way to Stará Ruda. Not a shot was fired there, but everyone knew about it, and not only because state television brainwashed them daily with images of B-52 bombers dropping napalm on the jungle. As during the Korean War, people knew that the Americans were helping the government of Vietnam and the Russians were helping the rebelling Communists. As an obedient portion of the Communist Empire, we were helping as well.

Some environments make wars impossible to win. For the Germans it was the Russian winter; twenty years later, Russians were trapped in the Afghan mountains; and the Americans experienced a fiasco in the tropical jungle. But at that time, none of the parties were aware of it, and everyone did their jobs as best they could. The Americans were bombing and the Russians were providing weapons and advisors. And somewhere at the tail end of the effort to help the heroic Vietnamese people was Czechoslovakia. Undoubtedly it had sent enough weapons and ammunition from its munitions factories, as well as food and medicine, but it also helped them in another way, by accepting a large Vietnamese community into the republic.

For the time being they were ordinary men and women who looked like children to the locals, even though some of them were over thirty. Was it this supposed youthfulness that prevented people from taking them seriously at the beginning? They worked in our factories and learned how to operate the machinery. These people didn't belong to the gangs that we were to experience in the third millennium, ruled by the Asian mafia predominantly active in the shadow economy of the Czech Republic. At this point they were quiet, inconspicuous people who had fought but now wanted to learn. Stará Ruda employed them in the Sanola factory.

That is where Anna encountered them. She had been moved out of the painting shop for health reasons as she began coughing more and more. The cough would attack her like a thief, jumping on her from behind and bending her so that she had to hold onto a railing to keep from falling down. The fit would pass in a moment and then she could go on.

Now she was working in a better environment. She checked tanning lamps while wearing glasses with an ultra-violet filter. She turned both lamps on, and the air immediately became fragrant with ozone. She loved that smell, remembering the evening when her husband brought a lamp home with a victorious smile. No need for expensive holidays! Forget about the beach on the seacoast! From now on, you can get that bronze tan in your living room!

That's how the advertisements of the time sounded, ignoring the fact that socialist workers could not really afford expensive holidays, to say nothing of holidays by the sea! More realistically they could afford a short break at a Moravian recreation center belonging to a sister company that at best was located near a lake, and at worst was deep in a woods full of prickly thorns and mosquitoes.

Anna brought home x-ray images wrapped in brown paper from the doctors. The district doctor sent her for a check-up in the regional hospital. Fortunately, a day before, Maria had called her from Bratislava. They called each other often. Although sharing the fate of being on their own, Maria still had her son Janko, while Anna had no one.

"How's your cough? How long has it been going on?"

"Three months."

"Anna, you have to see a doctor."

"I just came from one. They call him Doctor Aha. He never says anything, he just looks at the results and says 'aha, aha, aha.'"

"I can't listen to that. You're risking your life!"

"He sent me..."

"I'll get you a real doctor in Bratislava. He's Ferdinand's friend."

"It's been a year since..."

"Terrible..."

"I'm sorry I started ... please, don't cry..."

"You're coming to Bratislava and that's the end of it. Write down the name: Dr. Glauber."

On the way home from work the White Lady stopped at the post office. She was used to people not greeting her and turning away from her in embarrassment. Sanola had a new director, and an engineer whom Alex used to call "Natural Disaster" ran production. Who knew how good he was, but in any case Natural Disaster kept the company running and even received orders for dental equipment from Libya. Alex would say that all the dictatorships loved us, but at least we had someone who would buy our products.

Sometimes Alex and Petra reached her by phone, and they could talk for a long time without interruption. The two most important people in her life were constantly taking action to get her across the border. They wrote to the President and the Canadian Prime Minister. They visited all the organizations for refugees, but without results.

Anna was rushing to the post office to pick up a registered letter, walking faster than usual. She was almost running, in fact—a person who always walked slowly! She was looking forward to the letter against all common sense—people of her generation could expect nothing good from a registered letter. But who knew if Alex had not succeeded with some initiative of his? Maybe the letter contained documents that would allow her to travel. People can be so optimistic at times!

She walked by a Vietnamese hostel which the town had built in a redevelopment area outside the town center. As always she smelled the sweet aroma of unknown spices and the rice that they cooked all the time. She picked up the letter from the post office and hastily opened it right on the sidewalk.

Dear Comrade,

The Housing Committee of Sanola National Enterprises decided at a meeting on 20.1.1970 that you are not fulfilling the conditions for residing in a state apartment. Your apartment at General Dibrov Street 12 is too large for one person, and after consulting with the social committee of our firm, it will be assigned to a family with children. You have been assigned a replacement at Lenin Street 16.

Peace to the World!

Anna suffered a coughing attack that lasted a minute longer than usual, even scaring passersby, who stopped to ask, "Is anything wrong?" "Are you all right?"

But the White Lady just shook her head and slowly walked on. As she passed by a newsstand, the saleslady whispered to her conspiratorially:

"Hey, lady! Hey!"

She was waving an issue of *100 +1* magazine, which was especially popular thanks to total censorship. No foreign press was allowed in Czechoslovakia with the exception of *Volkstimme*, a paper published by Austrian Communists. *100 + 1 Foreign Curiosities* (as its full title read) brought its readers gossip from beyond the Iron Curtain and mainstream reporting from around the world every two weeks—from fast cars to British fashion, from snow-covered gorillas to the launch of the Apollo rocket and the break-up of the Beatles. Alex had bought it for years, and the lady at the kiosk faithfully continued to put aside a copy for him, even though he had emigrated a long time ago. Now she was handing Anna a copy wrapped in *Agricultural News* with a conspiratorial expression, as if engaged in dissident activity. But Anna didn't care.

"I don't want it. Thank you."

And she kept on walking. The woman in the kiosk was dumbfounded. She couldn't understand Anna's refusal and watched her with gaping mouth—a crown on tooth one, upper left, one cavity on tooth three, down right—everyone could see that in the city where dental equipment was produced. The White Lady was already far gone. She was walking by the Vietnamese hostel when she noticed a blue plate screwed to the wooden wall that said Lenin Street. Above the entrance was a number painted in black: No. 16.

She moved quickly, packing Alex's train, her clothing, pots and pans, the mixer, TV, and Petra's textbooks. She also took the kitchen table, chairs, and a small cabinet. The hostel would provide everything else, including a bed, shower, and built-in dresser. There was no place to put the rest of her furniture anyway.

She had always worried about what she would do with so many things when they would have to move to let their daughter take over the apartment with her husband and children. Anna had looked forward to her daughter's family but was afraid of moving.

Suddenly she found it easier than she had anticipated, perhaps because she had almost nothing worth moving. Her furniture with ebony veneer was definitely not worth moving. Someone at Sanola must have felt pretty bad about this, because they sent a moving van, but she didn't need it for the few things she was taking.

"But what should we do with the furniture in the rooms?"

Anna gave the men her keys.

"You can keep it."

And so the White Lady began her third life. The first was with her family, the second began when they left, and the third was without her apartment. She wasn't sad. She had no feelings about it. Her old apartment had become a minefield that she couldn't cross without being hurt; memories exploded at each step.

She couldn't be considered happy but she didn't suffer. The hostel still had a few empty rooms for social cases but nobody lasted very long there. It was because of the Vietnamese. They never did anything to anyone, least of all to Anna, whom they quickly learned to like. The problem was elsewhere. Not one of the locals would admit it, but they couldn't stand the newcomers.

"The bamboo bunch."

"Slanty eyes."

"The people from the reed country."

Racism was buried inside of people. On the outside they seemed happy and friendly, but given an opportunity, they would fight. Fights with the Vietnamese were so frequent that for a period of time a police car was parked permanently in front of the hostel. The drunken youth of Stará Ruda, who spiked their customary beer with a bit of juniper brandy, threw themselves into fights with gusto. The chivalric duels between Slovaks and Vietnamese always observed the rules of fair play: ten Slovak youths against one Vietnamese bamboo boy.

History is unwilling to record what happened at that time. People don't like to talk of their own racism. However, to be fair, racism resided not only in Stará Ruda, but in every place where the foreigners came. And they came not only from Vietnam, but also from Cuba, Angola, and other places.

Anna was glad that she had taken Red Cross training because sometimes her room became an emergency room. She treated head wounds, stabbed muscles, and scraped foreheads. The White Lady was like the old woman in the fairy tale who would blow on your wound, gently caress it and heal it.

An outsider in the town, here she was among equals. For the first few weeks the Vietnamese ignored her. They'd seen others who came and then went away. But when she didn't go away, and even greeted them and tried to talk to them, they thought she might be different. And once she started treating their wounds, it all became clear to them.

Because of that she didn't have to cook. Although she couldn't eat their Asian food every day, they always offered, and after a while she got used to it. She grew closer to them and saw what she had known all along: they were not different. They were just as unhappy or happy as we were, and among them were wise people as well as idiots, pleasant people as well as disgusting swine.

Just as with us.

Father

Tereza and Milan were living with Milan's aunt in London. A strict lady, she assigned them separate rooms. There was no way they could sleep together before the wedding! They felt like they were living in a secondary school dormitory.

"I'm afraid to touch your hand."

"She knows we're dating."

"I'm afraid she'll bite my finger."

"You should be glad you don't have to climb here on the lightning rod cable."

"You think I couldn't do it?"

"Don't even think of it, something might happen to you!"

Milan was working for a distribution company, delivering frozen food to schools. In the cold damp of late winter, he had to carry paper boxes of frozen food from a refrigerated truck. The boxes contained frozen French fries, steaks, vegetables, and fish. Even when he wore gloves, the frost passed through them and his hands were soon icy cold.

With the arrival of spring, the work improved, and during the sweltering hot summer months it even became pleasant. He would catch envious looks from passersby who would have happily traded places with him in that heat. Even the cold from fish sticks was more pleasant than the sultriness of the street. But Milan didn't get to enjoy London for long because things turned out differently than expected.

They both felt like foreigners there. Of course they were, and that was fine. They were glad they had a place to stay, but their surroundings made them sensitive to their position. They were in the underclass on the social ladder, and there seemed no exit from it. They wanted to go to school, but not there. They didn't want to again start something without finishing it.

It took them a relatively short time to solve two problems: they decided to go to Canada and to get married before moving there.

So even London became a temporary address. Many of their friends had already settled in Canada, and a letter that Petra had sent to Israel had been forwarded to them by Milan's friends. Reading the letter confirmed their decision to move on. They had improved their English and could converse, but would they understand English in a specific field? They had to finish school as soon as possible, or else deliver frozen peas forever.

Milan's aunt had lived in London for twenty years already and served a typical English breakfast, but her guests couldn't handle the combination of sausages, scrambled eggs, warmed beans, and toast with marmalade. Tereza switched to oatmeal, but Milan had to eat beans as well in order to have energy to work all day.

"The oatmeal is half a truck, the beans are a full truck unloaded."

After this comment Tereza began calling him Mr. Bean. The hard work meant something: it gave them enough for the airfare to Toronto. Milan's aunt refused to give them money. Instead, she pelted them with questions like all mothers and fathers: You don't like it here? Where will you go? You have no one to help you over there! When are you going to stop running? You can't run away from yourselves!

They certainly had made many of their decisions intuitively, but this was a clear and rational decision. They weren't running from themselves. They were not the problem; it was the people around them. England was too close to the Continental Europe that had disenchanted them. They believed—however naïvely—that distance would solve some problems, and that as in a fairy tale, being behind seven mountains and seven valleys must be different. Blessed are the ignorant, for theirs will be the kingdom of peace. But without a bit of naïveté they might well have jumped out the window. They planned their wedding for a weekend when his aunt was away from London.

She, who insisted that they stay in separate bedrooms, could not bear the thought of them being alone in her place. That was why she had paid for them to spend a few nights in a hotel, even though it was absolutely clear that they would be there together the whole time. But not in the same room! Feeling that she had done as much as she could to maintain the proper etiquette, she left for Liverpool.

On the way to the hotel, they walked around London. Feeling like tourists for the first time, they went to Trafalgar Square and lost themselves in the flocks of pigeons and people. Then Tereza saw him: his typically bent figure. He was walking away from her, but he kept turning his head towards her. She stopped and watched him. Every now and then a pigeon would fly up, and people moved their heads to avoid them. The wind from their wings tickled her face.

"What's wrong?"

"I think I just saw something..."

"What?"

"Oh, nothing."

"Really?"

Tereza took a few steps and then turned quickly toward Milan. She looked into his eyes.

"I think I just saw my father."

Milan looked where she was pointing. He didn't see her father among the hundreds of people sitting, rushing around, or posing for pictures.

"Where?"

Suddenly she wasn't sure and felt embarrassed for saying any-thing. Milan took her in his arms.

"It's normal. I've had the same thing happen with my grandmother. Quite often."

They went straight to the hotel from there, but as they passed through the revolving door, Tereza couldn't help but look at the busy square again. He was no longer there.

The hotel was a very simple one. The lower two floors were rented to people who could take care of themselves. It was a sort of informal seniors' home and looked quite depressing, but they overcame their distaste and entered. At the desk sat an old gentleman in a tweed suit who came joyfully alive as they handed him their passports.

"Ah, Czechoslovakia! Beneš!"

He registered them in his neat hand and gave them, unsurprisingly, two keys. The rooms were next to each other, and after going in they both broke down in laughter: the rooms looked like tiny dollhouses.

"Nice closet."

"I would say it's an elevator."

"No, it looks like a closet."

"And what about those buttons? It reminds me of an elevator."

They spent a while discussing what the little rooms looked like. They were no wider than their outstretched arms with a couple more fingers added on. Each room had a wrought iron bed with a thin mat-tress on sagging bedsprings that reminded Milan of the big sieve they used for sifting stones for stucco when they were fixing their house in Šamorín. When they lay down, the mattress almost touched the floor.

The tiny room had a window looking out on the opposite wall, made of the red bricks that the British love so much. There had been an unsuc-cessful attempt to raise the standard with a narrow armoire in which a few hangers were screwed to the rod. There was also a washbasin so small that it made those in railway cars seem like swimming pools. Above it, as elsewhere, were two typical British specialties—separate water taps for hot and cold water. But the tiny rooms were spotless, and each came with clean towels, a small bar of soap, and starched pillowcases, and everything smelled of a somewhat archaic sanitizer.

"Like in the times of Oliver Twist."

"Just be happy that we don't have any cute little pets here."

"We'll see."

In truth, no creatures appeared. The kitchen produced food that matched the housing. The scrambled eggs and sausages, familiar from their aunt's place, were accompanied by overcooked vegetables and fish, omelets and oatmeal. The food had to be soft enough that the old ladies who were the hotel's main customers could chew it.

They had a table reserved for their wedding dinner, definitely not a banquet, at the Park Restaurant two streets away from the hotel, but they shared their breakfast with the grandmas in the hotel. Since it was the weekend Milan didn't have to be Mr. Bean and decided to have granola with milk and fruit and toast with marmalade. They met a nice engineer from Bonn at the table, who congratulated them on their wedding. Tereza was surprised.

"How did you know we're getting married?"

"You talked so loudly about it that only the deaf wouldn't hear you. Pardon me, I understand Czech, as my grandmother was from Liberec."

"You always think that when you're abroad nobody can understand you."

"Well, good luck to you!"

The engineer waved at them and ate his sausages. They returned to the fourth floor in less than ten minutes when there was nothing left to eat in the dining room. Tereza shouted. The door to Milan's room was ajar and his suitcase was lying open on the floor.

"Our money!"

Milan started looking for their savings, which they kept in a small tin peppermint box. He looked under the pillow, lifted the mattress and searched through the suitcase again but didn't find anything. All the money they'd saved for airfare was in that box. They hadn't wanted to leave the money in their aunt's apartment; it seemed safer to take it with them.

Tereza sat on the bed crying. For the tenth time, Milan searched through his things, swearing with his eyes. He said nothing but was clearly very angry. Then he embraced her.

"We have to tell Beneš."

They thought of the owner who smiled at them all the time from his cubicle. He looked like an elegant cockatoo, always dressed in a flawless suit. As Milan jumped up, Tereza grabbed his sleeve.

"Do we want to involve the police?"

Milan sat down. They were the victims, yet they feared the police. Neither of them trusted the police of any state, who they believed would suspect foreigners with temporary visas or refugees from the communist bloc. The police were less trustworthy than an Englishman, crazy or not. Who knows, maybe a cop could really help them, but they were from the generation that didn't believe in uniforms.

There were many guests in the hotel that day. The grandmas had visitors. Here and there they saw strange young people who had definitely not come to see their grandmother out of courtesy, but rather to get a few pounds from her. Maybe one of those so-called grandsons had cleared out their suitcase.

It would be embarrassing to suspect anyone. They would never go downstairs to face Beneš and ask him if he'd seen anyone suspicious and then tell him not to call the police. The only thing left for them to do was cry. Tereza exercised her right to be emotional, which is not guaranteed in any constitution, but is the one used most often to address the world's injustices.

She wept with such intensity that a few doors in the hallway opened, but then closed again when they saw the couple embracing.

The young ones had had a falling out and now they were making peace. The story of love. Well, we weren't so different, were we? Those who love suffer. After the rain the sun will come out. And that's the way it is.

The German engineer stopped by as well. The hotel had no elevator, so he had to walk through the floor of tears. He came to the door like the others and hesitated as others had, but unlike them, he stayed. These people who were so happy a minute ago at breakfast, laughing so lovingly, could not have gotten mad at each other so soon. Milan told him everything that had happened, and without discussion, the German took his wallet out and handed them money as a loan. After all, they didn't even have money to pay for their wedding dinner. It was no time for pride, and they accepted with joy. Right away they invited him to meet them at three o'clock at the Park Restaurant. He smiled and accepted.

The recently robbed Tereza and Milan got married with the feeling that things could only get better.

Their aunt soon found out that they'd gotten married over the weekend. When the German engineer came to her house on Tuesday to say good-bye there was no point in keeping it secret any longer. She ended up thanking him. She was a bit offended, but they quickly made peace with her. The theft inspired Milan and Tereza to work harder. He kept working as a deliveryman and she started cleaning a ballet school in the evening. There was no thought of studying. That would happen over in Canada.

They were happy, believing without any rational basis that Canada would be their last stop: that the word "transient" would turn into "permanent." A few months later they had enough money for airfare. But during that strange wedding weekend, when so many good and bad things happened, when they lost everything but found themselves again, another strange thing happened: something that Tereza kept secret for a long time.

She talked about it as the Boeing aircraft peeled off Heathrow's tarmac and gained altitude on the way to Toronto. The plane was shaking, the undercarriage was pulling up noisily, and warning signs were flashing. Everyone was buckled up and the lights were dimmed. Heavy smokers suffered as they waited for the plane to reach cruising altitude so they could pull out a cigarette.

It was at this moment right after lift-off, when most of the world's airline crashes occur, that Tereza turned to her husband and started to talk.

"My father came to me."

"I beg your pardon?"

"We talked that night, after the wedding. While you were taking a shower."

"Your father?"

"I was lying in my bed and suddenly he was sitting there on the chair under the window. He was smiling. I was telling myself: what a nice dream! But I wasn't sleeping. It was him, but he was somewhat transparent. He was wearing the shirt he always wore, and I could see the chair through his shirt. It was dark outside. He looked like he was made of mist. I thought that I was ill, that I'd gone crazy. I was telling myself: you need a doctor. And suddenly he says: 'I didn't want to scare you.' He was speaking, talking normally. And he asked me if he should go. I just shook my head. I wasn't able to say anything. He was happy that he could see me, he continued. He had an opportunity because I thought about him so much. During our wedding I felt sorry that none of our parents could be there. Yours could have flown in, but mine... I knew from the beginning that I couldn't see my mother or brother that easily, but once it hits you... and suddenly he was there. I stopped being afraid. Not afraid of him, I wasn't, even for a second. I was afraid that something was wrong with me. You've lost it, Tereza, I said to myself, but the longer he sat there the more certain I became that I was normal and this wasn't a hallucination. I don't know if he was actually talking. He kept opening his mouth, I remember that. It was speech, but was he talking? He looked at the dresser and smiled, saying that we had one like that at home... when I was learning how to play the violin... my hands hurt and I was stubborn and refused to practice... and he remembered how he placed me on top of the dresser with my violin... and I sat there and played because I couldn't run away... and I remembered how I cried and how my nose started to run on top of that dresser on Panenská Street... my parents wanted me to have the best education, they said: what you know will protect you, what you have in your head, nobody can take from you... promise me, Tereza, that in Canada you'll go to university... I nodded, sure, that was what we'd decided a long time ago. We understood each other... it took a few minutes and suddenly he was no longer sitting in that chair. Then you came out of the shower, and you smelled like Oliver Twist... and you kissed me. I didn't want to scare you. It's been two months and I kept putting off telling you."

Milan took her hand and gently squeezed it. He belonged to her. She would have him. She could rely on him. She made herself comfortable in her seat at last. Up until then, her body had been in a spasm of tension. Now she felt the pressure subside.

"At the end he told me... 'You can do it, Tereza. You can.' And he disappeared. So what do you think? Is your wife crazy?"

Treason

Alexander started receiving letters from Czechoslovakia. Not only from Anna—those were rare, and they were always signed as Anna, meaning that she didn't write them on her own.

He was still always glad to see her writing even though he couldn't believe her words. At least when they spoke on the telephone he could hear her voice. After so many years of marriage he could tell, like a doctor, the source of her problem from the tone of her voice. The problem was not her lungs. The disease came from the heart and darkened her voice. He felt that something was killing her, and the new letters that began arriving in the spring of 1970 were killing him.

Dear Comrade Director,

We're writing to you as the former colleagues with whom you spent many years in the Sanola Company. We're very disappointed by your decision to leave our country. You abandoned your homeland that made it possible for you to study for free and also gave this opportunity to your daughter. You betrayed the people from our town who trusted you. We expected so much from you, but that was evidently not enough for you. After your cowardly escape production suffered. Now we no longer believe that you were sincere when years ago you pretended to be a man who loved his work and hometown. You were a specialist, true, but you abandoned your mission at the worst possible time.

Fortunately there were new people whom you did not trust in the past and whose progress you tried to slow down. These are the people who have taken over your work and are performing it at the highest level. We're ashamed that we come from the same town as you and that we used to sit at the same table as old friends do. Nothing is more hurtful than betrayal by a person you trust. All of your former colleagues, engineers, and designers are disappointed by your behavior. Could it be that you sold your honor because you needed dollars so badly? We feel sorry for you.

Maybe there would be a chance for you to return, but it would have to start with you. Maybe we could take you back as a former colleague and maybe we could forget about the harm your desertion has caused. Reflect on your actions.

For the Construction and Development Unit,
Engineer Ulman and...

There were a dozen signatures. Alex knew all of them. They were his friends. They were connected by endless days in the company for which they had sacrificed the best years of their lives, and often even nights, like when the Brno Exposition was coming up and they had to shine with a new product and it didn't work out as it was supposed to. They'd spent many Sundays in his living room, drinking cheap sparkling wine and eating heavenly sandwiches made by Anna, smiling and sharing the mutual feeling that they lived as well as they could under difficult circumstances...

There was no doubt that the signatures were real. And the writing was Ulman's. Alex knew him, as Ulman had been his deputy. He wasn't a complete idiot, but neither was he a top specialist. God protect Sanola if it had to be led by Natural Disaster. He knew who was responsible for this letter; he could imagine the elegant man in the leather jacket and loafers, though this might be beneath even him. He knew what they wanted to achieve with this letter, and he could analyze it rationally, but even so, they got to him.

Gutted, he sat with the envelope in his shaking hands. And that was how Petra found him in the kitchen.

"Dad, what's wrong? Father! Are you all right?"

He silently pointed to the letter. Petra scanned it and threw it on the table.

"Please, you can't take this seriously! You know they're dictating to mother what she can write. And every time you came back from a foreign country, State Security would question you, you told me yourself. They told them what to write and they signed it! They chose the people who liked you on purpose. They want to destroy you! Please, don't read it!"

Petra grabbed the letter, crumpled it up and threw it into the wastebasket. Alex looked at her, his eyes shining.

"But I did betray them, Petra, I truly betrayed them. They're right, whether I like it or not. I left them in the lurch..."

"Father, you didn't betray anyone. Maybe you left them in the lurch, but not me! You helped me!"

"I know."

"And maybe they would have fired you half a year later. They're doing this everywhere. Anyone who won't go along with them is gone."

Alex knew very well what was going on in Czechoslovakia. He'd heard it on Voice of America. They were replacing people one after another. Do you agree? Sign and you can stay. You don't? Leave! If you're not with us, you're against us!

He knew all that, but this was his second year away. He, too, was idealizing his past, and was unable to imagine how bad it had been at home. He was an honest man, and those are the people who worry most. He didn't have a clue how much he'd irritated the others with his sports car, good suits, and elegance, and how they'd secretly called him "playboy," even though he'd never been unfaithful to his wife. He stuck out, and when the time came for weeding, those were the people who got mowed down. Off with his head! All they had to do was to throw the sickle over the ocean, their aim accurate enough to hit the mark.

It wasn't enough for them that he'd lost the work that he loved and the country of his birth. They had to spit in his glass of memories and spoil the feeling that he'd managed to accomplish something good through his work back home and hadn't lived his life in vain. Something like this could break a good man like him.

Petra was completing her studies and the date of the licensure examination was approaching, but she sacrificed half a day and took her father out. She had needed him in Vienna, and he needed her in Canada. The city was holding an exhibition of the Group of Seven painters, classic landscapes that managed to capture and immortalize the Canadian wilderness. Petra was not that interested in art. Some medics write poetry and visit theaters and exhibitions, but she was not one of them. She preferred to stay home and read. The only exception was her love of skiing. Sometimes she would skate on the frozen Rideau Canal, but that was busier than the Bratislava promenade that locals called the Corso, where everybody admired ice sculptures by local artists. While skating, she thought of the beautiful loneliness of the skier, the wind and the snow... She promised herself that if she passed the examination and was hired by the hospital she would take her first weekend to go to the mountains. In the meantime she went to the gallery to at least see them as the Group of Seven saw them.

Seven artists: seven windows into the country. Lakes, trees, moss, and fallen leaves. And also snow and ice. Petra unconsciously released her father's arm; he didn't need her physical support. She walked past the paintings by herself. At first she scanned them quickly as if on an express train. She was sitting in the compartment, and beyond the window flashed a Canada the likes of which she had never seen.

"Where are you rushing?"

She didn't hear her father's voice. It took twenty minutes for her to scan all the paintings, and then she returned to the first one, where she found Alex. He was surprised by how much the art touched his daughter. When he and his wife were still young they were in love with opera. From Stará Ruda they would travel to Bratislava and even Brno. In time these delightful cultural trips stopped, without touching little Petra in the least. Alex was moved when he saw his grown-up child standing awestruck in front of the canvases. He'd apparently neglected something in her education, he mumbled to himself as he moved on. It would probably be impossible for him to make up for it.

Petra was most fascinated by Lawren Harris, who painted icebergs, water, and snow, starting from his first realistic representations up to his pinnacle style. The fascinating geometric shapes in blue and white represented water in an abstract manner that was more realistic than a photograph. She could not tell how, but it was all there.

Petra's snowy heart awoke and started to knock on the doors of memory. She tried to remember the places where she'd skied. Her first runs. The skis her father had brought her from Austria. The ski outfits that Mother had clumsily tailored since there were none in the stores. The first real ski outfit made in Hungary. Knitted hats, scarves, and gloves. Ski goggles. Bamboo ski poles. And the whistling air that caressed her cheeks like an ice grinder. And the snow thrown by her sharp turns as she stopped down under the ski lift. And the hot tea offered by Alex, her trusted Sancho Panza.

She had to go to the mountains. She wanted to make her father think about something else, and she felt inflamed by a lifelong dream. She would strike out into the north! As soon as she got a position, she...

"Hi, is that you?"

Before her stood a young man and woman, both holding sketchbooks with a copy of the geometric iceberg that fascinated her so much. They seemed familiar, but where from?

"Excuse me..."

"We met on the train, back when..."

The end of August, soldiers, lots of refugees going to Vienna, and those two with their little backpacks. Rudo and Silvia. They embraced each other.

"How are you doing?

"We're teaching children to draw."

"We want to study at the Academy. Where do you live?"

They talked for a long time. She went through the exhibition with them, and they told her about the painters who used to stay in wooden cabins in the wilderness and how nobody took them seriously at first, and how many of them died in poverty. Alex came alive: their talk interested him. Petra couldn't take her eyes off them. They weren't much younger than she was, but the difference in their attitude to life could be measured in light years.

Petra was always uptight and Silvia and Rudo were free. She knew she was idealizing them but she envied the ease with which they took care of themselves. She had a father who made her feel desperate and for whom she would have done anything, but she couldn't help him. She had no idea that Rudo was suffering from remorse at abandoning his mother, who was sick with a heart ailment, and that Silvia was receiving letters from her parents filled with suppressed sadness, and that even their carefully formulated optimism couldn't hide how much they missed her, and how they regretted agreeing to her departure. But could they have disagreed with it? She would have left anyway.

Everyone was carrying a tiny devil in their pocket that others had no idea about. To Petra, her own seemed the biggest. She had no partner to stop the storm. She was alone. She never loved recklessly, only perfunctorily. She had never known anything but her platonic love in high school and quick sex in the shower during the potato harvest. The drunken medical student had utterly disgusted her, and she never looked for another relationship.

Now, surrounded by books, she had no chance to find a friend. If the emigrants were looking for partners among themselves, though some instinctively looked elsewhere, she didn't need a compatriot, nor did she look for Canadians. She had nothing against them but soon found out that she was simply happy to be alone. She wasn't looking for a relationship, only for friendship.

At that moment a lucky finger touched her, one that she had felt so many times before. Her aunt was taking care of her, something that others who had to wash toilets in the pubs at night would have given anything for. She could just study. She had a place to live and enough to eat. And in addition, the lucky finger provided her with Paulette and Reneé. P and R, as she renamed them, were friends of Rudo and Silvia. They were nurses working in the hospital where Rudo and Silvia often went to draw with the sick children. P and R were happy to see that Petra was their colleague, or rather their future colleague, and invited her to go boating with them at the lake. Only three days earlier she had dragged her father out of the house to pull him out of his depression, and now he was surprised to see how his daughter radiated happiness.

They returned from the gallery via a used car lot. They saw old Cadillacs and Lincolns, huge and ship-like, with fins instead of turn signals, and shiny-hooded Buicks that seemed straight out of a gangster movie, shot through with rust but still dignified nevertheless.

If those cars embodied the American dream ten years ago, they still embodied the emigrant's dream of today. The former drivers of Moskvich, Wartburg, Trabant and Škoda vehicles dreamed of driving cars like these. We know that Alex had realized his dream back home already, but the less fortunate were finally experiencing it now.

They entered the car lot. The owner was a phlegmatic, giant black man who let them look at whatever they wanted. Alex came alive. He was twelve years old again. He would sit in a car and steer, trying the suspension of gigantic seats that looked suitable for a bus. Petra had a small camera in her bag, and she took pictures of her happy father. Then he took pictures of her, and finally the helpful owner—Alex was astonished, as in Czechoslovakia they would have been thrown out long ago—took a few pictures of them standing together in front of a shiny Lincoln.

Alex became nostalgic about his Felicia, and for a while he felt like saving up for a gigantic Cadillac that was actually not expensive at all since it was a piece of junk, but the enthusiasm that had so suddenly overwhelmed him quickly faded. The light in his eyes went out, and he became stooped and submerged in his melancholy again.

He didn't want a car. He would never want a car again. But a little twinkle remained in his eye. In the courtyard of the used car dealership he spotted a piece of shiny metal, apparently a piece of junk that nobody would miss. Alex examined it for a while and then put it in his pocket with a guilty expression on his face. But this dealership that gradually morphed into a junkyard was full of parts, shiny pieces of metal, old hoses and errant nuts. Anyone could pick them up.

An hour later, when Petra had already forgotten looking at the cars, he took out the piece of metal and showed it to her.

"What does this remind you of?"

"Iron?"

Alex reacted with disappointment.

"It's the little bridge! The one near the thermal plant in Stará Ruda, behind the station."

It really did look like the one she liked to ride her bike beneath, but that was not a topic for conversation. Everything related to the town was also related to her mother, whom they'd left there. They went home in deep silence.

On Friday evening her new friends stopped by to take Petra out in their old Peugeot. Alex and Mariška saw them off outside the house like regular parents, and the car disappeared in the distance. Alex went in, but he thoughtfully caressed the piece of metal in his pocket.

During the trip Petra fell in love with Canadian nature. They spent two nights in a cabin near Little Redstone Lake in Haliburton and canoed on the lake. They were obliged to share a single canoe that seated only two, but Petra was always one of them. She had priority since she was new at it. They took pleasure from the amazement they saw in her face.

While cooking in the evening they talked for a long time. Petra hadn't realized how much her language skills had improved. She moved freely from English to French. In those days, for the first time, she started to dream in a language other than Slovak. In the morning she turned to Silvia.

"Where did I go wrong?"

Silvia laughed with gusto, but then she grabbed Petra by the hand, seeing this was no time for joking.

"You finally left your home."

That was her only comment. However, R and P talked non-stop. They were getting ready to go to Big Trout Lake, a distant community in Northwest Ontario, to work as nurses. They wanted to help Canada's original inhabitants, whose communities were spread across a giant territory and who were generally known as the First Nations. They didn't want to stay in a big city; they felt they would be most helpful in a place where there were few medical services. They were young, unattached, and idealistic, willing to move to an area where they would have to rely only on their own clinical skills and judgement with the occasional consultations with the physicians in Sioux Lookout.

That is when Petra first heard the name of the place that was to change her life: Sioux Lookout.

Toronto

Jozef went to a small parish in Toronto. When he left the United States his bishop came to say goodbye, shaking his hand and suggesting that if it didn't work out for him in Canada, he could return any time he pleased. Jozef thanked him. So much had changed since his arrival in New York. He had work and another child and a new address.

In Canada his church wanted to assign the family a small house occupied by the previous minister, who had retired. But that would have meant moving the old man into an institution, and they didn't like that idea. Instead, Jozef and his wife and children moved into a rented apartment.

Toronto was huge. Some parishioners drove a hundred kilometers to attend church. Older people didn't want to drive in the evening and preferred to come in the morning. Near the church was a building that hosted a summer school, evening events, lectures, and performances. Jozef had no idea that a few years later he would use his artistic education to direct performances in addition to his pastoral duties.

Among those performances was a play written by Josef Škvorecký, who had also settled in Toronto and, together with his wife, had founded the legendary publishing house Sixty-Eight Publishers.

When I was gathering material for this novel, I had almost everything—and the rest I could imagine. But what I didn't want to invent was the family life of a Slovak pastor in Canada. And who could provide me with better information than Erika?

That's why I asked Erika to write me a few lines. I'll get inspired, I told myself, and I'll have the facts. Of course, every writer knows of a few reliable gambits that help him avoid topics he knows little about, although he could guess. But I didn't do that, and I'm glad, because Erika sent me an email.

Now I had the facts I needed, and they fascinated me so much that I've decided to give them to you almost verbatim. So, Erika, go for it!

What is the role of the pastor's wife in the Slovak community in Canada?

To take part in the church service every Sunday and thus be an example for all.

To take part in the activities of all the church groups, whether cultural or religious.

To be the first in the kitchen whenever a church dinner or banquet is being prepared.

Always bring baked goods.

Lead the choir.

If the organist leaves, substitute for him.

Help out with Sunday school and lead the children's activities.

Dress modestly, since everything our family has is donated by the church community.

Listen to everyone, even if the person wants to talk because he/she has nothing else to do.

Help everyone, whether or not they are members of the community.

Be hospitable to anyone visiting the community.

*Make sure the living space is always tidy to receive visits from members of
the community, even if unannounced, at any time of the day.*

*Let anyone stay overnight if necessary; the duration will be decided by the
visitor.*

*When other ministers come to visit, treat them properly (one complained,
saying that his wife would bake a cake for a visitor like him).*

Be friendly to everyone, but not overly, as others might get jealous.

*Help your husband prepare material for the sermon, and if he's short on
time, help him draft it.*

*Teach the children to be an example to all the other children; they can
never miss a church service and must greet everyone and answer their
questions. They cannot dress too fashionably.*

*Never complain when your husband has to cancel the family vacation
because of the death of someone in the community.*

Hold Christmas Eve dinner if a family is in crisis and needs the minister.

*If the husband, God forbid, becomes ill, make him better so he doesn't have
to miss a single Sunday or holiday.*

*Do the Christmas shopping and preparations on your own. The pastor
always has too much work over the holidays.*

And to do all of this out of love for the husband, because you said, "I do."

Finally, Jozef was able to send an invitation to his mother to come to
Canada. She wrote back that the authorities wouldn't allow her to go as
long as he continued what he was doing. He had started broadcasting
on the radio, and thousands of people back home listened to him. While
just an ordinary emigrant, he hadn't mattered in Czechoslovakia as
much as he did now that he was a famous personality.

All of the professions that he'd had to learn out of desperation
when prevented from practicing his chosen calling now merged into
an unexpected trio in Canada. He had become a Lutheran clergyman,
but he also regularly worked in radio and occasionally performed in
amateur theater productions. It was strangely like the primal energy at

the time of the Slovak National Revival that, after all, belonged in the nineteenth century and had become passé at home. People like him made it work across boundaries of time and space, and it lived on in isolated communities abroad.

He didn't give up on his attempts to reunite his family. While he wrote applications on behalf of his mother, Erika helped Alex with the invitation for Anna. At one point it looked like Jozef would be successful, but Anna's was a hopeless case.

Jozef's mother had already received her visa and permit to leave and was even able to buy some Canadian dollars for the trip, money that her stingy government sold begrudgingly. However, just a day before her departure, two men dressed in civilian clothes visited her and said they had to add some stamps in her passport. Jozef's mother gave them her passport and never saw it again. She missed her flight, the visa became invalid, and she never made it to Toronto.

Jozef knew that his mother wouldn't be able to handle such a long flight much longer. His father couldn't even think about flying because of his poor health, but he wrote that Jozef's mother had gained some weight during the winter, as usual, and that she would lose it in the spring while working in the vineyard. Jozef loved his father's letters. As a good winemaker he started the letter with a bottle of wine. By the time he finished, the bottle was empty, and the writing flowed like grape juice from a wine press. He wrote about the rain at home, and how when it froze it became not "ice," but simply "hurt-ass," as it was called locally.

As soon as Jozef had finished the letter the phone rang. He picked up the receiver up and almost fainted, as if "hurt-ass" had formed on his carpet.

"Hello, Stará Ruda calling... Lajo."

"Hello. Lajo?"

"Yeah. Surprised?"

"Shall I call Erika?"

"No, no. I'll talk to you if you don't hang up."

"I'm listening,"

"I hear they won't allow your mom to go to Canada."

"How do you know?"

"Don't be naïve, Jozef. Your mom is old, you know."

"I know."

"You can't win against our authorities. No matter how hard you try."

"Why are you calling?"

"I can arrange for your mother to be allowed out, if you want."

Standing next to the phone, Erika was astonished. This was a call from the man who hadn't even said hello to his sister for years and had harmed them as much as he could. She motioned to her husband to hang up the phone, but Jozef was curious to learn what this was all about. As he later admitted, for a brief moment he trusted this notorious liar, who was trying to convince him that he could get his mother to Canada. It was clear that he could do it, but the question was why.

"You want something for it, right?"

"Me? I don't want anything. But our people want you to stop your activity against our country."

"What in particular?"

"Stop broadcasting. Don't attend all these émigré meetings and don't give speeches like the one day before yesterday in Toronto's Royal York."

"You're well informed."

"I know fuck all. Others know. But I don't wish you any harm. I just want you to think about it."

Erika was mouthing Anna's name—ask about Anna.

"How is Anna?"

"I haven't seen her for a long time. She's ill."

"What's wrong with her?"

"Something with her lungs. A frog, maybe."

Unpleasant laughter followed. Erika was a good person, but at that moment she would have gladly hit Lajo on the head with a frying pan. She had even run in from the kitchen carrying the pan she'd been using to make a roux.

"Well, I have to go."

"Think about your mother. There isn't much time, but you can see her if you're reasonable."

Then a long tone sounded over the receiver. Erika returned to the kitchen without a word. Jozef had to go and take a shower.

The Chair

Tereza bought two chocolate muffins. There was reason to celebrate: they had bought their first chair. It was a white, bent-legged émigré model distantly related to the Thonet chair. Who knows how many families had used it before them? In some spots the paint was so thickly layered that it resembled the sediment in which archeologists occasionally find trilobites.

Whenever someone moved or managed to buy better furniture they sold their old things. Besides the migratory chair Tereza and Milan had a migratory table, two soup bowls, two dinner bowls, and cutlery. They had been promised a bed. For now they slept on the quilts that Tereza's mother had sent to Haifa, and which they had brought with them in a big red suitcase.

Luckily the apartment was warm. At night they would arrange the quilts on the floor, which they'd covered with newspaper, and then cover themselves with a blanket and whisper:

"Is that okay? It is."

And it was.

Things had looked less optimistic immediately after their arrival from London. Milan phoned his friend who taught at the university, and the friend was waiting for them at his place. Exhausted from the flight, Tereza was vomiting, and colorful circles danced before her weary eyes. She was looking forward to lying down for a while.

But instead of an oasis of calm they landed in glowing embers. Their friend, who happened to be a professor of English, had invited a female student to his apartment. Milan and Tereza witnessed a peculiar ritual during which it was unclear who was trying to seduce whom. In a room filled with cigarette smoke, Janis Joplin wailed on the record player, and two cups of cold tea had been abandoned on a chair next to the couch where the couple sat wrapped in conversation. After welcoming his friends, the professor rejoined his student and started developing some complicated theory that seemed to concern the language of Shakespeare's era, but could also have been about irregular verbs, or an analysis of the social question in the novels of Dickens.

The student listened with religious zeal, nodding and occasionally uttering a word or two, and the professor continued while managing to light another dozen cigarettes, boil tea for Tereza, and also make three phone calls. By the time the student finally left around half past one, Tereza wasn't even sorry about interrupting their date with their arrival. She went to bed immediately. As she gradually sank into the sweet depths of sleep, she heard Milan talking with his friend about his work.

In the morning they set out to find a rental. The professor just waved his hand: it would be easy. There were lots of vacant rooms; people gladly rented them out. So they went with him to check some out. The professor always knocked at the door, the landlord opened the door, and then closed it after a brief exchange. The professor couldn't believe what had happened to good old Toronto after they'd been rejected ten times, but Milan had it figured out.

His friend was a typical hippie, wearing an embroidered East Indian shirt and worn-out jeans that only his pedagogical gravitas kept from dropping to his knees. In his wavy, shoulder-length hair he wore a headband adorned with coral chips.

From then on it was Milan who knocked at the door. Dressed properly and with his hair cut short, he managed to rent a place on his second try. It was in a wooden two-story house in a hippie neighborhood where thick electric wires criss-crossed old wooden telephone poles. Milan couldn't help showing off his knowledge as a light-current specialist:

"It looks like they just discovered electricity in this neighborhood."

Now they were in their own room. It was dark. The power was out. It was resting. They also were resting. They were playing an organ, Milan first and then Tereza. She recalled the garden in Panenská Street and how the instrument had always fascinated her. It was mysterious. So they bought one in Canada.

"Do you know this one?"

Milan began to play a Bach cantata.

"Of course."

Tereza continued, and the melody softly filled their lodging. The organ hadn't cost much, not even a dollar. It was a comb with a piece of paper folded over it. They played the serious music light-heartedly.

"Do you know this one?"

The room was almost empty, with a trunk doubling as a table, and their "organ." When they finished their studies in a few years, they would buy a real electric organ. And then spend years paying it off. And when Tereza pressed the keys, she would be able to imagine being on her street in Bratislava. And that was priceless.

Then came 1970: the year of the first divorces. Emigration tested marriages. Those who managed to stay together while escaping were unable to withstand the problems in the new country: the temporary accommodation, the used furniture, and the lack of money. These same problems drew other couples even closer together. Milan and Tereza belonged to the second category. But it certainly wasn't thanks to the culinary skills of the lady of the house.

For dinner they usually made bean soup, although their reper-
toire also included potato soup, and eventually lentil soup. But they
never made their favorite garlic soup. Canadians hated garlic and
were horrified when Czechoslovaks cooked in their rented apartments and the aroma of garlic wafted everywhere. Once this became
known, some landlords began stating in the rental contract that the
use of garlic was prohibited. Tereza and Milan responded in their own
way.

After dinner (lentil soup minus garlic), they composed an opera
called *Garlic*.

"This will be the overture!"

Tereza played a few noble tones on her comb, if what came from
this instrument could be called tones.

"Act One. The heroic tenor Maxim Garlic comes on stage and
sings. Milan!"

Milan understood and began singing in a soft but not tenor voice.

"I am Maximilian Garlic, from Roma,

I know a million kinds aroma!"

Tereza protested.

"Of aroma. It should be 'of aroma.'"

"Who's Garlic? You or me?"

"Okay, just sing!"

Milan took a breath and continued.

"And I know so many different aromas,

"That I could wreck this house of *phantomas!*"

Now Tereza got up and for a greater effect placed a sieve on her
head (we'll hear about the history of its purchase) and announced in a
theatrical voice:

"Next comes the landlady, the soprano."

"You mean the landlady?"

Milan pointed downstairs towards the apartment of the owners.
Tereza placed her index finger on her lips and shushed him, then took
a bow and began to sing, but not in a soprano voice:

"Under punishment of pulling the eye teeth
It is strictly forbidden to use garlic
In my Castle.
Whoever disobeys this law will be broken on a wheel
Dipped in chocolate
And sent to Cuba to harvest oranges."
Milan protested.
"That does not rhyme."
"Haven't you heard of free verse, the French key to modern poetry?"
Milan nodded his head. He lightly tapped his right foot to keep rhythm.
"The vampire is coming."
"Who will be the vampire?"
"I will."
"But you're Garlic!"
"You haven't heard about alienation, the German discovery by Bertolt Brecht?"
"If you like, alienate yourself."
Milan used his two fingers to create fangs.
"I'm a German vampire,
I'll suck the blood of this apartment's Sire,
and I call for help, help!"
Tereza took the sieve off her head.
"I wonder how you'll play both Vampire and Garlic."
Milan took a small mirror from her purse and pointed at himself.
"Alive, I am Vampire. In the mirror, I am Garlic. As you know, a vampire doesn't have a reflection in the mirror."
He played on the comb an interesting series of tones reminiscent of the Saturday radio play for youth that all children used to listen to in Czechoslovakia.
"I am Garlic Max,
And for Vampire, I have an axe!"

"Oh thank you, brave Garlic. Now that I have your permission,
To use you in food solid and liquid is my mission!"

From the next apartment came the sound of banging on the wall
and an irritated voice.

"Be quiet, please!"

Tereza and Milan had to hold their hands in front of their mouths
to stifle their laughter as they rolled on the bed and tried to muffle the
sound under the blanket. Just looking at each other was enough for
them to burst out laughing again. They covered their faces with pillows to keep from provoking each another, but the laughter kept reig-
niting like a piece of burning coal.

Her father arrived unexpectedly. He wasn't there when she was putting
the cutlery (they already owned a soup ladle) into the drawer covered
by colorful paper, but a moment later she saw him by the window. He
still looked like a sculpture made of steam, somewhat transparent, light
and immaterial. Outside the window, the sun was shining, and the light
passing through his body created the effect of glowing from within.

Shocked and surprised, Tereza leaned against the table for support. She was more afraid than she had been in London. Then she had
thought it was only her irritated psyche, exhausted before departure,
but when he appeared again here, she no longer attempted to explain
it away. He simply came, and she would be happy and not scared, and
would enjoy it, full stop.

"Hi Kitten."

"Hi... I have no idea if you can hear me."

"Of course I can. It's a bit distant, as if you're at the end of a hallway, but I guess there's no hallway here, right?"

"No, there isn't. This is our room."

"Actually, I can't see anything, sorry, so I can't praise it. It feels like
I'm walking around inside cotton wool. Are you angry with me for not
saying that I like your room? At least tell me what you have here..."

Tereza started to list items with her trembling voice, but the longer she talked about the furniture, the stronger her voice became. Finally, she took out mother's letter.

"Mother wrote to me, I'll read it..."

She stopped and looked at him.

"But you probably know that, right? How are they? Do you know?"

Father shrugged his shoulders.

"I'm sorry, but I don't even know if I know anything. Maybe I was there and I know everything, or I knew it, but a minute later I forget. The terrible thing is that when I leave you, I'll forget what we talked about. I feel joy only now. In this small moment."

He pointed to the envelope.

"Read something."

She looked at mother's writing.

"Janko has grown a lot, you would not recognize him. He's as tall as Milan. He plays guitar all the time, but I don't know if anything will come of it. Everyone wants to play guitar now. Luckily, he has also started to study hard..."

She looked at her father. He was smiling gently and looking somewhere beyond her. She kept reading.

"He also helps a lot around the house, shopping and cleaning up. Before Easter he cleaned the apartment. He cleaned and waxed the kitchen and hallway, and he also cleaned the carpets. Everyone tells me that he looks very much like his dear sister..."

He was looking into the open drawer where the knives and forks were.

"How should I ask how you are, father?"

"Like normal: How are you?"

"How are you?"

"I'm more basic than you. Simpler. In our world, we don't need cutlery. We don't drink or eat. We don't sleep. We walk all the time. Maybe we talk, but I don't know what we talk about. I remember nothing. A second after I leave, I'll forget about our conversation.

Sometimes I think I'm being punished, but there are no punishments in Sheol."

"Please, don't worry anymore."

He stood in front of the window once more, and it seemed that the sunlight was entering him. As he began vanishing, his voice weakened.

"A second later I won't know that I was worrying. Unfortunately, I won't know that I was happy, either. We take these excursions only to support you, the living. Don't give up! You'll definitely be happy..."

Photographs

Anna was leaning on the cool surface of the x-ray machine. Through the lead glass she heard the instructions of the laboratory assistant.

"Breathe in and hold it!"

The instrument made a sound, the red light went off, and the young man in the dirty white coat changed the film.

"Now, stand with your side to the front, like this."

Anna obeyed.

"Breathe in, hold it!"

The red light flashed and then the laboratory assistant pointed at the door.

"Wait for the images."

"Thank you."

Anna got dressed in the cubicle and went out into the hall. The hospital where they examined her had the same appalling appearance as other similar buildings in Czechoslovakia. It was somewhere nobody liked to go, even for a visit, let alone to be treated. In spite of that the hallways were packed. Everyone knew the popular slogan, "Stay away from doctors," but often there was no choice.

When we don't need health services, we curse them, but when it's our turn, the instinct of self-preservation on one side and family on the other pushes us toward the doctors. So we cross through the gate with the hospital sign that presupposes that we've already crossed the vestibule of hell that is the district doctor, and that a specialist has advised us to enter hell itself, where one smells iodine instead of sulphur, and the female staff of hell wear tempting blue-white uniforms.

But even that does not deprive us of our sight, and even though we're used to ignoring the pathetic interiors we've been living in for dozens of years, we're still disgusted by the look of the walls, painted an olive color to the height of our shoulders and then spilling on in endless white to the corners. This is the building where the question of your being or non-being will be decided. It is a hundred-year-old building that in its better days was misused as military barracks by previous regimes. We give up our personal property, they give us a too-small dressing gown, and if we're lucky we'll be fed for the first time in the evening.

The over-boiled matter on the plate is testimony to the love of female cooks for the starchy plant exploited in a hundred ways, and ours is called mashed. On top of it sits a charred sausage. Until this moment we, the patients, feel like characters in a pathetic satire because we are allowed to criticize failings such as "There's no meat," "You can't buy oranges," "The repairmen are incompetent," and "The sales girls are stealing." But the approved satire never touches on the fact that this state of workers and peasants holds its citizens hostage without the medicine and modern diagnostics that higher-placed comrades enjoy in the State Sanatorium, a luxurious hospital for the top Communists. The hospital in which we find ourselves has a different qualifier: "Faculty." We could speak of being lucky because it could have been a "Regional" hospital.

Despite all of this miracles happen here on a daily basis—despite the lack of medicine and the obsolete equipment, there are doctors who are good specialists and who haven't yet surrendered to cynicism. We still have a chance to encounter a doctor who will give us more than he has to. In a hospital in Bratislava, where Anna was, there were doctors like this, and patients from all over Slovakia came to see them. This is where Maria brought her that morning.

Whether Dr. Glauber encountered such people intuitively or was drawn to them by his empathy, it is a fact that his patients included many lonely parents whose children had emigrated years ago. The fathers and mothers worried about their children and worried that the logic of the Iron Curtain would probably keep them from ever seeing them again. Their bodies reacted to this with illness. Heart attacks and cancer hit them with greater intensity than the rest of the population.

Now he was examining Anna's x-ray images. In the right lung he could see irregularly shaped points, islands of sickness in its primary stage. Glauber looked closer. It was crazy. The cancerous deposits had taken on the appearance of heavenly stars, and in the front-view image they formed the constellation of the Great Bear.

He'd never seen anything like it. He could see himself typing: "Diagnosis: the Great Bear." He examined the patient attentively and then put the stethoscope down next to his unfinished cup of coffee. Anna looked at the cup.

"I interrupted you."

"Don't worry about that."

Anna talked a lot to hide her embarrassment. He knew that. People came from the countryside and he paid the same attention to them as to everyone else. But for them it was special, because on the outskirts there was no time, means, or even will for a thorough examination.

"When did it start?"

"I'm not in pain, Doctor."

"I mean your cough."

"About six months ago."

"You can get dressed."

"Is it cancer?"

"I can't say with certainty..."

"I know you're not allowed to tell me, but thank you for examining me."

Glauber was washing his hands.

"We'll start with therapy. Will you agree to radiation?"

"Would I have to stay in the hospital?"

"Of course."

"I want to stay home. But thank you very much for offering it to me."

How much would she gain? A year? Half a year? This way she could stay where she wanted to be, even though her time would be cut shorter. Otherwise there would only be the hospital and infusions and the view of trams outside the window, but she would gain six months. As a doctor he had to offer her those six months, but as a human being he understood why she rejected it.

"You'll still get medicine. For the pain."

He was writing a prescription.

"Maria told me you were a stubborn person. I knew your husband. He was a famous man in our circles..."

Glauber stopped.

"Is it all right to mention him?"

Anna nodded, and he finished writing the prescription.

"All the doctors wanted to meet him. He could find instruments that we never heard of here. They tested a lot of things at Sanola and were looking for clinics to do it. They paid no attention to the patents. They would get a German respirator, change a few parts and start production. We received the first products."

He handed Anna the prescription.

"We'll meet anyway, whether you like it or not. At least once a month, okay? Promise me you'll come."

Anna nodded. Glauber shook her hand, but somehow Anna was unable to leave. She opened her purse and took out a photograph.

"Here he is. With our daughter."

The doctor looked at the black-and-white picture. Alex was standing in front of a shiny American car next to a slender girl with Anna's features.

"What does your daughter do?"

"She's a medical doctor, studying for the licensure examination."

"Our glorious university is good for nothing outside."

Glauber had resolved his dilemma long ago. Right after the invasion, he was invited to the Oncological Congress in California and offered a position. Of course he would have to pass the licensure examination, but this would be a minor detail, considering his publications. But he returned. He had no reason to. He just wanted to stay home.

"Is that their car?"

"I don't know."

"It's quite a rocket."

He had seen dozens of photographs like this, repeated itself over and over again. His patients were often his friends. They would open their purses or look in their jacket pockets and take out envelopes with pictures of children. Jana at Niagara Falls. Peter and Maya at an ostrich farm. Olivia next to a totem pole. Rasťo and Mária near the Statue of Liberty. Milan and Tereza at the Port of Haifa. And Alex and Petra in front of a parked Lincoln.

Children took pictures in places they had thought they would never see. And when they saw a luxurious convertible or a parked Rolls Royce, they would take a picture next to it, for fun. They would do the same if they happened to be next to an extravagant mansion. They didn't say in their letters that those were only tourist pictures; they thought it was obvious. But many parents thought that their children were doing extraordinarily well. They wanted to believe it. Look at their gorgeous house! And check out their car! Drive carefully, my dear children! They had to do well. If not, then what was the point of all of this?

Used cars were cheap. Even when the new owners spent more time beneath them than inside of them, they were worth it. Emigration destroys one fantasy but liberates another one.

The Great Bear that roamed the vault of Anna's lungs didn't give her much time. Even Glauber had no idea how quickly those little stars would grow into threatening suns, only to collapse into themselves like black holes.

Now Anna was enjoying a cake. She was on Panenská Street, which she hadn't visited since moving her daughter there. She was drinking coffee as Maria bemoaned her rejection of a cure. But Anna wasn't listening, like a person who has already made a decision. The words came in and then flew out again.

Maria stopped. She couldn't be angry with the White Lady, nor did she wish to upset her with the news that she herself had lost her job. She was no longer an editor and now worked in a warehouse where she filled baskets with books destined for recycling. This wasn't Tereza's fault. Political testing had not yet started, and when it did, thousands of specialists would become snack bar employees and warehouse staff. Maria had brought it on herself with a comment she made in her editorial office. When the topic turned to 1968, which by now seemed such a long time ago, she referred to it as an occupation. Her colleagues asked her not to say anything; they didn't want to talk about it at all.

But Maria had a whirlwind in her, like her daughter. She even stopped telling her daughter not to write about political topics. It's your life, Tereza. So she was quietly transferred to the warehouse, and an educated editor and proofreader became an ordinary worker. Janko, however, had no problem gaining admission to high school, which unlike in North America is not compulsory, but an elite school. It was the same one on Metod Street where his sister used to study and was still fondly remembered. He was getting excellent grades. He had finally succeeded in starting a rock band, and as a first-year student was playing at the celebrations for the first day of school. Only three songs, but nevertheless, he could play.

He was practicing even now, paying no attention to what his mother was saying, or to the silence of the peculiar White Lady. On the couch was a book with guitar scores, and he was trying to sing *House of the Rising Sun.* He couldn't play like the Animals and didn't have a voice like Eric Burdon, but he still had something from the sun.

Landscape

"The original population of Canada suffered greatly because of the European visitors. On the continent that from time immemorial had belonged to them and generations of their forefathers, the Europeans behaved like the proverbial bull in a china shop. It was us who forced them to speak our language; who forced our culture and religion and our way of life on them because we were sure it would be best for them. The more sincerely we believed that, the deeper they sank into hell.

"The encounter between our civilization and their ancient culture resulted in enormous tension. The founding of residential schools for indigenous people in the 1930s is one of the tragic mistakes we committed. The government at that time gave a mandate to the missionaries, who often took children by force from their environment and their families and sent them to the residential schools. The result was not a new self-confident and educated generation of the indigenous population, but rather a cascade of tragedies..."

Paulette and Reneé had brought Petra to a lecture by a young doctor, and she was listening intently, not wanting to miss a single word.

She had been struck by how the doctor had begun his lecture by thanking the Algonquin nation "on whose traditional and unceded territory we are gathered today."

The young doctor continued, "Whole generations of such children lost their native language and culture. Many were sexually abused, and all of them suffered from not being brought up by their parents in their own communities. When they returned after many years, they couldn't get used to their own culture. They didn't respect the chiefs or understand the language of their mothers. They were isolated and disinherited. Many committed suicide. With our civilization arrived alcohol and drugs. As all too often happens, these negative things were accepted more readily than the good customs we could offer them."

Petra remembered the Roma community that lived in disused train cars behind Stará Ruda. As a little girl she had been afraid of them, fearing that they would take her bicycle. Her parents warned her not to play there. Nobody knew what to do about the Roma and the merry-go-round of social assistance on which they became increasingly dependent. They had the right to receive help because they didn't work, and they didn't work because they had social assistance.

"Just a few years ago our government made the decision to apologize for the persecution of the indigenous population. We still haven't reached the point of compensating them for the harm. This made First Nations people distrust all Canadians, who now have a different attitude towards them. Our benevolence is based on maximizing attempts to understand them and minimizing interference in their social structures. A global understanding does not exist between them and us, but many positive relations exist among individual Canadians and individual First Nations people. Our medical station in Sioux Lookout is an example of Canada taking steps to address the harm caused to our First Nations."

When he finished, Petra learned from P and R that the young doctor had recently married an indigenous girl from the Ojibway Nation.

They introduced Petra to him, and the two of them talked for a while. His name was Alexander and he invited her to come and work in the north, but she took it as just a polite remark.

She had passed her licensure examinations a month ago and had started to visit medical wards: internal medicine, surgery, obstetrics, pediatrics ... She was about to embark on two beautiful years during which she would turn into a real doctor, sure of her abilities. At the end she would have to prove her knowledge with a theoretical and practical examination equal to the Attestation in Slovakia. She started out specializing as a family doctor. As the doctor who had first contact with her patients, Petra would need to know something about everything rather than being tied to a narrow specialization. As a family doctor, she would also have the latitude to practice in rural areas rather than being confined to an urban environment.

Her original fear that she would not be able to talk to people subsided as she found out that many immigrants could not speak as well as she could. She could use the language anywhere, and only her accent betrayed her. She realized that communicating with patients was the key to being an effective doctor in Canada. In Slovakia, practice was guided by the expert opinions of senior physicians, but in Canada the emphasis was on developing the skill to critically appraise the evidence before her, as well as honestly informing patients of the health issues they faced. She recalled with chagrin how Slovakian doctors had to learn Latin so they could discuss a patient's diagnosis in front of him without making him "sad." Luckily she had not practiced long enough in Slovakia for these habits to become ingrained. Even so, while she was the equivalent of a professor in histology compared to her Canadian colleagues, she had a lot to catching up to do in clinical work.

The work swallowed her; she put it on like a coat. She took on the maximum of shifts, and her supervisor began to worry about her health. She planned to add another year of training in emergency medicine after her first two years. She was able to work so much because her father didn't need her that much anymore. He was busy and dedicated to his hobby—having once again succumbed to his miniature trains. Some time ago she had found him browsing through a catalogue of model railways. He even talked Mariška into letting him use one of the four cellars in her house. She agreed, glad that her brother had pulled himself out of the funk he'd been so stuck in up to now.

Alex didn't become carefree overnight. He still worried about his wife, and his helplessness in arranging to see her was destroying him. But he forced himself not to think about it, and with his modeling hobby he seemed to improve.

With Petra's help he cleaned out the cellar that had two windows, removing Mariška's old furniture and arranging the room according to his taste. He kept only a big expandable table with mahogany veneer that had been an elegant component of Mariška's interior decoration until water damaged it in 1958. Alex bought new boards, plaster, paper and glue. What he was working on became a secret; nobody was allowed into the cellar and he only hinted mysteriously:

"You'll see!"

In the evenings he didn't watch television, but kept drawing in his giant sketchbook, running downstairs when struck by an idea. Sometimes he even asked them to bring his food there. When Mariška's servant came to take his tray, she heard the sounds of sawing and hammering from inside. He often left the food untouched. The maid reported this to Mariška, and she hobbled downstairs to have a talk with her brother:

"Alex, you have to eat something. Do you hear me? Alex!"

"Yes, Mom, sure, right away!"

And he wouldn't open the door for the next half hour. His only reply was the sound of drilling, polishing, and sanding. Petra gave him an artistic name.

"Dad, I'm going to call you Leonardo da Stará Ruda."

She had no idea how close to the truth she was.

Their walks together were no longer so frequent. She was busier, spending long hours at the hospital, so her father would go out alone; Mariška had been walking with a cane since an operation on her hip.

He always returned home with a full bag making mysterious noises, and when asked what he'd brought back, he answered like a little boy: nothing! When father and daughter did manage to go out together, Alex turned treasure hunter. He looked more at his feet than ahead of him, and once in a while he would pick up a stone, a twig, or a bottle cap.

"Look at this. Interesting, isn't it? This one is beautiful!"

He filled his pockets with various rocks, pebbles, and stones; he became a collector of them. Petra tried to joke that these were national treasures protected by law, and that if he were to remove the main super rock by accident, Canada would collapse, because every country has a hidden rock somewhere that holds its entire natural world together like a keystone holding up a ceiling.

Alex just looked at her.

"I'm not a little boy."

He kept on collecting. And he was as happy as a little boy. Petra could not have been more content. Later on she would feel remorseful about it.

At that time, she had twelve night shifts per month and would take some cases home—if she had doubts about a case, she would look it up in her books. Often she went straight from the hospital to the university library, and her dinner consisted of a small portion of rice that she gobbled down in a nearby sushi bar. That's where she was when Mariška called her.

"Petra, I'm afraid."

"What happened, Auntie?"

"It's your father..."

"What happened?"

"Come home if you can."

Alex was locked in the cellar and was not responding to anyone. When they were about to call the gardener to help them break down the door, he opened it. He couldn't understand what they were worried about; he just hadn't heard them. His hearing wasn't very good anymore, and he may have been napping. Who knows, maybe the glue and paint made you sleepy; after all, modeling hobbyists are hidden drug addicts. He laughed, stepped away from the door and let them in.

That was when they saw the miniature landscape.

Most of the cellar was taken up by the table and beer cases connected by wooden boards. The model was not yet finished, and the connecting boards between the table—the main landscape—and islands of beer cases suggested more distant territories. You could walk not only around the perimeter; the creator had allowed some gaps here and there so he could move in and out to make changes, popping up in one part of the landscape and then another like a worm in an apple. Petra couldn't believe her eyes. This was no model railway, as there were almost no rails; it was a huge landscape. After trying hard, she did find a little railway station, but the trains were not the main point. A scaled-down Stará Ruda stood there in the cellar.

She immediately thought of the expressionist *The Cabinet of Dr. Caligari*. Alex's buildings were crooked and irregular, as in the German film. The landscape radiated something sick and discordant. None of the buildings had right angles, and the roads led from nowhere to nowhere, ending above a precipice—this was the real end of the world, an artificial world created by the author's memory.

Petra recognized her native town, but as if built by a crazy architect. The bent factory smokestacks were made of drinking straws, and the oil drums she'd played around as a child were made from glass yogurt jars. A red star from a cigarette pack shone from the highest smokestack above Sanola. Many buildings were cut from shoeboxes and painted with acetone paints. The rocks that he had been collecting all this time formed the terrain of Stará Ruda, along with dry moss that he'd ripped out in the forest. She recognized their street and their house. It, too, was made of painted cardboard, and in front of it stood a small rack for carpet beating that Alex had formed from a wire hanger.

"And do you recognize this, Petra? This is our store, where we bought our milk, and where the huffy saleswoman once argued that she'd given me change from the fifty-crown banknote when she hadn't. And here's the drugstore. It looks like it, right? I don't have the shop window ready yet; that's tricky, but I'll finish it. Here's the bridge you used to bike on. You know, that's the first thing I found on the ground, and I said to myself: Petra's bridge. And Mother's rock, what do you think of Mother's rock? That's where we would sit down and rest after a hike. Your feet hurt terribly and you cried and misbehaved. Luckily Mother always carried a chocolate wafer to pacify you, and it worked. Look, we're sitting here!"

Petra suddenly saw herself as a little girl, together with her father and mother, modeled from something. She reached out her hand, but was afraid that it might be made of clay and didn't want to damage the figures. Father encouraged her.

"You can touch it, don't worry, and so can you, Mariška. It's a new kind of clay sold in the yellow store. You model it, then throw it in boiling water and it hardens in a moment. And do you recognize this path? It's Baker's Lane and Lower Mill, and Hoštáky and Kujanovec. Rudník will be here. I haven't made the lake yet, and the scale isn't right. If the lake were to scale, I'd have to put it in Mariška's bedroom."

An alarm clock began ringing in the cellar.

"Ah, I'm sorry, the old man called a meeting and I promised the boys at Sanola that I'd have a look at some dental instruments. Did you make a snack for me, Anka? Thank you."

And in front of the terrified eyes of his daughter and sister, Alex put on his jacket and then took it off, smiled and jerked his arms, took a half-step forward and then stopped and stepped back. Mariška burst into tears.

Petra stood in silence. Her father was there, and yet he was gone.

A Week

Jozef enjoyed driving. He sat behind the wheel daily. If he had looked in the rear mirror to adjust his collar, he would have seen a thirty-three-year-old man in a white shirt.

A casual look would not betray that he was a clergyman. And it wouldn't have revealed that he was also a legal and financial advisor for his small congregation, and a psychologist giving advice to people who were about to get married and to people with marital and inheritance problems. He helped with cases of abuse and alcoholism, and with children who had drug addictions, and he helped find work for the needy. That was enough for a driver.

The engine purred like a cat that some kids had found yesterday. They promised to take care of it, but we'll see. With his hands on the steering wheel on Monday, our driver thought about the previous Sunday. That was when people would tell him who was sick, and he would plan to visit them. On Sunday people usually brought along documents when they needed help. He gave them advice if he could. On the first day of the week he chose a text from the Bible that he would use for preaching the following Sunday. He had the whole week to find something in the newspapers, or something that he noticed on the street that would make his sermon lively. And it would be lively, and that's why the driver week after week attracted more drivers who gladly parked in front of the church where he also parked.

His son was learning the multiplication tables in school, and as he pressed the accelerator he subconsciously tested himself.

"Seven times nine? Sixty-three!"

The whole family was multiplying and dividing, and he was calculating right along with them, although he had never expected to. Nine times nine? Easy. Eight times three? No problem.

Tuesday was the day that the driver spent almost entirely in his car. He was visiting the sick in hospitals. He could do only two, or a maximum of four before evening. Now he was speeding his Ford along Yonge Street. The longest street in the world at 1,896 kilometers, it clearly demonstrated the size of Toronto and its neighboring region. Jozef drove with familiarity, having covered this route many times. His mother's letter was on his mind.

She wrote that she would not be allowed to see him as long as he worked with "those clerical people." That's how they put it to her in their office. Poor woman, she had no idea who the clerics even were, although he, too, was a cleric—a clergyman. He knew this had been profaned in Czechoslovakia and that it concerned Catholics more, since they wore the clerical collar. But it was a shame that they were punishing an old woman for the actions of her adult child, over whom she had no control.

He braked sharply. In his excitement he had almost rear-ended the car in front of him. He turned towards the hospital, where his first patient, the most difficult one, awaited him. He knew that his end was near and that's why he wanted to see Jozef. It was an old man who had never learned English. All his life he had worked with lumber; his tortured hands testified to his years of toil.

When they met for the first time, the man told him: "You know, when I talk to Him, I speak our language."

He pointed at the sky.

"My God is Slovak."

He would die soon, but he wanted to talk to the pastor before he had his last conversation with the one up there. And the old man surprised Jozef as he had before.

After his confession he wanted to talk about meat.

"You know, I really miss hog-killing, the way we used to do it back home... that was a big deal and we looked forward to it for weeks. It's quite different here. My son and I tried it but it wasn't the same. We made sausages from the meat we bought from the butcher shop. The butcher, a man from Yugoslavia, made his own ham and sausages, but there was no comparison. It smelled different back home than here in Canada."

The smell of smoke and drying sausages turned into the smell of gasoline. The driver was back on the freeway because it was Wednesday. He was visiting a family from his congregation. He tried to visit each family at least once each year. The visits always took place in the evening, because people worked. In the morning he could only visit retired people.

As he sat and drank tea, the conversation turned to Anna: the people he was visiting were medical doctors. Erika had received the news that her sister was seriously ill. Jozef was asking about her prognosis, and comparing treatments in Canada with those at home, and his hosts, who were very familiar with the health services back home, were skeptical. When Dr. Glauber's name was mentioned, they paid attention.

"Oh, that one is very good. An excellent doctor."

"But what can he do without medicine? The best solution would be to bring your sister over here."

"They won't let her come."

"In this condition they would. Although, if she could handle the flight... Write and tell them about her poor health, and perhaps they'll take pity on her."

"They don't even want to let my mother come..."

In the evening the driver was free for the first time. The rumble of the engine echoed in his ears and he tried but failed to concentrate on a book. He was thinking of a sentence in his mother's last letter.

"That goose won't let me go," alluding to the name of the president, Husák, whose name meant "gander." The name of that lovely and useful creature was fitting for a politician who would never be punished for "normalizing" a country of fifteen million people. Nor would the next one, who would spend the rest of his life in Bratislava as an old age pensioner. And what about the rest of us? We're left with irony. Yes, we can call them funny names, but they'll still give us the finger even from their graves.

On Thursday the driver changed his tire. He'd done it once by himself but hadn't tightened the screws properly, and from then on he never employed the ability so touted on his pre-emigration radio show *Watch Out for the Turn*. This time a man from India in overalls did it for him perfectly and quickly for a modest sum. The driver sat down in his car, his office on wheels, and mentally ran through the theme for his Sunday sermon. Thursday was the day to visit people who were sick and homebound.

The congregation was aging fast, and the number of those who were no longer mobile was growing; there were a dozen of them now. He managed to give confession to four or five of them and the day was gone. Many lived in the green suburbs, as there was a lot of greenery in Toronto, and mile-long rows of little white wooden houses that all looked the same. A driver wouldn't dare to come here without a map. Most days he drove without a map, but today he needed one.

A white German shepherd ran out in front of the house. He only understood Slovak. The bedridden lady petted him and the dog kept listening.

"When we went to visit our children in Washington for a month, we had to leave the dog home, and a boy from Malaysia took care of him. He had to learn Slovak to be able to handle him. It was quite a sight to watch the Malaysian boy shout at Bela in Slovak: 'Stay! Sit! Lie down!'"

Guessing that they were talking about her, the dog barked.

"She doesn't like the mailmen. They're afraid to come here and prefer to leave my mail with the neighbors. I don't know what it is that she has against uniforms."

The driver was glad that he didn't fall into the persecuted category. Bela laid her head on his shoes and listened. She approved of him.

And now the driver's Fridays. If nothing extraordinary happened, the car stayed parked in front of the house. He, Erika, and the children lived in one of the green suburbs of Toronto. They had moved there just recently. He was attempting to focus on his sermon, writing notes and searching through newspaper clippings. Not wishing to disturb him, Erika looked for help over the phone.

There was a skunk that had moved into their garden. Jozef couldn't stand it and went out for a look. The animal was protected and liked their lawn, but he couldn't get rid of it without getting sprayed.

Erika reached the service. A young man in an old station wagon showed up and asked for a lot of money. For what? The young man pointed to himself—for the risk. If it didn't work, he wouldn't be able to go out for two days and would have to throw his clothes away.

He lay down on the grass and crawled toward the animal extremely slowly, advancing only four inches each minute. In his hand was a cage. The skunk sniffed the air and occasionally lifted his tail and then lowered it. Jozef was halfway through writing his sermon when the young man began slowly covering the endless backyard, his eyes communicating with the animal. By the time the sermon was finished, the skunk was sitting in the cage, the young man was safe, and Erika was content: "See you later!"

The driver's Saturday began in the parking lot in front of the church. Children were preparing for confirmation in the clubroom. In the afternoon he would see a couple who were about to be married. They would meet about six times before their wedding and discuss whatever they wanted to about their relationship. The rest was up to them. At lunch the driver didn't get enough to eat because his wife read a letter from her brother to him.

The food turned bitter in his mouth.

All of your mother's passport problems are taken care of. She can request a Canadian visa, but the Party is still condemning your work against the Republic. Could you promise in writing that you'll stop this activity? If so, your mother's trip to Canada will take place. I would ensure that you would resign from all your political activities against the Republic of Czechoslovakia in Canada.

Yours truly,
Lajo.

The driver stopped eating, afraid that listening to Erika's words would cause stomach ulcers, and he told her she shouldn't have read the letter during lunch, but then, when? When would have been an appropriate time to remind yourself that your home makes you cry enough to go crazy?

Even on Sunday the car had no rest. The driver first took it to church, where he performed the English and then the Slovak services. Afterwards he gassed up and left for Niagara Falls. Once a month he visited countrymen who lived on farms and grew fruit and vegetables and poultry around the nearby town of Smithville. Many of them had lived there since the thirties.

His experiences with these people, most of them more than eighty years old, were so powerful that they would stay with Jozef as long as he lived. These people were open and spoke to him in simple language. His later relationship with their children in the English-speaking community would become more reserved.

It was getting dark when he passed the sign for Toronto. The driver wore a white shirt that you would never guess had actually been ironed earlier. The car engine worked perfectly—proof that the Indian auto service was legit—and the driver was formulating a reply.

Dear Lajo,

When my mother arrives, I will stop working for Radio Free Europe, and I stand by that. However, I am unwilling to obey your party's orders in connection with her arrival. I don't understand what that has to do with her and my work here in Canada.

I have never worked against my country and I object to your accusation. Nobody can take from me the right to be a Slovak and to be proud of what I am. You know that I love my mother and want to see her. I have maintained a calm expectation up to now, but if they will not allow her to come, I will be forced to publish everything concerning this case.

I am a free man; I have my principles and will not back down from them.

Rev. Jozef Rola

University

Tereza registered at the University of Toronto, a downtown complex of neo-Gothic buildings with ivy-covered walls, gabled roofs, towers, dormer windows, massive gates, a library with wood paneling... She was enjoying the charm of a city that reminded her—without irony—of Cambridge. As the university expanded, it bought new land and built other faculties in modern buildings. She went to hear lectures in one of them made of poured concrete that reminded her of the Czechoslovak passion for this material. The building lacked the old English atmosphere and she felt lost in it. More than five hundred students attended the general courses.

They moved to the north end of the city when Milan found work there. It was a newly-finished apartment, and they were the second tenants; the first ones were mice. It wasn't quite clear how they'd made it to the eleventh floor. It was an austere high-rise, mostly inhabited by students. They bought their first set of furniture, no longer beaten-up items but straight from the store—two yellow couches. Mother's comforters were no longer needed to sleep on but served as covering.

In their new location Tereza registered at York University in the Faculty of Arts and Sciences. When they bought their Pontiac Firebird on monthly payments, she used it to drive to the university. Canadian winters bothered her. Milan had to push her out of snowdrifts a few times, and the infinite walk from the parking ramp to the entrance of her school building chilled her to the bone. She had to defrost herself before she could function.

The school had a so-called French campus called Glendon College, an old building overgrown with ivy. It looked like a chateau extravagantly placed in a gorgeous forest park. One day on the way to school she spotted a house in a little street that had the same balustrade as their old house on Panenská Street, and that made her even happier with the school. She caressed the cast-iron balustrade until it gleamed like the fingers on a bronze statue rubbed for luck.

She had to finish school as soon as possible to find a good job, so she also attended lectures in the afternoon. Slavic literature was taught by Škvorecký and world literature by Professor Foster. His summer evening courses for adults were outstanding. They weren't for students; only for her and some Canadians.

There were ten of them in a group. She loved those lectures, as they walked at sunset down the lawn of the French campus and read prose aloud and recited poetry. The words wafted over a valley that amplified not only the sound but also the meaning of the poems.

After they'd gotten to know each other better, the professor asked them to bring wine to the lecture. Students took turns, and even Professor Foster brought some. It was in this relaxed atmosphere that Tereza said good-bye to the sixties, as the year 1971 had already arrived. One day the professor brought some marijuana, but she refused to smoke it.

"Czechoslovakia is clean."

"Sorry?"

"My country is clean."

"Clean?"

"No drugs."

"Really?"

Tereza nodded. This spurred some interest, and from then on she became an unofficial ambassador for the country she was not allowed to return to. The other students had heard something about the invasion; some had seen the film *The Shop on Main Street*, others knew of Janáček and Dvořák, but otherwise... Her greatest success was with folk music. She, a person who could not stand folklore back at home! It was she who would turn the radio off the moment she heard fiddles being played by the folk musicians. The regime had used them so disgustingly and declared folk music the only genuine art form, thus robbing them of half of their sympathizers!

In Canada the situation changed. If Milan came across Slovak folk music on the radio, he would turn the sound up. They would both listen, and tears would flow from their eyes: this was the effect of emigration. But they weren't ashamed of it. Maybe they'd become less snobbish; maybe they needed to be tested by separation to understand that this music was something like Slovak blues that peasants sang while working hard in the fields below the mountains. And that this was simply their music, and that to feel ashamed of it was embarrassing, even if it was just a song about a sun that had to be pulled down by its legs to finally bring it down. She even started to teach Canadians our folk songs.

The megahit of the previous week in Glendon College was "I have a red apple in my little window." To hear local people sing it in their inimitable accent was a divine experience.

She continued her personal struggle with English. It was no longer as bad as before, when she didn't know the word for strainer and had to tell the store clerk: "Water go, spaghetti stop," after which he was able to bring it to her with a smile. Communicating was one thing, however, and studying the history of literature was another. In a subject that communicates hidden nuances through the perfection of language, even her own language was a problem. She would fall and get up. That was Tereza with her scraped knees; she would climb again and again onto the bicycle of language and hurl herself down the steep hill of grammar, only to tumble on the rocks of exceptions that English has plenty of.

When she couldn't manage to analyze a poem by Yehuda Amichai, she cut it up into individual letters and created an alphabet. Then she glued the letters to a canvas and searched for connections between them. Milan was working for an electronics company and brought her some discarded microchips. She used their thin wires to connect the letters into new words that expressed the idea of the poem. She decomposed the English poem into atoms and rewired them into a new one. At the same time, she communicated that a foreigner in an unknown country is like a child again and has to relearn the alphabet before she can name the things that surround her.

The professor was fascinated by her work and together with the other students studied the codes connected by the microchips. She received the highest grade. She created a labyrinth from the words of another poem. Milan brought her used sheets of computer paper, which she connected to form a giant space like an airport, and onto it glued words that you could walk on. One by one Professor Foster and the other students entered the poem with their heads bowed to the ground. They walked around in the text, between the lines, and oriented themselves with the help of arrows in the great labyrinth that hid the secret of poetry.

Again she was the best in class only because English words could not adequately express what she felt in Slovak. She studied physics and mathematics because the university professed the belief that a person has to be well versed not only in the arts, but also in the natural sciences.

Tereza managed it all without getting lost. How could we even think that she, whom I called the center of many universes and who attracted new friends, would burn out like a dead star in Canada? She dressed as well as she could with her limited funds. She came from a generation that was used to sewing and altering. Even without a sewing machine, a needle and thread could do the job.

There was no cafeteria at school. Tereza packed a sandwich and an apple for her husband, and yogurt and some fruit for herself. Others ate in small restaurants near the university, but she couldn't afford it. Only in the last year, when she managed to get work, were she and Milan able to order a pizza for dinner. Smelling the hot olives and oregano made them feel great.

Each weekend they had a party with their friends in their little apartment. There would be a dozen of them there. They would pool their money and buy sandwiches, fruit, and wine, and would all jam together playing music. Someone played saxophone, someone else guitar or trumpet, and others would play on their comb. Since their neighbors were also students, no one was disturbed by the music; rather it attracted fellow musicians and listeners.

The apartment was filled with flowers. The building was surrounded by fields, so it wasn't hard to find fresh flowers for the vases. They lived very modestly, but they had enough to eat; they had friends, flowers, and music. She always felt happy on those weekend evenings.

She was a bit woozy from the wine when she walked out onto the balcony to get some fresh air. The band inside was playing its original version of "Let It Be," where the main melody was played by saxophone and trumpet accompanied by six combs and Milan's guitar.

As soon as she closed the door behind her, she let out a scream. A figure was hovering in the air right opposite the windows on the eleventh floor and was looking inside with curiosity.

"Dad, don't do that to me!"

"I'm sorry."

And the figure of fine steam that moved like smoke, the trembling silhouette that spoke with the voice of her father, slowly moved to the balcony.

"I don't even realize it, you know. I see light and move towards it, and suddenly I'm looking through the window. You see, I can't fall down."

"I'm sorry, it's just that you surprised me... I haven't seen you for a long time."

Father spread his arms. A long time? What's a long time? One time was for him and another time was for her.

"I'm glad you're doing so well. Unhappy people wouldn't be having so much fun. Is it true that I haven't been here for a long time?"

"A year and a half...but please, I don't want to criticize, I'm just surprised...I should be happy to see you, and I am happy. I should have told you that right away."

"How is school?"

"We have a new classmate named Yossi, a bearded and deep soul. He has the same accent problems I used to have. He finished his military service and came to marry a Canadian. Everybody listens closely to him while he's searching for words and analyzing the topic, as they used to with me. Nobody at school ever told me that I was a foreigner and that I was holding them back. I've only fully realized that with Yossi. Father, I've bloomed here."

He looked at the room filled with flowers and smiled.

"When I was taking philosophy back home, we sometimes skipped a lecture."

"Well, good going..."

She had no idea if he was joking or angry. Suddenly she felt like a little girl. He never liked it when she skipped school. Ferdinand was a man of strict attendance and strict rules. He went by the clock and couldn't tolerate sluggards. Tereza quickly continued:

"But here it's so creative that we never think of missing class. Back home we would copy stuff from one another, but here nobody does. After all, they're paying for school, so why would they cheat, right? I had to go so far away to understand these things."

"I'm glad that you're studying and that you haven't wasted your talent. I always knew you could do it..."

Suddenly the balcony door opened, followed by a cloud of smoke. Milan came out on the balcony and kissed her.

"What's going on?"

She smiled. Everything was in its place. Father was looking at them. Milan should have seen him if he were there. But her father was there and Milan said nothing. She knew that she'd experienced an unbelievable event—spending a few moments with a man who had died after bringing a warm coat and food for her to Vienna. Father became whiter and more transparent, and a moment later he was gone.

Somebody inside was playing a guitar. It was a challenge without a guarantee and they were all trying to guess what song it was. It sounded like something, but because of the free form intro, it could be anything.

"Satisfaction?"

"Love Me Do?"

"Help?"

Milan had an idea, but by the time he translated the title into English, another three guesses were voiced.

"Go Home, Ivan?"

The guitar player smiled in confusion.

"What's that?"

In her mind Tereza heard a song that was once played by every radio station in Czechoslovakia. In the song, a certain Ivan was sent home by our girls because he came to see them in a tank. She'd heard the song while she was at the kibbutz. Oh my God, she thought, that was such a long time ago. As if it had never happened.

She and Milan entered the room. She sang with her friends until it got dark, and occasionally she went out on the balcony, but nothing turned into the speaking apparition made of steam that she had so much to tell.

Arrivals

Erika was rushing to catch a bus. Today they were expecting the arrival of Alex's friend from Stará Ruda with his family. When Anna phoned her Erika had difficulty suppressing her tears. Her sister's voice was weak and interrupted by coughing. She was forcing herself to sound happy but she was a bad actress. The fact that Anna never called Erika "little one" showed how serious her condition was. She just asked her to help this family and said that Petra would have looked after them if they'd gone to Ottawa, but they'd insisted on going to Toronto where the husband had arrangements in place.

Erika arrived at the airport just in time. The immigration formalities were done and the first passengers were filing out into the arrivals hall. Erika never forgot what she had promised Darina. She wanted to pay back what she had borrowed and now she had a chance. That's why she took in the family from Stará Ruda. He was a company psychologist and she was a hairdresser. They had one child: a quiet girl with ponytails who became friendly with Peter right away. It was more difficult for the adults.

The psychologist looked around the airport and said hello to Erika.

"What a bunch of black mugs around here, right? Let me kiss your hands!"

He looked disapprovingly at the Indian porter who wanted to help them with their suitcases.

"No, no, no!"

He covered the luggage with his own body, then personally loaded it onto his cart and pushed it to the bus. They had flown in from the Traiskirchen refugee camp in Austria and the psychologist bad-mouthed the Austrians all the way back to Erika's place.

"We arrived there late at night, and imagine it, my dear Erika—the camp was locked up and we had to wait until morning to get in! It started to rain. You have no idea how wet we got. A nice welcome to democracy, right?"

His wife tried to disagree.

"But the policeman..."

"He was sitting in the car, listening to the radio! When it started to rain, he just looked at us."

"But he took Lucia into his car."

"Yes, he did, but we were soaked!"

The psychologist was a trial sent to test Erika's patience. She was taken aback. She would have assumed that he would be grateful for asylum and a roof over his head, but eventually, after surviving dozens of such meetings, she became wiser: she realized that one group of emigrants would fall in love with the new country and the other would find fault with it forever. When she asked about her sister in Stará Ruda the man had nothing to say. He knew Alex from when he worked at Sanola. He had been invited to their home once for canapés but that seemed to be the only connection they had.

Erika consulted lawyers, wrote letters everywhere, went to the embassies, and tried to get a precise diagnosis with Petra's help, but nothing could get Anna to Canada.

New refugees were arriving in Toronto and she made a spontaneous decision to receive them in her free time. Thinking of Darina she did it gladly. How surprised she was when after some time the multicultural section of the education office not only officially thanked her but also started paying her a salary for translating. In this way helping refugees became her second profession. She would wait at the airport and approach the families. She helped them find accommodation, schools for the children, and work for the parents. She went shopping with the women and showed them where and what to buy.

She could never forget the first evening with the psychologist's family. As soon as they finished their steaks with baked potatoes—Erika tried to show off and they all loved it—the psychologist poured himself some Canadian beer that she had taken from the fridge.

"Well, they can't compete with our beer, Madame Erika."

Then he turned to Jozef.

"You know, Reverend, I admire you. How can you live in such an uncultured country? I read some statistics about how many people listen to classical music. What do you think? How many?"

Jozef had no idea.

"Thirty-four percent fewer than in Czechoslovakia."

He looked at the black light switch in Jozef's living room.

"These switches are disgusting, aren't they? They've started making crème color switches in our country. They're too noisy when you turn them on, but otherwise they're neat."

Erika and Jozef used eye contact to signal each other: "Help! SOS!" But the psychologist was just warming up.

"This is capitalism, Madame Erika: I know very well how it works. I'm not going to fall on my ass in front of them! They got me for free, a ready-made man! My education didn't cost them a cent and now I should give them my very best? Oh well, I will indeed, but they'll have to pay me damn well for it!"

The psychologist poured himself some more substandard beer and drank it in one gulp. His wife tried to stop him, but he paralyzed her with his look.

"I know my price and I won't let them exploit me!"

He belonged to those who had gone on company trips: to Bucharest and twice to East Berlin, once to Krakow, and even, for forty-eight hours, to Vienna. These trips formed his worldview. Jozef restrained himself and didn't argue; he commented politely but without interrupting his guest's monologue for even a minute. The visitors were tired and Peter gave them his room.

The guests became increasingly intolerable but fortunately the psychologist found some housing. Jozef had a very mild disposition—after all, his mission was to forgive people's sins—but on the last evening, when his guest's self-praise turned into an ode, he couldn't take it anymore.

"You have a great outlook, I have to admit, but it leads only from one Slovak village to the next."

The psychologist turned red, the conversation ground to a halt, and the National Hockey League replaced it. It was of course much worse than the Czechoslovak League but no one said that out loud. The next day the psychologist and his family moved out, and Jozef and Erika never heard from them again.

Erika helped newly arrived children with their schoolwork. She tested their multiplication tables and knowledge of English, and they were assigned a grade on that basis. They had received no education in the refugee camps, and some parents had started one-class schools to prevent their children from going completely wild. The quality of this education can only be imagined. In Canada additional tutoring was necessary. Many children arrived in the company of Red Cross nurses because they had emigrated after their parents. By the time all the formalities were completed, many children especially small ones, had forgotten what their fathers or mothers looked like.

Erika was sitting with a little boy who had flown in from Vancouver and was supposed to be picked up by his grandmother.

"Where are you from?"

The boy didn't know.

"Was there anything interesting in the city you came from?"

The boy considered the question and then produced a sentence that is not an awkward invention of the author but one that I quote verbatim: "There's a man sitting on a horse, and pigeons shit on him, and trams drive around everywhere."

Well, he came from Prague.

Jozef had been broadcasting for more than a year for Voice of America and Radio Free Europe. The recordings were made in his church and the meditations in the basement with the help of a technician. The tapes were sent to either New York or Munich. He was helping Erika, too, by organizing fundraising and collection drives for the clothing and household needs of newly-arrived families. Sometimes they made potato gnocchi with goat cheese and served it to everyone who brought something for the refugees.

Once a year they organized a Christmas bazaar. With the help of many others they made 300 kilos of sausages and paprika bacon, and someone made sauerkraut that vanished as soon as it was put on the tables. On Advent evenings they cooked a huge cauldron of sauerkraut and sausage soup that was a great success. The families baked wafers and Christmas cookies. Once the cinnamon and vanilla-scented holidays were over and everything was sold they'd made a few thousand dollars for the church.

Smelling of sauerkraut and smoked meat like butcher's apprentices after a successful bazaar, Erika and Jozef had just put Peter and Eva to bed and hadn't even had time to shower when the phone rang. It was shortly before midnight. A desperate voice came over the receiver.

"Good evening, please don't be angry that I'm calling you this late, but I'm from Brezno and have just arrived in Toronto, and I don't know where to go."

"Where do you want to go?"

"I have a hostel, but I don't know where I am."

"Where are you calling from?"

"From a phone booth."

"Take a look at what street you're on. Read a sign for me."

There was silence in the receiver, and then Erika heard a voice with heavy breathing.

"It says 'one way.'"

He was reading a traffic sign.

"You have to find the name of the street."

The phone went silent again, and after some time he syllabified the name of the street.

She finally managed to direct him to the metro. Hers was the only contact he had. He'd found it in the washroom of the Montreal YMCA. The phone number was scratched into the wall, and underneath it was a sentence that they could place under their coat of arms, if they ever got one:

"At this number, they help everyone, not only Lutherans."

Sickle

T he White Lady died quietly. It is not known if she was conscious when it happened or asleep. It was hard to guess which shore she was on at the moment. The last few days she had been lying with her eyes closed and hadn't reacted to her name. The hostel had a common phone in the hallway that Petra tried to call. It would ring a hundred times every day without her reacting, but the moment her daughter called, the White Lady would open her eyes.

"That's Petra."

Then she would once more submerge herself into sleep or non-sleep, sooner than anyone could confirm that there was a call from Canada. Young Vietnamese women took turns taking care of her. One had returned from work when the others went on night shift at Sanola. It was necessary to work at night because no matter how hard we slaved, we couldn't catch up with the West, let alone overtake it.

The last time Petra called her mother was no longer able to come to the phone. It was always early morning in Ottawa, while she was drinking her first coffee before going to the hospital, that she called

Stará Ruda, where it was already afternoon. She no longer nagged her mother to seek medical help. She knew that Anna was an Aries, the sign of a stubborn personality who always gets what she wants. How many times had she tried to reprimand her for not going to the hospital! She was the mother of a medical doctor and taking chances with her health! But the child knew it was all in vain, and that her mother's illness had begun with her departure. What was she going to blame her for? Anna was already standing with one foot in the light and one in the darkness. She was leaving one shore and reaching her bare foot out to the other.

During her last visit to Dr. Glauber, forced by Petra and Maria and aided by a phone call from Erika, nobody had much to say. The patient was silent and the doctor looked at the x-rays of the approaching stars. On the first, the Great Bear was stepping out of the dark Universe. On another one the stars were much bigger, and on the third one bigger still. In the last two big knots of deadly matter exploded right into the camera, showering hundreds of meteorites that destroyed everything around.

"May I call you Anna?"

"Of course."

"You have advanced metastasis in multiple organs. You have to stay here."

"Thank you, but I can't."

"I beg you, tell me why?"

"I don't want to inconvenience anyone. What do I sign so you won't have any problems, Doctor?"

"I won't have any problems. But if it hits the nerve fibers..."

"I can take it."

Glauber knew there was no point in persuading her. While the nurse behind the screen prepared the next patient—the hall in front of his office was filled with sick people—he wrote a waiver stating that the patient rejected institutional treatment and claimed her right to die at home. That was how he literally put it because that was what she wished.

"You know, this is the last right I have left."

She signed the paper and slowly left the hall while the other patients opened a way for her. She didn't know that many were there with the same diagnosis as she had: that a crazy universe was exploding in their bodies only because a long time ago they had lost their children. Not all of them were like her; Anna was the only Canada. On the way she noticed, but did not recognize, two Germanys, one United States, and one Argentina. As she walked down the stairs, she greeted a tiny lady whom she occasionally met during her check-ups—Australia. But that, too, she never found out.

Outside a tram bell clanged and the White Lady walked briskly towards the bus depot. Her bus was leaving in a few minutes.

Stará Ruda looked different in 1972 than it had dozens of years before. City fathers had long studied the polystyrene model of transformation. It was decided that small agricultural housing from the nineteenth century would disappear and be superseded by panel buildings. Sanola was growing and exporting medical technology all over the world and its new employees had nowhere to live. The children of farm workers moved to the cities and settled in the new buildings, forgetting their roots. Here and there some still kept chicken and rabbits on their balconies, but socialist coexistence would soon put a stop to it; only flowers were tolerated on the balconies.

The Czechoslovakia of this time was a big sugar bowl, trying to make life as sweet as possible for its citizens. The government did what it could to make them forget the consequences of occupation, the lack of freedom, and the fear. Every day fewer people thought about the past and enjoyed what was actually there in front of them: work, happiness, satisfaction, and proletarian internationalism.

There was also this: a telephone call for a few pennies, a portion of ice cream for a nickel, lunch in the cafeteria for a dime, and everywhere the chance for a million.

There were also loans for newly married couples, fridges on an installment plan, and a few years later, color TV.

And there had to be and would be: agreement and enthusiasm.

The population traded their personal opinions for a standard of living. Never mind that it could not be compared. They could see that it was better at home than in Poland, Bulgaria, Romania, and the Soviet Union: for these countries, Czechoslovakia was like a little Western paradise. Tourists from socialist countries came there to buy everything: alcohol, down comforters, carpets, ceramics, and chandeliers. Hungary was also doing fine: Goulash socialism put them all to sleep. Now the Czechoslovak Communists copied the same recipe.

As to what life was really like beyond the Iron Curtain, nobody would find out. The Western press was not sold here, and films from the West were usually those critical of their own society, where the mafia killed a courageous prosecutor or neo-fascists beat people up in a progressive café. By some miracle a few decent films appeared, and one day in Stará Ruda *The Yellow Submarine* was shown. The Beatles had broken up long ago and the world had new pop icons, but John Lennon was tolerated as a "fighter for peace." They preferred to write about his symbolic planting of acorns rather than about his bedroom press conference with Yoko. It is nonetheless true that *The Yellow Submarine* sold out in Stará Ruda, and in the squeaky wooden seats of the town's cinema another generation of hormonal teenagers fell in love with the Beatles, including the author of this book.

Minimal information about the world filtered through but the author, like most of the population of socialist countries, had a talent for reading between the lines and gaining pleasure from small things. The psychedelic musical film, an excellent work of animation, started a chain reaction that ignited new fires in the forests of youthful imagination. Soon this turned into a blaze, and kids left the movie theater as lit up as Christmas trees. They started listening to music, and their burning heads shone on a new world that from outside looked like a small town. It was filled with construction sites full of trucks, excavators, and panels, but from the inside it was a happy place where they were destined to spend their childhood.

The author tried his first cigarettes, refusing the cheap brands and switching to those with filters. He didn't inhale, but let the smoke enter his mouth, which irritated his tongue and made him cough. He led boyish fights against neighboring boys, organized a competition to see who banged the door of a store the loudest, which made the saleswoman livid, raised a white-and-brown dog from the last little house that managed to escape demolition, and observed the buildings grow tenfold before his eyes, the dirty-white panels with holes displacing moss-covered roof tiles.

The author had no idea that in the Vietnamese hostel not far from his panel building the White Lady, whom he had occasionally met and somewhat feared, was dying. He was not aware of any limitations except his mother's prohibition against buying a battery-powered machine gun imported from China. He watched with curiosity as workers installed wooden boarding next to the highway entrance to the town, and poured in concrete under the supervision of a man wearing jeans. The man was a sculptor, and for observant children he remained the typical example of an artist for many years to come. Greying hair, sports jacket and jeans, a style that everyone would want but parents would forbid. Everyone wore clothes made of polyethylene, called *tesil* locally. A few days later, a concrete fist emerged from the wooden box. It held a sickle in front of a concrete star emblazoned with the words: GLORY TO THE COMMUNIST PARTY OF CZECHOSLOVAKIA.

For years, the author thought that the function of artists was to create concrete stars and hammers along the roadways, and because of that, he didn't want to become an artist. He turned to natural sciences and studied medicine. But that's really stepping on the gas, because it's years in the future.

In the meantime the population of Stará Ruda and the population of the district, region, and of all of Czechoslovakia, was covered by the fine layer of sugar from the state sugar bowl. Everything looked neat and clean, like in the wintertime when it snows and the crystalline water mercifully covers up the junk piles and dug-out walkways.

The dirt would be uncovered in the springtime, but that was still far away. In the meantime a higher standard of living, higher than the country could afford, poured ceaselessly from the sugar bowl. Why not, if it brought temporary peace? Though it encumbered their children with debt, and their children's children would have to pay it off one day.

The White Lady no longer cared. She quietly passed away. A huge grey sickle circled over the town and ended her suffering. Then like a silent boomerang it returned to the concrete fist and calmly watched the procession walking by.

It was a bizarre funeral, silent, without music. A few female colleagues showed up, women with whom the deceased had worked at Sanola, but most of them were Vietnamese. They felt it was only right to come and honor the dead woman who had helped them and nursed them on so many nights after fights with local people, or when their children were sick.

In a parked Škoda car sat a tall man with curly hair. He was not parked there by accident. He waited for the procession to pass and then started his engine and slowly turned around. It was Anna's brother.

Neither her husband nor her daughter walked behind the hearse. Her husband no longer remembered who he was, or who the lady nursing him was. Mariška took care of him as well as she could, but she was close to sixty and preferred to pay for a nurse. Petra would come straight from the hospital to see him, read the newspaper to him and talk with him. The psychiatrist recommended persistent contact. Her father listened attentively, but she had no idea whether he understood anything. He couldn't even name the blackbird he saw sitting on the branch of a cherry tree outside his window.

"What's the name of this... person?"

They never told him that his wife had died. Petra was not allowed to go to the funeral. The Czechoslovak Embassy denied her a visa. She was not welcome, and if she had returned she would have been immediately imprisoned for her unauthorized departure from Czechoslovakia.

That was why she sat in the kitchen with Mariška and looked at the candle flame. They tried to imagine the route of the funeral procession. Mariška imagined a little village with straw roofs where geese fed alongside a muddy road. Petra should have seen tall panel buildings and Škoda cars, but try as she might, she was unable to imagine her hometown. She could only see her father's construction of paper, stones, and moss. She saw dancing walls and roads leading from nowhere to nowhere. You could get there neither by car nor by walking.

The actual procession had just turned onto the little bridge that Alex represented with a piece of discarded metal. A train with a motor locomotive had just crossed it, honking twice for the semaphore. But we know that the train was saying goodbye to a woman who kept a model railway under her bed for years out of love for her husband.

The funeral procession proceeded up a steep incline to the cemetery and disappeared among the branches of linden trees that silently covered it all.

Guest

Erika was sitting in a dark living room. Keeping the lights off, she strained her eyes looking at photographs of her sister. She didn't have many, although she had packed them all before she left Bratislava. Anna didn't like to be photographed.

Jozef took the children to the swimming pool. Usually she would take them but he saw that she needed to be alone. Loading the water wings, towels, and hair dryer into the car with Peter and Eva he felt a quiet admiration for his wife, who handled such demanding chores so easily and in such a matter-of-fact way. After they drove off to the swimming pool, Erika remembered Anna and their childhood games, Anna's singing and the young men who courted her, always in greater numbers than those who pursued Erika.

She had been in the dark for no more than twenty minutes when the ringing of the phone interrupted her reveries with the most unbelievable call of her life. It was her brother.

"Hello, this is Lajo."

There was a silence that Erika imagined as a big cube that someone was slicing with a knife as the small pieces fell on her like snow.

"What do you want?"

"You should stop that."

"What?"

"The antagonism."

"I didn't start anything. How did you know it was me?"

"Jozef would talk right away. Actually, I was calling him."

"He's out with the children."

"Don't hang up. This is important."

The silence returned. Erika couldn't decide whether to angrily bang down the receiver or to magnanimously listen to him. This caller didn't deserve magnanimity.

"It's enough for you to listen. Things are beginning to move here, and some people I know would help. There's a real chance that Jozef's mother could be allowed out."

"My husband won't sign anything."

"They'll let her go without anything. I'll take care of it."

"What do you want for it?"

"Nothing. Just invite me to your place for a week."

There was nothing left to slice now, and Erika saw only the knife moving above her. Her brother wanted to come? Him? Lajo knew what was going on in his sister's head. He was speaking calmly, as if ready to lower the price on a used bicycle if someone bought him a beer.

It was so unexpected that her ability to speak fell out of her mouth and shattered like glass dentures. She looked at the shiny fragments with tears in her eyes, weighing the situation and thinking of Anna, who was no more. That's why she remained silent while her brother persisted.

"Look, talk it over with Jozef, and I'll call tomorrow at the same time. The deal is that either I come for a week and his mother after me, or nothing will ever happen. And don't worry; I'll pay for my ticket. One more thing: you're not doing me any favors, is that clear? I'm helping you. So goodbye. I'll call tomorrow."

There was a click followed by a busy tone. Erika could imagine how many other receivers were listening in to hear whether her brother said what he was supposed to and whether he said it well. It was clearly a game, but she had no inkling what the game was about.

More and more visitors were allowed to come from Czechoslovakia. For the first few years after 1968 it had been almost impossible, but the pressure was relaxing. Sisters were visiting brothers and grandmothers finally saw their grandchildren. Most of the visitors told their hosts not to invite anyone during their stay and not to do anything publicly that would be critical of their old country because the relatives had to report everything after returning home.

It was a business transaction: something in exchange for something else. The Czechoslovak government was preparing for the unpleasant gambit that was launched a few years later, called Adjustment of Status. If the emigrant paid for his education and for everything he'd gotten from his government "for free" prior to his emigration, he would be allowed to return as a tourist to Czechoslovakia. The comrades would determine the price of the "pain money." At least it was now obvious that ideology was of secondary importance and that the main thing was to get some dollars, which were in short supply in the Communist paradise. Nothing unusual: it was materialism, clearly of the dialectical type.

The adjustment of relationship didn't involve people like Jozef, who was considered an enemy of the state for his work in the media. Surprised by Lajo's proposal, after a long phone call the next day he agreed to the trip. He had nothing to lose and everything to gain. He might be able to see his mother again. Erika finally also agreed, for her husband's sake.

Three weeks later, Lajo was dining in their backyard. The situation felt unreal to everyone who sat around the gas grill at sunset. Thanks to his confessional practice Jozef had heard everything, so the visit didn't shock him. Erika, however, had difficulty overcoming the barrier that had grown between her and her brother. She was stand-offish, while Lajo lacked even a modicum of humility and had no intention of apologizing for anything. He said that he had gone to Anna's funeral, and although Erika didn't believe him, we know that he followed the procession from his car.

"She didn't want music. I've never seen such a thing—that she wouldn't want the brass band that used to play for May Day."

"But she was in a coma. How could she say what she wanted?"

"She wasn't in a coma. She talked now and then."

"Did you visit her?"

"That's what they said. Apart from me, it was mostly Vietnamese there."

That was the first evening. They just ate and drank a bit, and then their guest went to bed to catch up with jet lag. The next day they took him to the fruit market, which was a second culture shock for Lajo. The first one he'd experienced the day before, but without saying anything. He'd worked his whole life and all he'd managed to achieve, as far as housing was concerned, was a three-plus-one state-owned apartment in a panel building, while they, starting with nothing five years ago, already had a house with a garden!

That bothered him, but he kept his cool. He resolved the dilemma by telling himself that he wasn't exploited like people in Canada. At home he was governing along with the workers and peasants, working honestly, unlike Jozef, who'd prospered by hoodwinking the masses with religion, the opium of the people! He'd no sooner carried out this ideological vacuuming of his mind when they arrived at the market.

His mind was blown by the colors, aromas, and shapes of the fruits, many of which he was seeing for the first time in his life. He suddenly felt utterly confused. He'd arrived from a country where bananas and oranges were available only at Christmas and occasionally around May Day. Here they were available all year round, along with avocados, pineapples, kiwi fruit, and dozens of colorful beauties that he caressed and sniffed in a trance while Jozef told him their names.

On the way home from the market they stopped at the bank, which Lajo entered with a look of disdain on his face. This was, after all, the seat of capital, the temple of the dollar god. Jozef took out some cash and cordially greeted an elegantly dressed middle-aged black man. The man shook Jozef's hand, they exchanged a few words, and Lajo watched the man go behind a glass door.

"Who's he?"

"He's the manager of the bank."

Lajo grabbed the counter for support, alarming Jozef, who was afraid he might faint.

"Are you all right?"

Visibly pale, Lajo nodded and walked out of the building. The black man was manager of this incredibly rich bank, this palace of chrome and glass? And he was younger than Lajo! How was this possible? Shouldn't he have been assigned, at most, with cleaning the sidewalks or running a mop over the linoleum? There was racism in the West! Blacks were exploited, unemployed, and living in slums! At best they might play the ukulele and drive a bus! How could he be a manager?

Then they went to a Toronto shopping center. Lajo walked by shop windows filled with gold, clothing, appliances, and electronics. He felt like he was dreaming. Around him flowed a colorful mass of people: white, black, Hindus and Chinese... They passed exotic restaurants and small cafés. On a corner a young violinist played Vivaldi while a mime performed a few feet away, and a few hundred feet beyond them a young girl was improvising jazz on a saxophone. People streamed by freely like a river, enjoying themselves, laughing aloud, sitting on benches and in little bistros, kissing, engaged in earnest discussion or reading a newspaper. Gone was the grey shroud that covered Czechoslovakian streets and pedestrians. For a moment Lajo thought—and he doubted his mental health—that even the air smelled different here.

They had lunch in a Japanese restaurant. He agreed to try sushi but rejected the chopsticks, piercing the rolls with a fork in a dignified manner. He chewed in silent confusion. He couldn't understand anything. Everything was different. He was hurt. Then, by mistake, he took too much wasabi, which he'd mistaken for a harmless vegetable. Now he could finally cry freely.

Jozef began to fear for the health of his guest. For two days after this outing Lajo did not say a word. Even Erika was beginning to feel sorry for him. He just thumbed through some magazines and kept flipping through the TV channels, including those from the U.S. He went out for walks in the quiet neighborhood with white wooden houses, and twice, with some hesitation, they let him go downtown, and he didn't get lost.

After forty-eight hours, he said his first sentence to Jozef.

"They've lied to me all my life."

He continued browsing through the magazine. Jozef began to think that some miracle had occurred, but then Lajo retracted his confession.

"Don't think that everything is so great here."

He closed the magazine and looked with pleasure at the cover photo of a young woman in a swimsuit recommending a sun tanning lotion.

"I'm not as mean as you think. Your mother will come. I'll see to it personally."

Only Jozef and Lajo shared the farewell dinner. Erika excused herself because of the children and spent an unusually long time putting them to bed. Preferring to spend as little time with her brother as possible, she gave Peter an extra portion of the stories from her youth that the boy found extremely entertaining. Little Eva fell asleep early on, but Peter was interested in everything: What did you wear? What did your bicycle look like? You really didn't have a battery-powered robot? Soon it was almost eleven o'clock.

The men sat in the living room drinking aged Canadian whisky and looking out at the maple tree beneath which the skunk had been caught in that memorable adventure. Lajo did most of the drinking: while Jozef was still nursing his first glass, Lajo downed almost half a bottle and became sentimental.

"Jozef, do you realize how hard it is to be a class act? You have it easy because you have the church behind you, and that makes you a classy fellow. But I'm going it alone, and I have to be damned careful to stay classy. You wouldn't believe the kind of swine surrounding me and just waiting for me to make a mistake. Everyone wants to climb higher but they haven't got it, and I do, and you know why? Do you? I have class, because I'm careful. No worries: your mother will come, and I won't report anything bad about you. Just a little bit. I can't make you into—you know—a hero. That would look suspicious. I have to put in something negative. After all you're overthrowing our state down to its roots, but that's none of my business. They know it and I'll confirm it, but watch out! Watch out, I'll tell them, he is not lost. I mean you're not lost. That they can work with you."

He continued, "Oh, don't worry. I don't want anything. They're not dumb. They know that you're Jozef the Just. You don't want money and you don't want broads. They won't try to break you. They have class. Jozef, listen: you're a clergyman and you're not allowed to disclose anything people tell you, right? That's why I'm talking to you so openly. If the guys back home knew I told you this I'd be screwed. But you have to keep it secret, right? Like this whatshisname... Nepomucký; I know he was a Catholic, but he kept it secret. He never revealed it. They cut him up and threw him in the water, but he didn't say a word. You clergy never reveal a secret. So in fifty-two I was with this pastor—don't worry, it wasn't me who beat him, we had Sergey for that. I didn't even interrogate him: I just went to look. He kept quiet like Nepomucký. Jozef, I have to tell you something about myself. This isn't a confession; don't think that I'm going to shit my pants over your Toronto or your maple syrup, no. I'm still a Communist, but a classy one. This isn't a confession: I just want to talk. Sometimes I behave like a swine, but only sometimes, because I have class. I wrote to Erika's school that you were getting married: I mean, a student and a clergyman. They knew it anyway, but I was new to the party and had to show them how good I was. So Erika was thrown out of her school. They would have done it anyway, but that wasn't very classy of me.

"I also wrote about Anna, that her husband was an opportunist and a Trotskyite. I had class then: that was why I said Trotskyite. You know, we also read, we have class. Maybe that wasn't the right thing to do, but it happened. I don't want what you call a pardon or anything... I just wanted to tell this to you as a man of the cloth. I don't want to keep it in my head. Let someone else have it in his head, someone who can't tell it to anyone. I know that it wasn't good that I sometimes... well, you know...it wasn't good. But I did it because I wanted to have class. Can you understand, a little bit at least? Can you?"

The next day Jozef drove him to the airport. Erika went along to wait for a group coming from Germany. Lajo's head ached from the night before, since he'd followed the five-year-old whisky with two-year-old wine and only a five-minute-old coffee as refreshment. It didn't help. He slept through half of the flight and even refused the beer offered by the flight attendant, spending the second half of the flight in the washroom.

He wasn't the kind of guy who would vomit into paper bags in front of everyone. People with class don't do that.

Graduation

One moment it was a city and the next moment it was a broad plane. For a moment mountains towered over the horizon, and then after a while one could see the waves of the sea. Sometimes one felt a sandy beach under one's feet, and other times stones polished by thousands of steps and grooved by carts.

Ferdinand was in Sheol, the world below the world, where those who'd left the world above would gather. For a few moments he saw ahead of him city fortifications that reminded him of the old Jerusalem described by the rabbi in *schul*. Taking a few steps, he felt his shoes were wet and found himself on the shore of a sea. He looked down and saw that his feet were bare. He had no idea how long he had walked through the city or along the seashore. Time was lost; nobody needed it and nobody measured it. He could have lived hundreds of earthly years or only a second and he wouldn't have known the difference.

The land below the land was mostly mist. He had no idea what to call this constantly whirling and flowing mass that comprised everything: the sea, the fortifications, the city, the beach, and finally himself as well. It sometimes reminded him of something familiar.

He was standing on a railway platform as a train approached pulling cars from the Austro-Hungarian Empire. The steam locomotive, itself made of mist, stopped with a hiss of steam, and the doors of the train cars opened. In one stood a conductor who was on the train with him, too. But he had no idea when it happened. Time didn't exist anymore.

Ferdinand couldn't remember precisely how they had met. He didn't remember the face of this man bending over him on the train that had taken him from Vienna while Tereza waved on the platform. He no longer remembered the man trying to help him and finally calling an ambulance in Bratislava. He couldn't be sure if this conductor had brought him to Sheol along with the others today. Every day new people arrived from up there, and their friends waited for them. The platform thronged with men, women, and children.

But today it was not very colorful; it was much more monotonous. Crowds of soldiers were pouring out of the Art Nouveau railway cars. They were also light and unfocused, wearing transparent uniforms and carrying weapons with barrels twisting like snakes. More soldiers waited for them on the platform, greeting them loudly, slapping them on the shoulders and laughing, but Ferdinand couldn't understand their language.

Not recognizing any of the new arrivals he turned around. He seemed pointlessly happy—happy because the train hadn't brought anyone he loved. From day to day—or more precisely, from perception to perception, since it's audacious to talk about a day in timelessness—he felt less certain of his feelings. He no longer knew what was sad or what was happy, what it meant to suffer or to be content.

In the world of whirling mist it was difficult to distinguish anything specific, as he could see not only people and things, but also the millions of people and things behind them. He could actually see all of them at the same time as transparent layers. He could recognize neither faces and places nor emotions. Everything was transparent. Nothing could make him feel enthusiasm or joy.

Now he took a moment of rest on a wooden bench in a huge sauna. Around him and above him were thousands of similar benches, on which everyone was wrapped in a white sheet, sitting in the steam and sweating. It was very warm there. Sometimes Ferdinand felt thirsty and got up to reach for a jug of water. But there was nothing there except whirling steam, and in fact he no longer felt the sensation of thirst. Hundreds of people got up from their benches, just like him, and walked towards their jugs, and then sat down again.

Suddenly he recognized a man next to him with his characteristic full lips and forelock of hair. He'd seen him in a photograph somewhere, but where... Ferdinand knew he respected the man for some reason, but didn't know what for. Maybe his picture was on the cover of a book that Maria had brought home? Yes, it was a white book with black stripes, and people in the world above were fighting to have it, and Maria would bring home more and more faulty copies from the publishers that people would gladly accept, and they would copy the missing pages and glue them into their books, because there was no other way to buy it.

The world in which books were made of paper and not steam emerged before Ferdinand. He saw the book again. A young girl with brown hair was reading it. He was looking at her, he wasn't sitting in the sauna, and her image was sharp compared to the shadows in the steam; it seemed too concrete. Something about her attracted Ferdinand, and he wasn't sure whether it was the girl or the book, because he didn't recognize the girl.

Now he saw clearly. The man in the sauna was the man on the cover. He read the title of the book. Some doctor...Zhiva...Zhiva...go? *Doctor Zhivago*. He couldn't remember. Was the man next to him a doctor? He saw him less and less clearly. Someone increased the pressure of the steam and the people in white sheets disappeared from view. Ferdinand felt a gust of cold air. It was refreshing.

Suddenly he knew where to go. Instead of being led by light, he followed the fresh air. He walked briskly toward the girl who was reading the book, not because of the book but because of the girl who was reading the book. Suddenly he had sandals on his feet and was wearing his favorite old suit with the comfortable jacket that bulged at the elbows. He didn't know exactly what he felt, but walking with his feet on the grass felt different. What sort of feeling was that? He was unsure. After all, what was—a feeling? He was remembering. He might be happy.

When Tereza was twelve, she had her Bat Mitzvah. Afterwards her father took her to Café Stefania, where he met his friends on a weekly basis. Although a railway man he loved literature. He always invited writers to his table, and they would talk about new books.

During Tereza's first visit she drank yellow lemonade with a straw and felt as if she were drinking absinthe at Café Les Deux Magots, with Verlaine and Rimbaud arguing next to her. She paid no attention to what her father's friends were saying, simply enjoying the grown-up atmosphere which she was finally experiencing, and deservedly so, now that she was twelve years old!

Who knows what made her think of these moments at Café Stefania, that Parnassus of Slovakia that was experiencing its few years of glory. She had often gone there since that first time. Another memory emerged of everybody excitedly discussing Pasternak, his novel, the Nobel Prize that he had refused, the freedom, the truth in fiction, the religion that upset so many critics, and the author saying that he'd purposely included Christian symbols in his prose to warm people like a fireplace in a house...

Tereza was standing in the university courtyard with hundreds of other students, wearing a black robe with a diploma in her hand. She didn't know why she kept looking around so much.

She did know. She was looking for her father. Everyone had someone there. Students from India, China, Congo, and even Malaysia all had relatives there. Only she and Milan had no one.

At least they made phone calls. Milan called Haifa, and she called Bratislava. Maria wept. Her daughter was graduating from the university! After so many obstacles, after so much traveling and on a different continent, she had managed to graduate. At least she was able to hear her mother's voice through the receiver at the Toronto post office. There were twenty cubicles next to each other, and in each someone was talking on the phone.

Tereza put the receiver down, went to the counter to pay for the call, and waited for Milan to finish his call to his parents. It was an hour before closing, and the cubicles gradually emptied. Tereza sat under a huge map of the world that flashed with red lines connecting the places where phone calls could be placed. As she sat below the lit-up world that talked to itself, suddenly the air around her grew warmer.

He was sitting next to her. He was almost invisible, barely more than nothing, but it was he.

"Dad, I graduated today."

"I missed it...forgive me."

"It doesn't matter. I'm happy to see you."

"I hear you less and less distinctly where I am...I almost thought I wouldn't make it... Somehow I couldn't do it, and not because of my heart, I don't have one...I think this may be the last time..."

"Don't say that..."

"I was very lucky that I could see you. You no longer need me. You've made it. Do you hear me? You've made it, Tereza..."

He was slowly disappearing; the warm mist gradually dissipated and turned into a cool draft just as Milan came out of his cubicle.

"My folks send their greetings."

She nodded.

"Where shall we celebrate? This calls for a great dinner for my academic."

"There are two options. Either I'll go with my academic to the French restaurant that you liked so much last time..."

"Only by looking through the restaurant window."

"Yes, but you liked it. Or there's a second possibility: the female academic will warm up chicken soup, on the way home they'll buy that good bottle of wine that they've been eyeing for the last six months, and after dinner they'll get a bit drunk."

"But only a little bit."

"Will one bottle be enough?"

"Make it two."

"We won't have any money for the gas bill."

"We're only graduating once."

"Right, then: two bottles."

North

Alex died in 1973, and two months later Mariška died as well. Petra was taking her examinations in emergency medicine at the time. She'd been working in the emergency room where stress, blood, pain, and very little time teach doctors to act quickly and accurately. The emergency room was filled night after night with victims of car crashes, fights, mundane fractures, food poisoning, and drug overdoses. As a family physician she was gaining invaluable experience.

She lived between two hospitals. She practiced in one and lived in the other. For a time, along with a hired nurse, she took care of both her father and aunt. Mariška would go to church every day, even during the cruel Ottawa winters. Although Petra or their gardener, who became a driver in wintertime, always drove her, it didn't save her from falling down. In the five meters she had to walk from the car to the church door, she fell and broke her pelvis. They took her to the hospital and kept her there.

Alexander was home alone. He no longer recognized his daughter and spent most of his time sitting by the window and watching the falling of the leaves, the rain, or the snow. He refused to eat, living from infusions, and after some time he followed his sister to the hospital as his organs began to fail.

He died about a month after he was admitted. It was morning and Petra was just finishing her night shift. She visited him several times a day. The staff knew her well, and as soon as she entered the room they would give her a brief description of her father's condition. They shook their heads. Doesn't react. Didn't wake up. It's worse.

She sat with him as always and bathed him, even though he couldn't have been washed better; the nurses really tried their best. She told him what was new since she was sure it was necessary to talk to him. What if he could hear her? What if she mentioned a key word that would force him to open his eyes? That morning she sat with him longer than usual; she didn't want to leave. Finally she got up, said a few words to the nurse, and went home.

As she opened the door of Mariška's house the phone rang. She knew right away who it was. She accepted the news silently and returned to the hospital. Before leaving home she mechanically and tearlessly took out things for the dead man: Alex's best suit that he used to wear while sitting outside the house, watching the sky, as well as his shirts, socks, tie, and everything else that was needed, including the cuff links Anna had bought him for their twentieth wedding anniversary.

The service was at the crematorium. Considering her father's life, it would have seemed strange to have a pastor preside over a church service for him. She discussed this with Jozef.

"You know, Petra, as a clergyman I should persuade you to have a church funeral, but as a man, I understand when you say no."

Only Jozef and Erika came to the funeral, along with Mariška's gardener, who admired Alex because of his model of Stará Ruda. When it was clear that Alex had swum to the other shore of sanity, he would patiently go with him into the basement and listen to him explain the model and who lived where. At least that's what the gardener assumed was happening since Alex spoke Slovak and the gardener English, but they always had a good chat.

Now Mariška was all that Petra had left. She was like her mother and Petra never forgot how much she'd helped them after they'd arrived helpless from Vienna. But the grey sickle from the concrete hand was already flying over the ocean. After being bedridden for so long, Mariška caught pneumonia, and diabetes kept her broken bones from healing. Despite the excellent care she received, the inevitable finally happened.

Petra met Jozef again, but this time at the cemetery, the way Mariška would have liked, with a church service and a pastor. As she sat in a restaurant afterwards with her Toronto visitors, as Peter and Eva were running around, Jozef asked Petra what she planned to do.

She answered with a look. In her eyes was a compass that pointed in one direction.

She had been driving for six hours already and had to take a break. At a small highway restaurant she ate a sandwich and took the coffee to go. The trip to Sioux Lookout was supposed to take twenty-one hours; she was prepared for that. The doctor that Paulette and Reneé had introduced her to was still working in Northwest Ontario. Petra made a quick decision. She had long wanted to go north, and now she had no reason to stay in Ottawa. Mariška's house was rented out to a Belgian family except for Petra's room and one cellar, which she carefully locked. This cellar fascinated the new tenants' children for many years, because through the keyhole they could see houses made of paper and long smokestacks made of straws with little stars glued to them.

Petra was going for only a year; she had no idea how long she would last in the wilderness. It was supposed to be a transitional place before she made a final decision what to do with her life. She left to forget. For a moment she felt relief at being free again, but later on she felt remorse. After all, it was because she no longer had her father or the aunt who had done everything for her that she could now sit in her car on the Trans-Canada Highway.

They really needed her in the new place, since a female doctor had recently left for Vancouver; they avoided telling her that her predecessor had torn a ligament when fleeing a bear while she was out jogging.

The longer Petra sat behind the wheel, the more beautiful nature became and the more abandoned the small towns looked. They looked like ghost towns, with shutters nailed down on the houses for sale. People had left harsh nature for places where life was easier. She was doing the opposite. She was a bit scared, but joy at the beauty all around her balanced it out. Here was the landscape in the colors that had fascinated her at the Group of Seven exhibition. She spent the night in a town called Wawa, where she was greeted by a statue of an enormous Canadian goose. Poised to take flight, the gigantic bird seemed like a good omen as she continued her journey the next morning.

Sioux Lookout, with a population of a bit more than a thousand, had a stop on the Canadian National Railway. They called it the Gateway to the North. It was the administrative center for the local native communities, mostly Ojibway and Cree. She was lucky. While other doctors lived in engineered homes near the hospital, her friend Reneé, an expert negotiator who knew everyone in town, had found her a beautiful log cabin on Abram Lake whose previous tenant, a pilot, had just left for Montreal to fly with a commercial airline after completing her compulsory flight hours.

Airplanes provided a critical connection to surrounding settlements, some of them hundreds of miles away. During the winter months communities could be accessed by "winter roads" across frozen lakes that could bear the weight of cars and large trucks. Some could also be accessed by small roundabout roads but for the most part, especially during the warmer months, they could only be reached by air.

The little town had a main street with a few hotels and a restaurant, a community center, two food stores, an ice rink, and a pungently malodorous cinema. There were two hospitals, commonly referred to as the Town and the Zone. The Town hospital primarily served the non-native population of Sioux Lookout, while the Zone hospital, where Petra was working, exclusively served the Aboriginal population. The district comprised twenty-six communities that were inhabited by a hundred and fifty to fifteen hundred people. They had their own school and a health center with a nurse. The territory that belonged to them was as big as France.

The Zone hospital reminded Petra of a building in Vyšne Hágy in Slovakia, where she had worked as a student. The radiologist was a quiet Irishman, semi-retired, who had left McMaster University to serve the population of the north. He had trained many community members to be x-ray technicians. He and Petra understood each other right away. They had both fallen for the endless sky that seemed higher than any they had ever seen.

She experienced a feeling of freedom that she had never known before. It must have been due to the space, its expanse; to the air, the lake, and the snow. Her only disappointment was her distance from the mountains, a five-hour drive to Thunder Bay. She settled for cross-country skiing which gave her the solitude she craved, if not the wind brushing her cheeks. Like her father's model railway, it was a diminutive version of the reality we love and that we yearn to return to all our lives. And she had managed to achieve it. She was back.

Since the doctors of Sioux Lookout often flew to see their patients, they had to complete survival training. The goal of the training was to be able to last twenty-four hours in the wilderness without any help in case of a crash. They were provided with an instructor, a sleeping bag, matches, and a saw.

The training started at the end of January. Everything was covered with snow and the thermometer showed minus 38 degrees Celsius. Petra's group included several colleagues from the hospital. She was forced to pair up with an internist who was always unhappy, who criticized everything and never agreed with anyone.

They spent two days together and one frozen night outside. They ate only nuts and drank melted snow. The instructor fried some dough on his gas stove that tasted like her mother's doughnuts. The internist constantly complained about everything. Petra understood that the most difficult thing in survival is that you cannot choose who is with you when you crash.

Those forty-eight hours in the dazzlingly white snow and the cold that penetrated their lungs like a knife had a curative effect on her soul. If there was a wound, it had been cauterized. Petra felt relief. Her head cleared and her thoughts were freed. She spent her first night without dreaming about anything connected with her father or Mariška. She woke up feeling light and clean, and when she heard the helicopter coming to take them back, she was almost sorry to go.

Baby Jesus

Jozef had just finished his phone call with his mother. It seemed that nothing was moving with her trip to Canada, even though Lajo, who they finally managed to catch on the phone and who they suspected was avoiding them, said that she would have come long ago if not for the "trouble." What sort of trouble they soon found out.

Before Christmas of 1973, when Jozef was snowed under by work and Erika was organizing collections for children, they each received a present from the Czechoslovakian Consulate in Montreal.

Decision. The Ministry of the Interior of the Slovak Socialist Republic in Bratislava, according to Paragraph. 15 of the Law of SNR No. 206/1968 of the Code...

Although expecting this letter for years, she suddenly felt surprised.

...has terminated the citizenship of the Slovak Socialist Republic of Erika Rola, born...

Like every other refugee, she had dreams of being back in Bratislava and unable to get out. At the same time she desired nothing more than to have one more look at the place, if just for a day.

Reason: Erika Rola left on 15.11.1968 for four days to Austria. She did not return from this trip, and since 21.11.1968, she has been living abroad without the permission of the Czechoslovakian government...

Jozef opened his letter a moment after her.

...and after his arrival abroad he worked as an announcer for Radio Free Europe...

They both stood and read the papers with the round stamps again. The stamp depicted a lion with two tails, with a burning flame on his chest and a star gleaming above his head.

Considering that the public activity of the named person is oriented against the state and social system of the ČSSR and that he has resided abroad for more than five years without a valid Czechoslovak document that would entitle him to stay abroad, the resulting decision is...

Erika folded up her letter.

...to remove the citizenship of Erika Rola... Jozef Rola... in accordance with the aforementioned legal stipulations.

Jozef sat down; Erika walked into the kitchen and straightened the glasses in the cabinet. They were silent and thoughtful. They knew that home is where you feel good and where people are decent to you. They knew that Canada had become home for them, and that this was only the formal removal of something that a person carries within him and that cannot be taken away.

Even so, they felt as if only an hour had passed since the white and red barrier had lowered behind their car, and that in the distance one could still see the lights of Bratislava.

When during the hot summer of 2007 I collected material for this book in Toronto, I met many young Slovaks who had tried to solve their personal and financial problems by staying in Canada. They were all from the generation that had left after 1989. I was struck by the fact that many had doubts whether they had made the right decision. They had work and made more money than they would have in Slovakia, but they still felt something was missing.

Some said that they actually envied the older generation that had felt compelled to go to Canada because of the Russian tanks. They envied the clarity of their decision since they had no choice, like many other foreign-born people in Toronto who had escaped wars, starvation, or crazy dictators.

Today's migrants from Slovakia, thank God, don't leave because of threats against their lives. They can return any time without a risk of prison or a life of poverty. The moment they arrive in the new country that they have idealized, they find something that bothers them and start criticizing it and thinking of how to go back. And many have returned, only to complain about the impossible Slovakia and to start planning where to go next.

In the years when my novel takes place, many people from Czechoslovakia escaped by airline trips to Havana. They paid for the trip to Cuba, and when the airplane stopped in Montreal for refueling, people would get out and immediately ask for asylum. Airplanes often arrived in Cuba half full. The Czechoslovakian government solved the problem in its own way: during the layover in Canada, despite international rules, passengers were forced to stay on board. There were no stairs to let them out, and their lives were at risk while surrounded by highly flammable jet fuel.

People kept escaping anyway. They would open the door in spite of protests from the flight attendants and would jump from that height to the concrete runway, breaking their legs and injuring themselves and their children—but they were free.

Today nobody can imagine what we were once prepared to do for freedom. Since then many things have become more expensive, but things spiritual or intellectual have somehow become cheap. So why would freedom not lose its price?

The last Czechoslovakian refugees of 1973 flew in before Christmas Eve. They flew to Quebec, but the airport would not allow them to land because of a snowstorm, so they landed in Toronto. The Immigration Office decided that they would spend their Christmas there and then continue to their original destination. This involved around forty people, mostly families with small children who had met for the first time in France, where they had gathered over the course of a few weeks. They all applied for placement in the francophone part of Canada.

Erika always did her work as if meeting refugees for the first time. She took nothing for granted. Each planeload was, in a way, her first one. In each she had to deal with unique destinies that would overlap with her life over the years. Unfortunately, this sometimes happened in a sad way. She remembered a young man from Žilina for whom she found work and housing. A year later she met him in court. He had joined a gang that specialized in stealing valuable carpets. She gave the court an account that was both brief and to the point, since his arrival was no different from that of hundreds of others. She can still see his eyes watching her as his sentence was read. They begged for forgiveness. No, she will not forget him.

Nor will she forget the Christmas plane from Quebec. They gathered all the passengers in a room that had been quickly rented, and planned to drive them to a hotel before they continued their flight. She worried most about the children, who were tired and scared but looked with curiosity at the Christmas decorations around them. She talked to one of the boys.

"Hi! Are you looking forward to Christmas?"

He nodded hesitantly.

"Baby Jesus won't come to us this year."

"Tell me, why not?"

"My parents told me so. It's because we've moved too much and he doesn't know our address."

Erika smiled.

"I wouldn't be too sure of that."

They gave the people water and sandwiches, and while her colleagues were helping them fill out the immigration documents Erika went to the nearest phone booth to make a call.

"Jozef, listen: call everyone who has time and tell them to make sauerkraut soup. Marika can make her potato salad... not for us, for forty people... yes... send Peter to the toy store we went to last time and give him money to buy toys for ten boys and fourteen girls... from four to seven years old. Is the hall free? For Christmas Eve... yes... someone should bring tablecloths and cutlery. We'll need plates... And tell Ludmila that I beg her to bake some Christmas wafers for us...yes...see you soon!"

Their friends exceeded Erika's expectations. They festooned the room, brought tablecloths, cutlery, and dishes, and the next day drove the forty surprised people to the hall. Someone bought a tree, while others lent their Christmas tree ornaments and placed the presents for the children under the tree.

She never saw those people again, as they continued their journey to Quebec the very next day. She made a point of looking for the boy she'd talked to at the airport. He was holding a toy police car in his hand. She winked at him conspiratorially, and he enthusiastically showed her his present.

That evening the Baby Jesus reportedly arrived in Toronto. There were at least forty witnesses. According to one of them, he looked like a lady in a checkered skirt, but there's no way to prove it.

Wilderness

The First Nations people she treated never looked her in the eye. According to their custom that was not polite. They never thanked her. Most of the time they kept silent. At first Petra found it difficult to take, but fortunately the outpatient ward had an advisor, more like a "cultural translator," who shared her patients' background and language.

The most important thing was to reflect on everything, speak slowly, and not answer right away. Everything had to be said after a pause. There was no way to quickly come up with a diagnosis. She had to pause between words. It was no wonder that finding out what preceded the illness could take an hour, and she would learn nothing.

An example: "Are you in pain?"

Pause. The patient reflects.

"A bit."

Pause. The doctor reflects.

"Where does it hurt?"

Pause. They point to a certain place. The doctor wrinkles her forehead. She's thinking. A pause.

"What sort of pain is it? Does it burn?"

Pause. The patient shakes his head. The doctor makes an expression of thinking hard.

"Does the pain shoot into the left hand?"

Pause. The patient moves his head in a way that suggests neither yes nor no. The doctor sighs.

"Does walking uphill make you breathe hard?"

And so on.

While the doctor's brain gathered the signs of an ischemic disease that flowed like tributaries to the great river of diagnosis, she knew she had to talk to the patient for a while. Reaching a conclusion too soon would make her untrustworthy.

At least one thing was certain: everyone who showed up was ill. It could be generally assumed that every injury was serious; otherwise people would not make the long trip to the hospital that would take them away from their daily work and hunting.

Indigenous women sometimes hid their pregnancies to avoid giving birth in a hospital, which would mean a stay of at least a week. Who would take care of her children while she was away and her husband had to go out to work before daybreak? So the women preferred to remain at home, and a doctor would be summoned only if there were complications. That would often be too late, and the fate of the patient would be decided by the weather. If there was a snowstorm, the airplane would not fly, and there would only be a nurse to take care of the woman.

The indigenous people did not bestow their trust lightly. Many doctors didn't stay long enough for local people to get to know them. Why should they talk about themselves when new doctors would come a year later and start asking the same questions all over again? With the best will in the world doctors were not always able to save a life, and the suspicion inevitably lingered that they had misunderstood the problem or had not tried hard enough.

An important rite of passage was learning to pronounce patients' names. When cases were discussed during rounds a newcomer to the Zone was sure to stumble over a surname like Angeconeb or Ashpaneqestum. The more experienced doctors would all titter mercilessly and move on to the next presentation.

The doctors of Sioux Lookout were a colorful group. All of them were young, the oldest only thirty-nine, and many had traveled the world, working in India and Africa before venturing to this wilderness as the next place where it was worthwhile practicing medicine. Some looked like hippies and Petra, who initially turned up in regulation doctor's attire, looked like a bank clerk in comparison. Her colleagues jokingly called her Boss even after she began dressing more casually.

One day she went to eat in a local restaurant, which was actually a log cabin filled with stuffed bears and beavers. A moose with antlers looked at her from the opposite wall, its glassy look making her lose her appetite. She wanted to turn her back to it, but then a toothy beaver gazed into her plate, its teeth so prominent that it could finish her dinner along with her table and all the chairs.

Only fried food was available in this establishment, and everything was drowned in a nondescript sauce that her colleagues dubbed the Revenge of the Mountain Spirits. Only two kinds of drinks were served: coffee and beer. Anyone who ordered something else or, God forbid, didn't want sauce with his meal was immediately moved into the category of "suspicious foreigner." Petra's colleagues wondered why she even went to that tacky hole, but it was a necessary experience. Since then she had cooked her own meals or eaten in the hospital cafeteria.

Paulette and Reneé had recently left to study at the university, so they called each other now and again. Petra didn't feel alone; the intense work brought an intense feeling of life. As long as a person didn't become run down, the work was deeply satisfying. The oldest doctor in the Zone hospital was Alexander, the Chief of Staff, whose life's purpose was to serve the community. He would get so excited when speaking about the problems of the local population that their discussions reminded them of parliamentary arguments.

Sean was the internist with whom she had to "crash." He was still trying to figure out his personal life, and Petra learned more than she wanted to about his on-and-off relationship with a hot-blooded brunette named Rhonda that brought both of them a lot of stress and pain. There was also Kyle from Nova Scotia, who seemed very laid back until Petra once ventured to pull a CD out of his extensive collection and received a sharp reprimand for disturbing his meticulous alphabetical arrangement. A lot of people here seemed to be trying to find out who they were and what they wanted. Petra believed she had resolved this question; the children she helped to bring into this world were also, in a way, her children.

Her more experienced colleagues warned her that local women would not show any sign of pain, and as a result it was difficult to find out if they were already experiencing the onset of childbirth. The head doctor gave her some good advice.

"Petra, look at their forehead. If a bead of sweat appears, that means they're fully dilated and ready to push." The silent stoicism of the indigenous women in the face of agonizing and unmediated pain contrasted sharply with Petra's experience among the assertively vocal urban population.

During her first birth up north, Petra found herself confronted with two silent indigenous women. One had sweat on her brow. The head doctor handed her a green surgical gown, scrubs, hat, and mask.

"Get going."

With some surprise Petra took the clothing, which was normally used only in the operating room. The standard attire for a Canadian doctor was corduroy pants, a white shirt, and a stethoscope around the neck. Petra quickly dressed and entered the birthing suite. She didn't feel comfortable in her clothing, but Alexander told her it was done this way here. She was certain that everything would go well. The woman giving birth was already crowning, and the baby's head was visible. Next to her stood almost all her colleagues, and it didn't occur to her to wonder why they were there as she concentrated on the birth. Finally the little boy came out. He breathed in and started to cry.

It was a large child, much larger than any she'd delivered before. She waited until the last blood passed through the umbilical cord and then clamped it. When she handed the boy to his mother, the others started to laugh and applaud. She looked around in surprise. They all had on their street clothes; only she looked odd in her greens. It was her baptism. She pulled down her mask and laughed with them. She felt she would get along with these people.

Colonialist civilization extended its reach to indigenous people for better and for worse. Life connected to nature could be idealized only if one didn't crave the survival advantages of electricity, clean drinking water, and sanitation. But with these advantages came the diseases of well-being. Before, indigenous people had eaten only seasonal meat, but now they had everything from the freezer. Hunters stopped hunting and lost their purpose in life, succumbing to depression. Families had a washing machine, radio, and television, but also alcohol, cigarettes, and sugary foods and the maladies that came with them.

Petra had twelve- and twenty-four-hour shifts during which she had to answer telephone calls from the wilderness. Every reserve had a nurse to consult about treatment. Some were just beginners, while others were excellent diagnosticians who could do x-rays, EKGs, and blood tests. They would then report the results to a doctor, who would decide whether the ailment could be handled long distance, or whether the patient had to be brought in. After each shift, Petra whispered her mantra:

"We survived. Thanks. I only hope I didn't make too many mistakes."

After a year had passed, she signed a new contract without hesitation. She took a short vacation in Ottawa, lit candles on the graves and checked Mariška's house. She went to the movies and theater, walked around Parliament Hill and had dinner in an Indian restaurant, but continued to impatiently watch the time that separated her from the north. The big city no longer interested her. There she was one of many, lost in the crowd.

Only in Sioux Lookout was she a Boss.

Beard

t's going to be a surprise."

"Can't you tell me?"

"Then it wouldn't be a surprise."

"You're such a..."

Peter was pouting, a sign of resistance. His father was taking him on a trip and didn't want to tell him where. They got into the car and drove for a while through the side roads among dozens of wooden houses like the one in which they, too, lived. He couldn't stay offended for long.

"Is it outside of Toronto, or in Toronto?"

"Both."

"Both? In Toronto and out of Toronto?"

"A bit like that."

Confused, Peter stuck out his lower lip even more. Not wanting to make him angry, Jozef added:

"We'll be there in half an hour and you'll be very happy. You'll see."

What Jozef had given up hoping for had happened: Lajo had kept his promise, and Jozef's mother was flying in from Vienna. They hadn't seen each other for six years, not counting the meeting below Devin Castle where, separated by the river, they had waved at her from the Austrian shore. He'd never overcome his remorse for not being able to say goodbye before escaping from Czechoslovakia.

When she'd asked him a few days earlier what she should bring him, he said: "Yourself. Come healthy and in good spirits." But then he remembered something. As a former winemaker, he wanted to start a vineyard in Canada! So he asked his mother to bring a few roots. Besides her, that would be the most precious gift he could get.

"Daddy? Do you want to grow a beard?"

"What gave you the idea?"

"Just asking."

She would arrive by herself; his father's health didn't permit him to fly, and he was spending more time in the hospital than at home. Now he was feeling a little better, which was why Jozef's mother decided to fly; otherwise she wouldn't hear of it. The best evidence that his father was getting weaker was his flagging passion for reading. Gone were the days when he would read a book a day and then discuss it with the author over a glass of wine.

Jozef could see it from another side as well: it wasn't only his father that had changed, but also the books. There was nothing to read, no one to talk to. The free publishing houses had moved abroad, one of them even to Toronto, and their owners could unfortunately not have a glass of wine with their reader from Modra.

"You should grow a beard, Daddy."

"If you give me one good reason, I'll think about it, Peter."

"Will you tell me where we're going?"

"Don't mix two things up. The beard is one thing and the surprise is another."

Why a beard? Now? Maybe in a few years. A few years... what would happen in a few years?

Well, he would celebrate the tenth anniversary of his ordination. Ten years would have passed, and his life was tolerable; in fact, he wasn't afraid to admit that it was even good. He had no idea that in a short while someone from the Canadian government would notice Erika's many years of volunteer work on behalf of the refugees. On the recommendation of the Queen's Privy Council the Governor in Council would appoint Erika to the Immigration and Refugee Board of Canada. As a member of this independent, quasi-judicial tribunal, Erika would make decisions on claims of asylum for people from all over the world. We know already that Erika would be the right kind of person for this work, but she had no inkling of it yet.

She could see only a few hours ahead, like any ordinary mortal. She knew that her mother-in-law would soon arrive by air, so she was doing her best. She was preparing her table for a festive occasion, frying the schnitzels, mixing the potato salad, cooking the chicken soup, cooling the pear brandy, and polishing the cutlery, all the while helped by little Eva, whom she had to watch like a crystal glass.

"I actually have two good reasons."

Peter had been quiet for ten minutes, and Jozef had already forgotten what they were talking about. Traffic was getting heavier as they approached the freeway.

"You need a beard. It's a natural thing; hair keeps growing, right? It's not natural to shave, but it's natural to let it grow."

"But it would scare everyone when I climbed into the pulpit. Give me a better reason."

Peter couldn't hide his family background. He took a deep breath and fired his large-caliber weapon.

"Even Jesus had a beard. He was the Son of God and you are only his servant."

Jozef suddenly understood what it meant to be speechless. He drove quietly, hit by the heavy artillery of his own son, who fifteen years later would become an excellent doctor. Fifteen years... but he didn't know that yet. Only the author knows and is enjoying this knowledge.

"That was the second reason. But I have another one. Every Sunday you're perfectly shaved. What if you offered your congregation some variety? At least for a while."

Jozef couldn't help but laugh out loud, which helped him recover his ability to speak.

"I would have to ask them if they wouldn't mind."

"Would you, then?"

He really would. He rather hoped that they would reject it, but they didn't. And so after his agreement with his son, he started to grow a beard—until the son's birthday. He made it a game, but also a little sacrifice for his good luck today. The car turned off the freeway toward the airport.

"We're going to the airport? Who's coming?"

Jozef waited a minute to answer. He found a parking spot and turned to his son.

"Grandma's coming."

Peter began jumping in his seat and shouting with joy. Jozef remembered at that moment how she used to pray with him in the evening: "Now I lay me down to sleep, I pray the Lord my soul to keep. If I should die before I wake, I pray the Lord my soul to take. This I ask in Jesus' name, Amen." Jozef continued that prayer every night with Peter and Eva, with a special prayer for their grandmother as well.

He repeated her words in his mind. It had worked. Peter was jumping in front of him, around him, he was everywhere. Before they reached the arrival hall, they saw in the distance three beautiful, white airplanes as they landed. According to Peter, Grandma was in each of them. As another landed, he corrected himself, and on it went. The planes that landed ranged from the smallest Cessna to a gigantic Boeing, and this was his reason for placing her in each.

But she really was in the biggest one.

Refrain

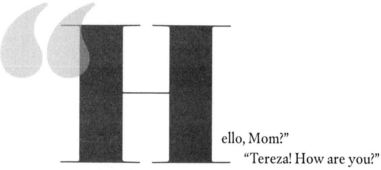

ello, Mom?"

"Tereza! How are you?"

"Happy birthday!"

"You didn't forget?"

"I remembered and it's in the calendar. What are you doing?"

"I finally have some time to go to the garden. How's your health? Is Milan home?"

"He has a new job installing sound equipment for the Philharmonic. What is Janko doing?"

"You can't hear him?"

"We have Mick Jagger at home?"

"He's graduating this year but spends more time with the guitar than books."

"Please, let me talk to him."

"Hi Sis! We have a concert on Saturday."

"At the Culture Park?"

"Hardly! It's a competition among amateur rock groups in Vajnory Street."

"Play something for me."

"It'll cost you a lot."

"Who's making the phone call?"

"I'll let you talk to Mom."

"He went to practice. He said he has to play it again."

"Do you need anything, Mom? What should I send you?"

"You can send Janko those pants, you know which ones."

"Jeans?"

"He doesn't wear anything else."

"We're going to move; we're buying a little house, really small, but you would like it a lot. And Jozef lives nearby. They send their greetings. We saw them last night."

"Thanks, send them my greetings, too."

"We were laughing so hard, because they took his mother to see Niagara Falls and were looking forward to her reaction, after he gave her a lecture about it being the biggest waterfall in the world, and then his mother just looked at it for a while and said one word: water; nothing more than water. Oh, by the way, Petra and I are writing to each other, do you know where she is?"

"She sent me a postcard with polar bears."

"Isn't that something? Our Petra is now a northerner!"

"I'm not saying that it's good that you're not here, girls... neither of you..."

"Mummy, don't cry."

"It has to do something to you, I'm telling myself, it has to change you somehow."

"Do you want to hear some big news, I mean really big news?"

"Something good?"

"Some excellent news."

"I do."

"But you have to stop crying, Mummy."

"Fine."

"I'm pregnant. Mummy! You promised..."

"I'm sorry... I have to cry..."
"Sis? I'll play for you."
"Great."
"This is just the refrain... Mummy, hold the receiver...
na, na, na, naaaah, naah, na, na,...
Every window has a light,
Why is yours dark?
Meteor shines so bright,
Come to me tonight,
na, na, na, naaah, naah, na, na..."

Happiness

Dear Tereza!

Congratulations on the awesome news about your pregnancy. What a great woman you are! If by chance you are looking for a godmother, then you have a northerner available! Greetings to Milan, he must be really happy. I'm married to medicine; you know that. I only have a dog, but you know that as well. I'll have to leave the poor creature alone for a week; the Chief of Staff promised to take care of him.

Tomorrow I'm flying up north again; each of us does that once a month. We fly there on these little airplanes. The pilots are young, and they look even too young for a driver's license. But they fly well and they land on a strip no larger than our school playground in Stará Ruda (you don't know it).

They pack food for me for a week: salad, tomatoes, chicken meat, cereal, tea, because I'll cook for myself. There's a store over there, but everything costs three times as much as in an Italian deli in Ottawa. I'm flying to Webequie; I've been there before. They have an excellent nurse over there: she's indigenous, knows everybody, and also knows *everything about the community (health, children, animals, including the fish they caught). A woman like that could have a meteoric career in the capital, but she doesn't want to move, because she's at home there.*

The last time I flew in a bigger plane they were transporting fish. It was great, if you can imagine. They removed all the seats and left two for me and loaded large plastic containers full of fish. The locals did the loading, but the containers weren't properly closed and our bush pilot had to maneuver (you can't fly normally here, there's nothing but lakes and valleys around), and when we landed there was water up to our ankles, and I wasn't the only one getting off the plane, the fish were too.

I wouldn't have it any other way for the world. I've been running away all my life. Here I'm at the end of the world, and thank God, I can't go any further. And suddenly it's all over. I feel good here. You and Milan and the baby have to come visit someday.

The sky really is endless here. And in winter it's illuminated by the northern lights. Aurora borealis. The kind of light I've never seen before. I've found calm and peace here. I'm making wickerwork furniture. It's big over here, and I started on a little table, but it turned into a flowerpot. I won't become a folk artist in this genre.

Do you remember the deer in Stará Ruda? We used to feed it cigarettes when you came for a visit. Here there are only moose. I'll see if they like tobacco, but only a bit. I don't want to make addicts out of them. Back then I showed you my father's railway under my parents' bed. When I was a little girl he used to buy me toy trains for Christmas, but he played with them alone. I liked it when he turned the current on and I'd put the engine on the rails, still holding it in my hand. Its wheels would slide on the rails and then I'd let it go and it would shoot ahead. That's how I feel today. I have no idea whether I deserve so much happiness.

But, enough about myself. Write to me how your baby is growing, about the new house, about Milan, Toronto, Uncle Jozef, and Aunt Erika. Write about everything!

Lots of kisses, your Petra.

ACKNOWLEDGMENTS

This novel is based on the stories of real people. I changed their names and let their doubles live their own lives. Any similarity to persons living or no longer living is no accident, even though much occurred differently than depicted here. I would like to thank the models for my characters for the faith in me that they demonstrated in Toronto during the hot summer of 2007, when they recounted their life experiences long into the night.

It was then, for the first time in forty years, that they found the courage to communicate the stories that you find in this book. As a listener I was startled, amazed, and ultimately moved by the power of the events that changed their lives overnight.

Here they are:

DUŠAN TÓTH—Pastor and theater actor who started everything by arranging my meeting with others and asking me to write a play that was performed in Toronto and Slovakia.

VALERIA TÓTH—his excellent wife and fellow organizer, who was the first to find out that I was writing this book.

Peter Tóth—their son, a medical doctor, who told me everything about the Canadian North.

Sonia—thanks for her frankness, confidence, and energy in overcoming evil.

Ivan—her husband and a great person.

Juraj—Sonia's brother, who did not live to see the novel, but still lives in it.

Eva—who inspired me to write about Petra and Alexander, even though her fate was different.

Ady Strážovec—the architect and artist whose name was deleted from film credits after 1968 and did not return to them after 1989.

Jarmila Filipko—a dentist, whose "model" swallowed her fillings during the dentistry exam, requiring Jarmila to retake the exam.

Katka and Mato Bíro—they escaped in an Opel Record, but they are not this novel's Alex and Anna.

Sylvia and Štefan Galvánek—the artists who told me about the fascinating gallery with the works of the Group of Seven.

Ivan Rázl—who introduced me to the White Lady.

Stanislav Jančiarik—who told me about Argentina under Peron.

Yuri Dojč—who gave me the notebook that I used to write the first lines of the novel.

And my thanks to others from the Toronto Slovak Theatre who contributed their ideas, statements or even just a word.

I particularly want to thank my aunts Anna de Cortes and Maria de Dominguez, both born Klimáčková—who moved to Buenos Aires before World War II, but without their brother Ivan, to whom I was born a quarter century later. That would have been another novel—or, maybe not.

—Viliam Klimáček

◆ ◆ ◆

My wife Valika was always full of great ideas. She packed one for me as I prepared to travel to Slovakia in the spring of 2007. "Find Viliam Klimáček (the playwright) and ask him if he would write a play for our Toronto Slovak Theatre to commemorate the fortieth anniversary of the occupation of Czechoslovakia by the Warsaw Pact countries."

Well, I thought, an appealing idea to be sure. But I had no idea how to make this possible? I had never met Klimáček in person nor had any contact with him. I had seen one of his comedies and read a dozen of his plays. The prospect of just calling a famous Slovak playwright and asking him to write a play seemed far-fetched.

When I arrived in Slovakia I happened to look at the Slovak National Theatre's program and noticed that one of Klimacek's plays, *Hypermarket*, was playing. I decided to call the theatre office and simply ask to speak with the staff there about the production. Maybe they could provide me with a contact for Klimáček. When I called, a woman answered. I introduced myself and explained my reason for calling. After an initial pause she told me "I am actually Viliam Klimáček's wife." Only God Himself could have arranged this, I said to myself! Encouraged by this opportunity, I called "The Master," Viliam Klimáček. At first he was pleasant, but I noticed he was cautious as I explained the reason for my call. He did, however, promise to meet with me.

At the time he seemed quite preoccupied. Later I found out that the issues of emigration were very personal for him. During the interview I invited him to come to Toronto with the promise that I would introduce him to several refugee families that had settled there after 1968. Believe it or not, everything went according to plan! The play was born, and on the fortieth anniversary of the Czechoslovak invasion the Toronto Slovak Theatre presented its first performance to fans in Toronto. The play then continued with six performances in Slovakia. A year later it was published in book form in Slovakia and was later translated into Arabic, French, and Lithuanian. The idea that the novel would be translated into English was yet another dream for Valika and me so that the continent that welcomed us so many years ago could share our experiences.

We knew that for any publisher to consider this endeavor we would have to have the novel eloquently translated. We were sure that Dr. Peter Petro, Professor Emeritus and formal Chair of the Program of Modern European Studies, University of British Columbia, was up to the task.

Thanks to the generosity of our children Peter and Andrea we managed to raise funds in order to move forward. Editing was then lovingly provided by Stacy Mosher who gave us so much good advice, resulting ultimately in the birth of this book.

We lacked the means for funding so that the book could see the light here in our adopted English language. This was Valika's last project. Unfortunately she did not live long enough to see this last stage in the novel's development. It was the many donors who so kindly offered funds in her memory that helped us to bring this project to fruition. We treasure them all with thankfulness and love. She would have been very happy to know *The Hot Summer of 1968* will be read in English.

We especially remember the family of Darina Rasmussen, who welcomed and took us under her wings when we first arrived in Milwaukee almost fifty years ago with our son and two suitcases. Their son Carl Rasmussen and daughter Jarmila Koepp and their families gratefully and generously contributed to *The Hot Summer of 1968*, bringing this book on its way to English readers. Carl was especially instrumental in helping the novel find a publisher, Mandel Vilar Press and Dryad Press, who saw the potential of this story and its appeal to the English reader.

We thank the many people who have made it easier for us to integrate into life, first in the USA and later in Canada. The list is rich. For us, and for many other refugees, good people opened their doors and hearts and accepted us. This way we were able to ultimately find a new home, friends, and community which continues to enrich our lives and the lives of our children!

—Dusan Toth, Toronto, Canada, June 2020

PUBLISHER'S ACKNOWLEDGMENTS

*Mandel Vilar Press and Dryad Press would like to dedicate
the publication of this English translation to the memory
and accomplishments of Valéria Tóth.*

◆ ◆ ◆

The publishers would like to thank Reverend Dušan Tóth, Valéria
Tóth, Peter Tóth, Andrea Tóth, Doris Huber, and Stacey Mosher for
supporting and contributing to this important English translation and
publication.

We would also like to thank the author, Viliam Klimáček and the translator, Dr. Peter Petro, for their permission to publish and distribute
this English translation throughout the English reading world.

Finally, the publishers are grateful to Dr. Carl Rasmussen and Dr.
Cathy Rasmussen for their assistance in making this project a reality
and a success.